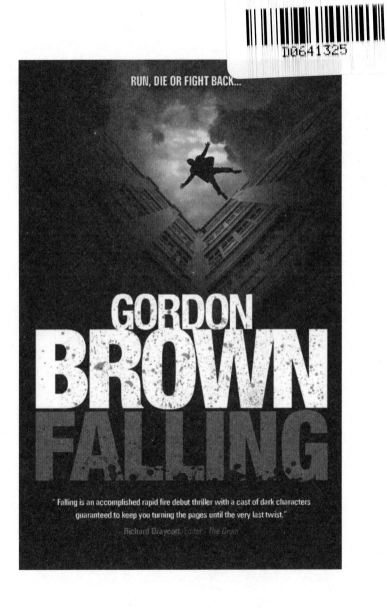

RUN, DIE OR FIGHT BACK...

GORDON
BROWN
FALLING

" Falling is an accomplished rapid fire debut thriller with a cast of dark characters
guaranteed to keep you turning the pages until the very last twist."

Richard Draycott, Editor - The Drum

FALLING

Gordon Brown

W R

Blythswood Square

8/3/12

Fledgling Press 2009

First published in June 2009 by Fledgling Press
7 Lennox Street, Edinburgh EH4 1QB, Scotland
www.fledglingpress.com

All the characters in this book are imaginary. Any
resemblance to real people, living or dead, is purely
coincidental. Some places are real, others are in the
imagination of the author.
Any errors are those of the author.

A CIP catalogue reference for this book is available
from the British Library

ISBN: 978 1 905916 23 8

Cover produced by 999 Design.
Printed and Bound by Thomson Litho Ltd,
East Kilbride, Scotland

About the author

Gordon Brown was born and lives in Glasgow.

He is married with two children - having spent twenty five years in the sales and marketing world working on everything from alcohol to global charities and from TV to lingerie.

Gordon started out life packing shelves for Sainsbury's before moving to Canada to join the brewery business. He set up his own marketing business in 2001 and has an honours degree from Strathclyde along with an MBA from Nottingham Trent University.

Gordon has been writing for pleasure for some twenty years and this is his debut novel

Dedication

This book is dedicated to my wife Lesley for putting up with her husband battering a keyboard when he should have been helping out and believing that one day a book would emerge.

To Scott and Nicole for letting Dad write in peace.

To Richard, Fiona, Doug, Tracy and Julie for taking the time to read my rough manuscript.

To Alison for all the support and advice.

And to Zander for being the one who said yes when I most needed it.

Prologue.

The door to the toilet slams open and I turn to the noise. Two men in suits, one tall, one small, barrel across the tiles and pin me to the wall. The tall one is grinning like a cat on speed and he grabs my arm, spins me around to connect with the fist of the short one and I go into stun mode.

They are strong and the tall one kicks my feet from under me and they haul me out of the toilet and onto the fire escape. I try to resist and receive a slap to the head for every word I utter. Seven slaps - I'm a slow learner.

We hit the roof at full speed and I'm lifted clean off my feet and hurled over the edge.

Chapter 1

Tina needs a break.

'Get your own tea'

God I could spit. You wear a skirt, sit next to a computer and some male tosser thinks you're the office slave. Why the hell would I want to make tea? When was the last time someone made tea for me? It's not in my bloody job description. I know - I looked. Bad day already and it's not even past ten. Time to take a cigarette break.

Even a ciggie break is a pain in the rear end. When I started work, smoking was almost compulsory. By mid morning the fug in the office was so thick that it blurred the edges of the people, my wonderful work colleagues, who sat at the far end of the office. Crashing fags was a given. It was an unwritten offence to come to work with less than a twenty pack and you were in the mire if you came back from foreign climes with anything less than a box of two hundred.

How it's all changed for us lepers. First we were banished to a hell hole of a room in the basement. Just an awful place! No windows. No decoration and rock hard chairs. Like a secret meeting of some perverse society we sat, drawing in, in turn, your own cigarette smoke and then someone else's. But at least it was a place to go and, crappy or not, you could escape from work for ten minutes.

Then we were relegated to the street. Correction, relegated to a spot in the lane round the corner from our front door. There we would huddle rain, shine, snow, wind. Backs to the elements - drawing sustenance and complaining. Complaining, complaining and complaining. Complaining about our bosses, our work colleagues, our staff, our spouses, our neighbours, the newsreader on BBC1, the girl in reception with the worst dress sense on the planet, the security guard with the breath of Satan, the pay, the conditions, the weather, the lack of toilet rolls last Tuesday, the smell of urine in the lane, the size of Mars Bars (yes they were bigger in the past), the price of a cup of coffee in Starbucks, the taste of a cup of coffee in Starbucks, the unisex toilet in Starbucks (but we still go to Starbucks), the cost of petrol, the cost of living, the cost of smoking. Complaining is what we do best and the time to do it is during a fag break. And now in another clampdown by the cigarette police we are to be banished from the lane.

It seems our mounting doubts (the ciggy kind not the mental kind) and the sheer number of addicts that congregate to partake have caused other people to complain - ironic or what! We have been told to find a spot away from our building.

As a group we are fairly sure this is illegal but it gives us something else to complain about and has, to be fair, given birth to an unforeseen opportunity. An opportunity spotted by yours truly.

I had been talking to Satan Breath about the ban on smoking in the lane and to my surprise he informed me he was also a smoker. Since I hadn't seen him in the leper colony I asked where he smoked. 'The roof' he informed me. And so was born the mile high club.

Smoking on the roof is strictly against company policy and no doubt it is against safety regulations, local bye laws and the civil liberties of the pigeons that now have to inhale our waste products. But for a short window it is also glorious.

The roof could have been custom designed for smoking. Stunning views, plenty of shelter, easy access and the world's largest dustbin - just chuck the ciggies over the edge. Satan Breath has assured us that the twenty storey fall will put out the burning stub well before it hits the ground. Just to be on the safe side we sling them into the lane. This will no doubt confuse the hell out of the office manager. No smokers in the lane but lots of used cigarettes. It won't last. Can't last. Someone will blab and we will be ejected. But while the going is good, let's smoke.

It's just warming up on the roof today and there is no one else around. Unusual for this time of day! Maybe we've been found out and I'm the last to know and, any moment now, someone will burst from the fire escape to arrest me.

I think I'll enjoy my moment of solitude on the west wing today. Not the best view. A forty storey office block sits just across the lane but there is a small sun trap and a vent that can be used as a seat. An uncomfortable seat - but a seat none the less.

I light up, look up and nearly throw up. Above me on the block opposite there is a man falling from the roof. One foot on the roof - the rest of him hanging out in space.

Mother!

Chapter 2

Charlie learns to fly.

Falling is the last thing I wanted to do. You really don't fancy it when you're standing on the edge of a forty storey building and all that stands between you and the road below is a few hundred feet of fresh air. But, hey life's not all a bed of roses and sometimes it throws you a dodgy one and you either fight it or bend over and wait for the bad news to arrive.

In my case the bad news was on its way. If you've ever stood next to a large drop and possess half the vertigo that I suffer from then, that feeling you get in your bowel, the one that resembles a full on food mixer, take it, triple it, add on some brown sauce for seasoning and you might get close to what I was going through.

Not that I wanted to be stepping out into the wide blue. Far from it! I had a million other things I would rather have been doing. Don't ask me for the full million long list - but you get the gig. I didn't want to go freefalling without the benefit of a safety net or at least a parachute.

What I did want to do was to move four feet to my left and stay there. Simple really! Not much to ask for. No great demand of life, God and the universe. Not as if I'm asking for a win on the lottery or a weekend with Cybil McLean. You won't know Cybil but trust me if you are male, straight and alive you would like Cybil.

It's not even as if I'm asking to add a hundred years to my lifespan. Ten minutes would be good. Ten seconds would be a starting point. Anything other than the three or four seconds between now and the concrete waiting below!

On the plus side I can see a lot from up here. Not that its registering that well but it's still a hell of a view. On a better day it would be worth trying to grab a few photos. Maybe even a video. I heard once that the last image you see before you die stays embedded on your retina. Maybe I should pick out a good landmark, stare at it and close my eyes. That way the coroner can stare into my dead eyes and view a pleasant snapshot from five hundred feet up - one for the morgue wall maybe.

I still have one foot on the roof but no chance of redemption. One foot, in this case, is one foot too few. A fully planted foot with all my weight would give me hope. Unfortunately I have less than the tip of my shoe left on the building and even that is about to go airborne.

I also resemble something of a windmill at the moment. Arms flailing. Leg flailing - leg singular - not legs - my tiny connection to the roof prevents my left leg joining in the fun. My head is flailing. My heart is flailing. Hell even my dick is flailing. Not that this excess of flailing is making a blind bit of difference to my fate - but then again what would?

Maybe a man can fly? Maybe world class flailing precedes the ability to soar like a bird and I'll soon find myself buzzing around the sky.

I'm also screaming. Not words. Just sounds. Strange, I would have thought that words such as 'No' or more likely 'Noooooooooooo' would have been up there as a more likely response to my situation. But I seem to have reverted to a high pitch wail.

Wail and flail that's me.

My name is Charlie Wiggs and I'm fifty four years old. I planned on making fifty five until less than ten minutes ago when two gorillas entered the toilet, picked me up and threw me off the roof of the building I have happily worked in for some thirty years.

I can see them both now, watching my impending demise, dressed in tightly fitting grey suits, muscles pressing hard on the material. Gorilla number one is shorter than me - and that takes some doing. Hair cropped to the bone and a handlebar moustache that was last seen on the Village People. He hasn't uttered a word but growls a lot from the back of his throat.

Gorilla number two is taller. A good foot on me. Long greasy hair and designer or just lazy-man stubble. He seems to be the more articulate of the two although this only stretches as far as shouting 'Shut the fuck up' on a regular basis.

I'd guess the gorillas are both in their forties and their guts, nicely hanging out over their waistband in best beer belly tradition, suggest that brute force rather than physical fitness is the order of the day in their line of work. People that like their pop and food and rely on muscle built up many years ago to get by in their day to day work.

Both are surprisingly fragrant. If I'm not mistaken gorilla number one is wearing L'Eeau D'Issey Pour Homme by Issey Miyake. A favourite of mine. Gorilla number two is more a Lynx man. Even their breath has a fresh tinge. Nice to know I'm being murdered by hygienic people.

None of this helps with the key question that has bounced round my head since leaving the toilet in such a rush. Why? Who the hell would want to murder a fifty four year old accountant with a life that would bore a saint?

Why go to the bother of killing a man who, if asked politely, would clearly apologise for whatever it was he had done and point out that it couldn't have been him in the first place as he had never really knowingly done anything to warrant execution.

Alternatively this could be a new form of impulse killing akin to 'drive-by shooting,' only this is called 'walk-by throwing.' It could be a new craze that I have missed. Unless it was widely reported on Radio 2 there is a good chance I don't know about it. Individuals being thrown from high points all across the UK. Happy chucking not happy slapping.

Gorilla number two is now holding a phone in my direction. Filming it for 'You Tube' no doubt. Well maybe in death I'll achieve a level of fame that was denied me in life.

'Hope it was worth it you thievin' prick.'

That was gorilla number two demonstrating his range of vocabulary. The comment was aimed at me. Me who once lifted a Mars Bar from the corner shop when I was in S3. Me a boy that crapped himself for a month after the incident - expecting the police to descend at any moment. It was two years before I had the guts to go in to the shop again and even then I felt that the shopkeeper was staring at a neon sign above my head saying 'Him - it's him. The Mars Bar Boy'.

'Thievin' prick?'

Give me a break - even my tax return has to be the most honest in history and I should know - after all my speciality is tax. I'm never off the bloody hotline when it comes to my own dealings. So much so that last year I received an irate call from the call centre supervisor asking me to come in for a chat as I was causing some distress to the staff with the frequency of my calls.

'Thievin' prick'? When, how? Who from? I couldn't. I wouldn't.

Did I?

I'll be dead soon but it would have been nice to know what the gorilla is referring to. Who I stole from? What I stole? Why I stole? If I stole?

The wind is getting up, trying to push me back towards the men in grey. Not hard enough to make any difference to my fate but it's cool on my face, drying the sweat. Pleasant almost. It's ruffling gorilla number two's hair and if I'm not mistaken there is more than a hint of a toupee about the way his hair is moving around. He half turns away from me to let the wind sweep over him from the back, protecting his wig from the next big gust. I feel like shouting out *'Hey wiggy!'* - but I don't - my screaming is getting in the way.

10

He keeps filming. At least I assume he is filming - either that or he is focussing on a particularly important text. I hope not. I hope he hasn't placed my demise below his girlfriend's request to pop into Tesco for some milk on the way home.

I'm falling.

Chapter 3

A gorilla gets suspicious.

The accountant is on his way - job done. A few seconds to check he hits the concrete below and then home. Another day - another dollar.

I never intended to become a criminal. Not really. Not deep down. I intended to be a lazy. That was my real aim in life. Work shy - that's what my mum called me. She called me a lot worse than that over the years but you get the drift. At first I'd cut school, hang around the shops, noising up the locals. Occasionally getting pulled by the police. No big deal. A slap on the wrist and 'don't do it again.' Of course it escalated. I remember the detail. Hard to forget given the outcome.

Craig Bradley, a friend of mine from primary school had a brother who was into some serious shit. Drugs, knives, porn, gambling, booze - he had the full set as far as I was concerned. He lived in a flat with three other guys, having been flung out by his mother the day he hit sixteen.

Craig's brother was a bit of an anti-hero to the gang I hung around with. When he was in the right mood he let us peruse his extensive collection of video art. A real eye opener for a thirteen year old. If he was in a very good mood he would chip in a few cans of lager and a packet of Embassy No 1. If he was in a shit mood he would slap you round the back of the head and demand cash with menaces.

His name was Darg and life around him was always a bit of an adventure into the unknown. That adventure hit a new high point one Saturday night.

Darg was in an ace mood. Drug induced - but I was too naive to know that at the time. It was closing in on midnight and we should have been tucked up at home but Darg's generosity had fuelled us with a constant stream of drink, fags and porn and we were in seventh heaven. When the doorbell rang and a crowd of Darg's friends piled into the flat we were left to our own devices as they retired to the bedroom.

Twenty minutes later, just as the woman on the tape was trying to accommodate three men at once, the front door crashed to the floor and half a dozen of our finest men in blue stormed the place. We froze at the sight but Darg's friends came out fighting.

The battle lasted for ten minutes before back up in the form of six more police and two police dogs swung the advantage. Next thing we know we are slung in the back of a paddy wagon and whisked off to the local police station.

It goes without saying that when my mum turned up to bail me out I wasn't flavour of the moment. Only Darg's insistence with the police that we had nothing to do with the drugs got us out of there. My mum didn't believe this - not for a second. From that day forward her attempts to put me on the straight and narrow pushed me the other way. There is nothing like teenage rebellion and sheer stupidity to set someone on a criminal path.

I left home on my sixteenth birthday. Getting a job was low down on my list of things to do and I needed other ways to earn some cash. It didn't take long before I fell in with the type of people who had all sorts of opportunities for a young and willing man. Especially one with few scruples and a desire to obtain a bit more of the folding stuff.

I realised from the outset that I was never destined to be a criminal mastermind. I became a drone and this suited me. But I quickly learned three rules that have served me well: always have a plan B up your sleeve; never have any illusions over your indispensability; and stash enough cash to keep you liquid through the lean times.

So I muscled up, learned my craft and buckled down to a life that relied on my brawn, a bit of my brain and long stretches of boredom.

At forty four I'm past my prime in the thug stakes - it needs day to day energy to be a real pro in my line and that went a long time ago. But I'm respected enough to be trusted with some decent jobs and my tan is testament to three regular holidays in the sun a year and a deposit on a flat near Malaga. Today is just another dollar towards my retirement fund and the little prick that we are throwing off the roof is worth three grand in my back pocket. Jim, my colleague, is on a third of that, but to be honest I doubt Jim knows enough maths to figure out he is getting stuffed.

I have no idea why the little prick is going for a Mikey. So named after Mikey MacDonald who - high on some designer drug - went base jumping off the Wallace Monument in Stirling without a parachute.

I don't care either. It's not good practice to get into dialogue with the vic. In the same way farmers don't give their beasts names, I bestow the same courtesy on the vics - that way I don't see them as people - just pay-packets that scream.

'Hope it was worth it you thievin' prick.'

I hear Jim shout it and it dawns on me that my intellectually challenged colleague is off on one or, more worryingly, knows something that I don't. The former I can deal with, the latter I can't. As I said I have no idea why the vic is earthbound.

Jim takes a swim in the deep end of insanity on a regular basis. He is not my favourite partner on these jobs but he is cheap, strong as the proverbial and doesn't seem to baulk at any instruction you give him. He does, however, lose the plot more often than Coronation Street, drinks like a guppy in the Sahara and is given to breaking down in tears at the most inopportune moments.

'Hope it was worth it you thievin' prick.'

Not a good sign. What does Jim know that I don't? Jim's standing in my world is low and information is the currency that keeps you higher up the food chain. As a result he should know sweet fuck all about this deal.

In simple terms him knowing something and me not knowing might signal a little change in our relative statuses. Not a good thing. Not a good thing at all.

And why is Jim videoing the bloody thing on his phone. Was he told to do that? If so by whom? I took the instruction on the hit from 'the Voice'. Who the vic was. What was required. I was given the choice who to work with. How would Jim know any background?

I'm the nervous sort and the thought that Jim might be taking a step up in the world I live in, at my expense, has no upside at all.

Jim knows something. Jim knows nothing. Jim is on the inside on this. Jim is off on Planet Jim.

'Hope it was worth it you thievin' prick.'
'Hope it was worth it you thievin' prick.'
'Hope it was worth it you thievin' prick.'

I come to the conclusion.

Jim knows something!

Chapter 4

George cleans up.

The moon was bright last night. A silver fireball in a coal cellar sky. No city lights to dull the sky. No orange tinge to mask the stars. Ice cold. No wind. Air as fresh as a slap in the face. Ground firm. Chilled. Bird song rare. The occasional rustle from the forest and the distant sound of a truck on the road below. Other than that my heartbeat, my breathing and silence. A gold dust moment in life. Dark water below. Hilltops above.

A real gold dust moment.

I shake the thought from my head and look down at the mop in my hand, the bucket by my feet and the pool of vomit - dried vomit. The faint smell of alcohol still lingers and it will only get stronger once I introduce the vomit to mop and water. This is the third pool this morning (two dried and one wet). So much for a 'quiet' office party.

On top of the vomit we have, in order of treatment by yours truly, the following:

- Three blocked toilets - two blocked by excessive toilet paper, one by a cushion from the sofa in reception.
- One smashed window - lower left panel on the Managing Director's office door.
- One busted tap in the ladies – it leaked all night and has caved in the roof on the floor below.
- Unknown quantities of glassware, bottles, cans and plastic cups strewn across the entire floor.

17

- Suspicious burn marks on the blinds on the south side of the main floor.
- Door off its hinges in the medical room.
- Three used condoms - all in the old smoking room.
- Six jackets, three handbags, a wallet and a company logoed golf umbrella left behind.

The office is empty. It will stay that way. A day off for the revellers was part of the deal from the senior management as the company seems to be on a roll at the moment.

The MD, Simon Malmon, popped in earlier but he was hardly in a fit state to assess the damage and anyway he seemed more intent in retrieving something from his desk than talking to me. I wonder what was so precious that he drove in from his luxurious pad in the country with a killer hangover - and he was clearly hungover - the wet pool of vomit is his.

I need a break. I'm fairly sure by the time I knock off this afternoon that the damage list will run to three or four pages. The factor for the building will love this and I'll get the grief. He'll send in the troops to fix what I can't and then send in the bill. The bill will be suitably marked up and I will get it in the neck from Simon.

'George, George, George (always three times with him). I have a fucking bill for the day after our little party. Plumbers George, electricians George, glaziers George, specialist cleaners George. Maybe our factor isn't aware that you exist. What the fuck do we pay you for? Do you know what a maintenance man is supposed to do? Isn't he supposed to fix things? Eh? So why didn't you do your fucking job?'

Every time we have to get someone from outside to do some work, I get it in the neck. To give you an idea of how weird this can get, Simon once asked me if I knew anything about minor surgery. No joke - straight up. Amanda, her of too short skirts and too fat legs for the too short skirts, impaled her arm on a coat hook. Before sending for an ambulance Simon had pulled her arm off the hook, wrapped it up in a bandage and asked me if I knew how to sew up a wound? That is a perfect example of what I have to deal with on this floor.

Compared to this floor the rest of the building is a walk in the park but I swear this floor exists in another dimension. Last year they held what could only be described as an impromptu indoor tennis tournament using a cricket ball and two baseball bats and took out eight, count them, eight windows.

Next on the list is the mess on the fire escape. Wine stains, beer stains - OTHER stains. All leading up to the roof. Even CSI would struggle unravelling this one. My best guess is a rampant eight on the stairs alcohol fuelled orgy. I could be wrong but I bet I'm closer than I think.

I decide to make this easy. Start at the top. Mop down and slosh the mess over the edge. A forty storey drop down the stairwell will vaporise most of the falling liquid and if I'm quick I can grab a ten minute break and some fresh air up top before I need to check in with the head office.

'Ladies and gentlemen welcome to the annual Tyler Tower Facilities Management Games. Up first

is the individual stair cleaning - one hundred steps or less category'.

Mop, check. Bucket, check. Soapy water, check. Packet of chewing gum, check. Target time to clean three floors and get back to the top for a breath of air - ten minutes.

'Ladies and gentlemen going for a new world record is Mr George Dall. Anything under nine minutes fifty seven seconds will constitute a new world's best. Best of order. Silence in the arena. To your marks. Set. Go.'

'And stop. Nine minutes thirty two seconds. A new World Record. I thank you.'

Cheering and applause deafen the athlete and I take a bow. Now for a break.

I used to smoke but I gave it up ten years ago but I didn't give up the breaks. I can't see why a cigarette addict should get a break and I don't. As a rule I take four breaks a day. It's not in my contract but then again smokers have no contractual exemption either.

Across the road from my building they have closed the smoking room and even banned anyone from smoking outside the front door. This all seems a bit draconian if you ask me. Anyway I'll just sit up top. Grab a few lungfuls of the fresh stuff and drift back to last night.

The next task is to wash what looks suspiciously like a spray of blood from the boardroom wall. Now that will take time and effort. So it can wait.

I am half way back to last night. High up on the Cowal Peninsula looking down on the dark sheet that is the River Clyde. I have a flat in Innellan - a small village squeezed into a ribbon of flat land between the hills of the peninsula and the river. An hour after the sun set last night, I was high on the forest road behind the village doing little more than taking in the serenity.

In my mind I breathe in the Atlantic fresh air while trying to open the fire door to the roof. The fire door to the roof has always been stiff. The handle is hard to turn and my mind slips from the hills to thinking about the blood on the boardroom wall. There's quite a bit. Could be red wine but I've seen a lot of red wine stains and I've seen a lot of blood stains and my money's on blood. Class-leading nose bleed. Punch up. Ritual slaughter of a virgin. Overly violent paper cut. Probably punch up. You can bury yourself with the petty hate that flies around this floor.

I've been doing this job for five and half years and haven't seen a fight, hardly a word raised, on all the other floors put together. But on this floor I'd reckon on a flare up twice a week. Fisticuffs - at least once a month. Serious violence - a couple of times a year. Well you only have to go back to the Christmas Party: Police, Fire Brigade, Ambulance - we were only missing the Coastguard. Two arrests and Michael, the head of sales, spending a night in the Royal with a fractured skull.

I have no idea how the company makes cash. If they are not killing each other, they are ripping each other off. I'm sure Simon is on the major fiddle and Karen, the HR director, is well in it with him. I'm also fairly sure that Robin, the Financial Director, is riding shotgun with both. It's amazing how invisible a maintenance man can become and how much they can learn. By all accounts I am considered both hard of hearing and on an IQ band that equates me with a monkey. At least I have to assume this is the case by the way the majority of the occupants ignore or talk down to me on a regular basis.

As such I hear much but say little.

I open the door. Fresh air. Well as fresh as it gets in the middle of the city. This is the tallest building in Glasgow and the pollution below has thinned by the time it gets up here.

It's amazing where your head goes when you switch off for a second. Up here I can freewheel 'till my heart is content. Escape the job for a moment and focus on the more positive things. Positive things like my love life. A subject that is dear to my heart. My girlfriend!

Stop - let me say that again - slowly - my G-I-R-L-F-R-I-E-N-D. Wonderful. Sorry but I need to say it yet again. My Girlfriend and I. Sounds good. It is hard to fathom that a confirmed bachelor and a man on a ten year forced celibacy trip now has a female companion who seems happy to be referred to as his girlfriend. Hand holding, snuggling, smooching - even a little bit of fondling. To be honest I've not pushed things much further on that front. Patience is a virtue and after ten years I can wait a bit longer.

Not much longer though. I'm embarrassed to the core over the industrial scale masturbation I have embarked on as my preferred methodology to cool down after a night out with Tina. It is running out of control and has now become a matter of public record.

Maybe I should précis how this has come about with a little dose of mitigation.

I met up with Tina at lunch time a week ago. A highly unusual occurrence to be fair. Even though she works close by she is a home bird at lunchtime and prefers thirty minutes in her own home to an hour in the nearest Pret-a-Manger or munching at her desk. She phoned and asked the office manager on the fifth floor, an old friend of mine, to track me down. I called her back and we met up at the small park that backs on to my building. I had sandwiches and she bought a sub from Subway.

We ate and chatted our way through the lunch hour and at the end we kissed and for reasons known only to Tina she took the opportunity, just before we parted, to squeeze my balls. And with that she was off. Flustered I was left to return to work fully supporting the sort of erection that is nigh on impossible to hide. Half an hour later it was showing no signs of abating and I was struggling to get on with work.

Now common sense would have had me pick one of the hundred odd toilet cubicles that litter the building and relieve myself in secure isolation. Instead I chose a cleaning cupboard on the twenty eighth floor. To be fair it is a favourite haunt of mine if I want to grab forty winks mid shift and I have always thought it fairly safe.

What I didn't count on was the receptionist for Lader & Sons opening the cupboard door and finding me on my haunches, trousers round my ankles in full flow. I was surprised that she had a key to the cupboard. She was surprised at just about everything. She screamed and slammed the door shut and I fell back into the cleaning equipment behind me.

She ran to the reception and informed the first person she met. Unfortunately it turned out to be Mr Lader himself - a grizzled old man that made his fortune looking down his nose at people.

Realising all was not good I whipped up my trousers, grabbed a bucket, some Flash and a mop. Mr Lader flung open the door and I went into denial mode. Her word against mine. I had every right to be in the cupboard after all.

He asked why I had locked it. I didn't have a good answer.

He asked if this was something I did on a regular basis. I said yes. He meant masturbating. I meant getting equipment from the cupboard.

He called me a pervert. I took umbrage at this.

He threatened to report me. I threatened to call the union.

He asked why? I didn't have an answer to this.

I tried to leave.

He demanded an apology. I refused and we hit stalemate.

It's all got a little awkward since then. For a start the story spread like a virus throughout the building. I think I can cope with the sniggers, the pointing and the gossip. I'm not sure I can cope with the wisecracks.

'PULL the other one George.'
'Are you UP to it George?'
'George have you got time for a SWIFT ONE?'

'George something has come UP. Could you give me a HAND?'

To top it all the company that employs me is sending over an inspector to review my performance next week. There is not a cat in hell's chance that the inspector won't find out about the incident and when the story gets back to head office I'm dead meat.

The fire door opens and I step out, look around and freeze mid step.

That looks a lot like Charlie Wiggs being thrown off the top of my roof!

Why is someone throwing Charlie Wiggs off my roof?

Charlie Wiggs. Accountant. Cheedle, Baker and Nudge. Twentieth floor. Third office on the right. Always leaves his bin full of barely used Kleenex. Strange choice of person to throw off the roof I would have thought.

Why would someone throw Charlie Wiggs off the roof?

Chapter 5

The regrets of Simon.

I can't face it. I need someone to take a hammer and strike just above my neck - right at the base of my skull. A clean stroke. Out like a light I'll go. Deep, blissful, soothing, nothingness. Right now. Right fucking now. Please if there's any justice on this planet.

Three more aspirin. Make it four and I'll get on the road. How many is that today. Eight, nine. I've lost count. Too many? I don't think so. The last lot came up when I chucked up in the office. They won't count. I'll make it four. Four aspirin washed down with the dregs from a warm can of Coke. Foul!

God how did I get this bad and more importantly, much more importantly, what was I doing snogging Karen Lewis.

Man, but that will seriously come home to haunt me. What on earth was I thinking? Karen Lewis? Our HR Director. Of all the people to snog! What possessed me? I don't even fancy her. At least I don't think I do.

Something to do with a thong. That was it. She bet me that I couldn't squeeze into her thong without it snapping. Why would I do that? What kind of crazy bet is that? She is built like a stick insect. I have a waist that would do Moby Dick proud.

Did I really do it? God I'm struggling. Tell me I didn't? Please. Shit. I think I did. I'm sure it all happened in my office. Sometime late last night. At the office party.

She had her thong off in seconds and next thing I'm down to my y-fronts. Correction down to my bare BOLLOCKS!!! Down to my bare bollocks and trying to pull on a strip of dental floss. Then she came on to me. We snogged and...

...and I can't remember. But it sure doesn't feel like it stopped there. I woke up this morning, admittedly alone in my own bed, an empty feeling downstairs. I suspect that our snog was a bit more than a kiss. I can't cope. Not while I have a hangover of this scale. And then there was the camera. My camera. Her taking a picture of me trying on her thong just before things went black. The camera that I have just driven through hell to come in and get. The camera that now has no memory card in it. And that is down in the dirt bad news. I have no idea what is on that card. I doubt it will be good for my future.

I've known Karen for twenty plus years and she is a bitch of the first order. She needs to be in our business. Too many secrets. Too many opportunities for slip ups. When I want someone out of our business I want it now. No questions. When I want some gen on an employee it is Karen's job to dig up the crap.

She has two files on every employee. File A - the proper HR file. Reviews, personal details - the usual; and then there is File B or the X Files as I call them. The dirt on each employee. Their indiscretions - and they all have indiscretions. Who they are sleeping with, their drug habits, their other habits, their financial troubles and it doesn't stop there.

We've got knowledge on their families, their friends and some cases their friends' friends. We've used private detective agencies, local criminals, bribed people, threatened people - if you can name it we can probably own up to it. All to fill the X Files. For the X Files are my insurance. Do your job and you get a gold star in File A. Cause trouble and we dig out your X File.

Well you need to in our job. One loose mouth, one crying baby, one bleeding heart and we could be history. Fifteen years to life history if you get my drift. So there's no room to dick around.

Karen is my right hand woman, Robin my right hand man and I may have just had intercourse with the devil herself. I need to get out of here. Deal with this later.

I head for my car. It is parked down in the building's basement car park.

Concentrate. Engine on. Select drive. Crap. Select reverse. Pull it together. I suspect I'm going to chuck up again. If I do it will be an expensive vomit - this thing costs two hundred quid a pop to valet. Exit barrier. Ramp. Back lane and here comes last night's remains. Out the car, engine still running and my digestive system goes into reverse.

How bad must I look? Lying in the gutter of some back alley trying to throw up the lining of my stomach? If anyone sees me I can kiss my hard man image goodnight. What in the hell was I drinking last night?

I remember the wine - a nice bottle or two of Cote Rotie la Mouline 2004 Guigal, one fifty a pop. Then onto a bottle of Dalmore 18 year old. Then I think it went down hill.

Grey Goose vodka, Ron Coba 12 year old rum, Cascade Mountain gin. I remember a couple of bottles of Harviestoun's Ola Dubh and you have the makings of a stunning hangover.

Well at least it was all done in the best possible taste.

Can you be done for drunk in charge of car when you're not actually in the car? I don't give a crap at the moment. All I want to do is curl up and wish the fucking pain away. I think I'll flip on my back. Seems like a good idea. Can't think I'm going to choke on my own puke. I'm retched out.

I can see the sky framed between the buildings and smell the exhaust from my car. If I close my eyes the pain seems to lessen for a second or two. I'll keep them closed. Anything to numb the agony.

Karen and me. I am in so much shit from so many directions. Shall I name them? Let's start with my fiancée, Susan. She isn't going to be enamoured when she finds out. And she WILL find out. Next on the list of trouble. My sister. If Susan finds out then my sister will find out and then she will phone my mother. Carolyn's been crying out for a chance to get one over on me for years. The successful son. Mum's favourite.

Then there's Craig; Karen's husband. That will be a tricky one. Ex SAS. Bodyguard. Keep fit freak.

Oh and I think he has a black belt in something. Keep going.

Robin my best friend, our Financial Director and, unfortunately Karen's younger brother. Oh this is so sweet. Of all the things I could have done on this planet to screw my life up I would be hard pressed to come up with a better course of action than get into bed with Karen. Hard to think that things can go south from here.

'Excuse me sir.'

Wrong. I open my eyes and look up. Policeman.

'Morning officer.'

What the hell is that up there? Above the policeman. Hanging out over the edge of the building. Is that a person?

'Eh officer…'

Chapter 6

Charlie's flight is cut short.

For your information I no longer retain any physical connection between the building and my person. I have a mental connection but that doesn't count for much. As it's been said in so many ways 'Elvis has truly left the building'.

Flailing does not look like it has overcome gravity and, much as I might have hoped that I was to be the exception, it looks like Newton was right. A short downward trajectory followed by a somewhat ungainly landing is the sum total of my future.

I've never really contemplated this moment in my life. The end I mean. Sure I've talked about it, usually while drunk or in a state of serious depression, but not really thought about. You don't, do you? At least I don't. I kind of work on the life eternal thing. I'm now in my mid fifties and everyday I see or hear of plenty of people in their eighties and nineties. Knock off the first ten years of my life as little more than a dozen good childhood memories and I could have more good years in front than behind.

Makes sense to me.

At least it did until ten minutes ago. Now that my end seems so much closer I should probably be giving some thought to the hereafter or my loved ones or cherished moments in life or some such thing. Yet all I can do is dance around the 'thievin' prick' thing. No flash of my life in front of my eyes. No religious conversion on the brink of death. No regrets that rush forth to be announced. Nothing but a nagging desire to know why the hell I am being asked to join the bungee-less jump club.

It could be a case of mistaken identity. Maybe they have the wrong man. Gorilla number one and two hardly undertook a formal introduction. For all I know I'm not the man they are supposed to be teaching to fly. After all I wasn't sitting at my desk when they found me. A desk with my name emblazoned on the office door. Well not exactly emblazoned. Third name down on the brass plaque. Three points smaller than the top two names and point size means status in Cheedle, Baker and Nudge. So how did they know I am me? I could have been anyone having a pee.

Does it really matter? Even if I am the wrong person, is this the time to be thinking about such things? Hell even if I am the right person and had been caught bang to right with my fingers in some guy's till - does it matter? Would it not make a bit more sense for me to use these last few seconds a bit more constructively?

Pathetic. I mean I am truly pathetic.

This is the script to my life. I can write you a rock solid guarantee that, throughout my life and at any given time on this planet, whatever it is was that I was supposed to be doing was exactly the opposite of what would have been good for me. Study at school? - no - bunk off. Kiss Cybil McLean? - no - run away crying. Go to university? - no - go to a dead end college. Pass my exams? - no - fail my exams. Propose to the one person I have truly loved? - no - drive her away into the arms of another. Choose the right job? - no choose a dead end job. Ask for a pay rise? - no - accept a pay cut. Go to the pub? - no - go home to feed the dog. Go to football? - no - go to Ikea. You get the drift.

In my world if I was really destined to be jumping off a building then I would actually be standing on the pavement below wondering why I wasn't jumping off the building. It's the Charlie Wiggs way of life.

So for once in your life Charlie do the right thing!

So what is the right thing? Pray? Cry? Plead? Scream? Prepare? Pass out? Whistle the national anthem? I have no idea.

I see gorilla number one has taken a step towards me. To get a better view no doubt. It's not often you see someone head-butt concrete from forty stories up. Can't think what the mess is going to be like. Not good I suppose. Not the sort of job the council cleaners will be fighting over. But someone will have to do it. Either that or they will have to cone me off and let the local wildlife do a number on me. Probably the ecological way but not very PC.

Then again cleaning up dead people from the pavement, especially ones mashed and trashed by a big fall, must use some fairly serious chemicals if you want to get all the stains out. Serious chemicals that lack an environmentally friendly bent and if there is one thing you can say about the local council it is their impeccable drive towards an environmentally friendly future.

So my guess is a bin bag - biodegradable or recyclable of course, a scrubbing brush and some warm water and I'll be history. Such will be the sad ending that bears the title Charlie Wiggs.

Interesting how gorilla number one seems to want such a close view of events and gorilla number two seems content to film things from a distance. There will be a good deep seated psychological reason for this but the psyche of killers was never a strong interest of mine so I'll let it go at that.

Gorilla number one is ever so close. With a little effort I could almost touch him. Almost being the operative word in this case.

I look at him and then up into the sky as I twist in the air. High above me a contrail from a US bound jetliner scores a crystal clear sky. The view from the plane's windows must be stunning. I cock my head slightly and trace the dissipating trail as the jet stream grabs it and begins to whip it into nothing. I cock my head a little further and the trail peters out as if it was never there. Soon there will be no evidence of the passing of the plane. Three hundred people will have slipped by at a fraction below the speed of sound, wrapped in a metal tube flying higher than Mt Everest. It's so every day we don't even notice any more.

I feel myself gently turn and the sky vanishes as I begin to tumble towards earth. I see the lane below and I close my eyes.

The sharp change in direction doesn't register for the briefest of moments and then my arc changes and I am accelerating back towards the building. I feel someone grabbing at my leg and then I slam, upside down and head first, into the building and a dark world opens up.

Silence.

Chapter 7

The thoughts of a second gorilla.

'What the fuck are you doing?' I shout.

Bally has just grabbed the vic out of mid air. As cool as you like he has just leapt forward and snatched his left leg. What for? Good riddance to bad rubbish is my motto. Hello to a grand. I need the money. I don't need the grief. Doesn't Bally realise that we will get a right kicking if Mr Accountant doesn't end up with a short service in the local crematorium sometime soon. I don't want no kicking. I don't need no kicking. It's sore. Bloody sore. Like when I screwed up and duffed up the wrong jockey on the day of the big race last year. I got a real kicking for that one.

Shit but they all looked the same. Four feet nothing. Shiny clothes and the smell of horses. Not my fault. I asked the vic if he was the jockey for the favourite in the two thirty and he said yes. So I hit him. Four thirty not two thirty. I should have said four thirty. Turns out I beat the crap out of the country's leading steeplechaser. I don't even know what a steeplechaser is. I mean what the fuck have church steeples to do with horse racing.

Cost my employer fifty grand so I was told. Cost me three weeks in the ICU unit. They didn't even send flowers. I ain't going back to ICU. So what the hell is Bally up to?

'Easy job big man,' said Bally. 'Pick up a vic in the city. Do a Mikey and away before the police appear. A thousand quid for a thirty minute job.'

It was supposed to be that easy. And now he's rescuing him.

ICU. ICU. Hang on. ICU. That's not what Bally said would happen to us if we screwed up. He told me 'the Voice' promised something else.

Hang on I'll remember. I find it hard to remember things at times. If you just give me a second it will come back. It always does. I'm good at remembering things - given time.

Look I can prove it I'll name every player in the nineteen sixty seven European Cup winning Celtic side.

There was Simpson, Craig, Gemmell, Murdoch, McNeil, Clark, Johnstone, Wallace, Chalmers, Auld and... and... and shit. And. I know. I do. And I know I know. I'm good at remembering I am.

Estádio Nacional, Lisbon, Portugal, May 25th, 1967. First northern European team to win the European Cup. Come on I know this I do. Simpson, Craig, Gemmell, Murdoch, McNeil, Clark, Johnstone, Wallace, Chalmers, Auld and, and...

'Bally who played outside left for Celtic in the 1967 European Cup Final?'

No answer. I think Bally might be concentrating on keeping the vic from falling. Bally is good at concentrating. He says I'm not. He says I can't keep my mind on one thing long enough for toffee. Attention span of a goldfish. Bally tells me that.

I don't like to tell him that I don't know what an attention span is. I don't understand a lot of what

37

Bally tells me but I like him. He looks after me. He's a friend.

We went to the same school. At least we did until I got kicked out for setting fire to the headmaster's car. What a fuss over a battered old Morris Minor and how was I to know his stupid dog was sleeping in the back seat. It's cruel to keep a dog in the car when it's that hot. Anyone knows that and I was only getting my own back on the headmaster after he grassed me up to my mum about my drinking at the school dance.

There wasn't no need to tell mum. She got proper mad. Not about the drink. She didn't give a crap about the drink. What narked her was where I had got the money for the drink and why it was ok to spend it on me and not give it to her. Mum wasn't big on money sitting with anyone but her. My dad was scared of her. *'A busted pay packet will kill you son,'* he used to say. As far as I know he never brought home a busted pay packet.

I can see that holding the vic from falling is hurting Bally. He's as a strong as an ox but it ain't easy holding on to a man by the leg like that. He won't last long.

'Jim give me a hand,' he shouts at me.

Coffin. That was it. Coffin. Not ICU. 'the Voice' said if we screwed up we would end up in a coffin. See, told you I was good at remembering things. If I just put my mind to it I'm good at remembering things.

'Coffin,' I shout.

Bally is really struggling. I tried to hold a man like that once. Well not quite the same. I once had a man by the collar and dangled him out of the third floor of my gran's tenement. He'd been noising up my wee sister and nobody does that. So I dragged him up to my gran's house and hung him out the window. It really hurt. I couldn't do shit with my left arm for weeks. It didn't help that my gran was beating seven bells out of me with her walking stick at the time. Hard to hold a man and take a beating at the same time. No I don't envy Bally one bit.

Hard to hold a man like that.

Now if I could only remember the name from the Celtic European Cup winning team of 1967. Simpson, Craig, Gemmell, Murdoch, McNeil, Clark, Johnstone, Wallace, Chalmers, Auld and who?

Chapter 8

George gets involved.

Thoughts of Innellan are blown away. What are you supposed to do when you see someone being thrown off a high rise building? Phone the police? Nice idea but it kind of lacks the sort of direct intervention that is required.

I could rush over and try and grab the poor soul but there is forty yards of rooftop between me and the incident. There's no way I can make it before Charlie is long gone.

I could shout and that might distract the two guys in suits but Charlie will still head for the pavement.

I don't recognise the two men. One of them seems to be filming the whole thing with a mobile phone. Frightening. Well we all need to get our kicks somehow.

I decide on the police and reach for my mobile just as the smaller of the two men reaches out and grabs Charlie by the leg. He is trying to rescue him. I rush forward to give a hand. Maybe I have read this wrong. Maybe they are saving Charlie from himself.

The tall one is shouting something but I can't hear what as I am too far away. I run, head down and feel the bitumen roof getting tacky under my feet as the heat of the day kicks in.

The short one looks like he is asking the tall one for help. The tall one is saying something in reply but doesn't make a move to give a hand.

I rush past the tall one and get side by side with the shorter one and grab onto Charlie's other leg. I can see the look of surprise on the short man's face when I arrive but I don't have time for introductions.

Between us we put in some muscle and haul Charlie up and over the small retaining wall and drop him onto the roof. We are both panting and for a second or two neither of us has the energy to do anything but suck air. I slump to the roof with my back against the wall and try and take in what is happening around me. The tall one is open mouthed and if you ask me has the sort of eyes that suggest his picnic basket is missing a few Marks and Spencer's pre packs. He is putting his phone away but seems in two minds as to what to do next.

Next to me the short man is bent double and still heaving in air. He is also rubbing the bicep on his right arm and glances at me before looking over at his tall friend and then returns to massaging his arm.

Charlie is sprawled between us. His eyes are closed and dribble is running from the corner of his mouth. His head is bleeding and I notice stains around his crotch. His fly is open and there is a suggestion that his manhood is not as securely tucked away as it should be. I look away.

Above me the end of a plane's contrail provides a distraction as I take a deep breath before trying to stand up. The short man moves with a speed that belies his bulk. He leaps straight over Charlie and slams me back on to the roof - pinning me to the wall by my arms. His face is a few inches from mine and his fragrant mix of mouthwash and after shave hangs in the air before he lets go of my left arm and grabs my hair, pulling my head towards him.

I'm eyeball to eyeball. He has deep green eyes, not unintelligent but a little world weary. The stubble on his face is more designer than lazy and the crispness of the shirt collar and sheen on the tie suggest a not inexpensive attention to style.

He cocks his head to one side and after a second of studying me he looks round in search of his mate. I don't move. I'm not sure what's going on. He rolls off me and stands up and I stay seated. He walks over to the tall one and they begin chatting in a low whisper.

I flick my eyes back to Charlie. The pool of dribble is growing. I put one hand on the roof and start to stand up again. The short one spots the movement and is back on me like a shot. No words - just action. I slump back against the wall and he lets me go again. I get the idea and resign myself to waiting.

I look back at Charlie and the drool now has a red tinge. Blood.

'Excuse me.'

The short one looks round at me and walks over. He looks down, leans a little closer and slaps me across the face. Hard.

'Shut it.'

My cheek stings.

'But Charlie's got blood coming out of his mouth,' I say.

The short one looks at me with a quizzical squint.

'Who the fuck is Charlie?'

I look back at him - my own version of quizzical washing across my face.

'Charlie Wiggs. You know the guy we just hauled from certain death?'

The short one kicks me in the thigh and returns to the tall one.

Charlie's drool is getting redder.

Chapter 9

A gorilla realises his mistake.

I look at Jim and then back at the pair next to the wall. Charlie Wiggs? Who the hell is Charlie Wiggs? Jim looks confused but then again Jim always looks confused. It's what he does for a living.

Think back - the vic's name is Leonard Thwaite. Mid fifties, married with three kids, balding, beer gut - works as an accountant on the twentieth floor of Tyler Tower for Cheedle, Baker and Nudge. 'the Voice's' description was quite graphic.

'Gormless fucker, looks like a pervert.'

Lives in the third office on the right as you pass by reception - only he wasn't there. One of the other guys on the corridor thought he had gone for a slash so we had gone hunting and lifted him at the pisser.

I tilt my head slightly to get a better look at the prone body. He is a dead ringer for a gormless fucker. Balding, mid fifties - what's not to be Leonard?

I walk back over to the stranger that just helped me save Leonard/Charlie.

'Who the fuck are you?'

He tells me his name is George and he's the maintenance man for the building.

'And this isn't Leonard Thwaite?'

He shakes his head and tells me again it's a guy called Charlie Wiggs. Shares an office with

44

Leonard. He even tells me that they look a little like each other. Bingo. I walk back over to Jim.

'Fuck up time, Jim.'

I explain that we've lifted the wrong man. Jim starts talking about coffins - I tell him to shut it. I need to think.

Jim asks why I rescued the vic. I want to tell him it was because I was going to interrogate the vic to find out if Jim knew something I didn't - but I leave it for later.

Jim suggests doing a Mikey on both of them and then finding Leonard.

'Aye. Right!' says I in return and when the police turn up to investigate two dead bodies in the lane they won't figure to ask around just as we are trying to abduct Leonard. How easy will that make our job? This is a prime time, gold plated, diamond encrusted fuck up. Jim opens his mouth. Here comes another pearl of wisdom.

'Lennox. Bobby Lennox.'

I have no idea what he is on about. He has left this world.

'I knew I'd remember. Bobby Lennox. Simpson, Craig, Gemmell, Murdoch, McNeil, Clark, Johnstone, Wallace, Chalmers, Auld AND Lennox.'

I know Jim is cheap to hire but you don't need this kind of shit when things are heading for the back door in such an obvious fashion. I need to sort this out.

Three things to do.

Point One - deal with the maintenance man and Charlie Wiggs.

Point Two - find Leonard and give him the bad news.

Point Three - find out what Jim meant by 'thievin' prick'.

Intuitive improvisation. I try to live by the phrase. I got the idea from 'View to a Kill.' It's what Max Zorrin, the megalomaniac, tells James Bond is the secret to genius and it's what I need to demonstrate right now.

I tell Jim to go find some rope and be quick about it. I bend down to look at Charlie Wiggs and things are looking poor. There is now a large pool of blood around his mouth, his breathing is shallow and the blood from his head is matting what little hair he has.

I turn to the maintenance man.

'Do you know anything about first aid?'

The maintenance man shakes his head so I kick him. Charlie is almost lying in the recovery position anyway so I pull his left arm from under him and use it to support his upper body. That seems to accelerate the blood flow. I order the maintenance man to lie face down next to Charlie.

Where the hell is Jim?

The door to the roof opens and Jim walks out trailing a jumble of plastic coated wires. The wires are covered in dust and interspersed with connectors and switches.

Jim tells me he couldn't find rope but they are re-wiring the floor below so he ripped out as much wire from the wall as he could. I can't decide if this is clever or stupid.

I tell Jim to bind the maintenance man and Charlie by their wrists. Hands behind their backs. Probably not the best thing for Charlie but I need to get control of this whole thing quickly.

Once they are both tied up, I drag the maintenance man to his feet. The bindings are tight but messy. We don't have any decent knives to cut free the spare cable so the maintenance man is trailing a tail of wire a couple of yards long.

'Tell me somewhere safe I can put you for an hour or two?'

I have to slap him twice before he opens up. He tells me there is a cupboard three flights of stairs down. The keys are on the ring hanging from his belt. I tell Jim to take the maintenance man down to the cupboard lock him in and then come straight back. As they both walk away I'm hoping Jim won't fuck this up.

Once they are gone I turn to Charlie. I need to put him out of sight and give me as much breathing space as possible in case someone gets nosey.

Charlie coughs up some blood and I know he is not doing well but I can't afford the time to do anything else but dump him. I want to question Charlie but he is in no fit state and I need the time to bag Leonard and scarper.

I look round. A row of air conditioning units run out to the far side of the building. Beyond them there is a depression in the roof. I grab Charlie by the armpits and haul him past the AC units and towards the dip. It's hard work. Even on a good day it takes muscle to drag a man anywhere. This guy is sixteen stone of dead weight but he feels twice that.

My right arm is bitching after holding onto him as he swung out over the lane and I am sweating like a horse on the last furlong. I keep looking back to the door hoping Jim will re-emerge and give me a hand.

Far below I hear the whoop of a police siren. I freeze. One whoop and one whoop only. The way they do when a police car is coming to a halt. I drop Charlie and head back to the wall and lean over to look down into the lane.

It's too far to see to the bottom with any clarity but there is a car down there, but not a police car, and two figures next to it. One looks like he is lying down. An accident? I scan the lane and at the far end a police car appears and winds its way slowly towards the two figures. As I watch the police car stops and a policeman gets out and looks up. I duck back out of sight.

I hear the crackle of a police radio below. It's too far away to hear words but you can't mistake the noise.

I hope they are dealing with the car in the lane and haven't been called in by someone in one of the other buildings that happened to see Charlie take his short flight. The policeman looked up. Not unusual. Not unusual unless you've been told that someone is throwing bodies from the top floor.

I return to Charlie and pick him up again. The last of the AC units grinds past and I drop Charlie into the depression. There are no doors near by and no buildings overlooking. Unless you walked right up to him Charlie is all but invisible. He is still dribbling blood and there is a trail leading from the edge of the roof to where he lies but there is nothing I can do about that.

The roof door opens and Jim appears. He waves and I head over. I ask if the maintenance man is locked away and he nods. He starts talking about coffins again and I ignore him and move on to point two - Leonard.

I make a note to get to point three soon.

Chapter 10

Tina phones the police.

It takes me a few seconds to take in the enormity of what I am seeing. There was a man jumping from the roof or was he being thrown from the roof? I can't tell. Then I see a pair of hands appear and grab one of the man's legs and then a split second later another pair of hands appear and grasp the other leg. For an instant I see the faces of the men as they desperately try to pull the falling man back in but at this distance it is hard to make out detail. I stare harder and feel my heart skip a beat. I recognise the second helper. I'm a good ten storeys below but I think that... No it can't be. I try and squint to compensate for my short sightedness. I need new glasses but can't afford to even take the eye test at the moment. Cigarettes are a costly way to die.

I yelp.

George. That's George up there. I watch as George and a stranger pull the falling man back onto the roof. What in heaven's name is George doing? Then I remember - of course he's the maintenance man for the building. He must have seen the man in trouble and rushed to help. So like my boyfriend. A kind soul. He has taken our whole relationship a step at a time. No pressure. No rush to bed. Nice guy. Although a bit of rush now and again might be nicer. And now here he is acting the hero. My George.

I can't see what is happening now. All the figures have vanished behind the retaining wall. I walk back as far as I can on the roof and jump up and down but the retaining wall on the other building still blocks my view. I reach for my mobile, hitting the short dial key for George's mobile. It trips to answer machine and then I remember that the firm George works for doesn't allow personal mobiles at work. I look up his work number and punch it. It too diverts to answer machine.

I return my attention to the other building and I think I see some more movement but then it's gone. Should I phone someone? I can't think why I need to. If George is there he will have things under control. But that's not true. George isn't good at these things. He means well but there is a big difference between meaning well and doing well.

For a few moments there is no movement above and then I see George again. Someone is helping him up. It looks like George has his hands behind his back and then he is pushed out of sight. Not guided out of sight, or helped out of sight but PUSHED out of sight. My eyes might be crap but that didn't look like a friendly push. I haven't a blind clue what is going on up there but I'm sure that was a push and not a good push. Not a good push at all.

I should phone the police - after all I saw a man dangling forty floors up in the air. Even if the man is now safe I should report it and then I can tell them about George and the push.

I hit 999 on the mobile. I ask for police when the operator answers. The operator transfers me but stays on the line to repeat my mobile number to the police.

I try and stay calm and explain in simple terms what I've seen but it takes a while. I get George mixed up with the falling man and at one point they think my boyfriend was trying to jump. I correct them and once they have the address and the exact location they tell me they will send someone to investigate and to stay where I am.

It doesn't seem two minutes before I hear a police siren and when I look down into the lane I see a police car crawling along. A little further along the lane there is another policeman bent over a figure on the ground next to a car that is gently pouring exhaust fumes into the atmosphere.

I watch as the police car stops and a policeman gets out. He looks up. I follow his gaze and I catch a glimpse of someone disappearing behind the retaining wall above me. I look back down and wave one hand at the policeman while pointing the other hand to the opposite roof. He has turned his attention to the man in the lane.

What the hell is he doing down there. He needs to be up here. Or better still on top of the other roof. I shout but it is a long way down and my lungs were never the best and twenty a day hasn't helped. I want to scream *'Hey shit-head - forget him, go do your job.'*

The two policemen meet up and look down at the man on the ground.

For God's sake get a move on. Just get a move on.

I make a decision. I'm going to see what is going on up on George's roof. Police instruction or not, I'm not waiting while they pass the time of day with some guy in a lane. I walk then half run back to my floor and grab my coat. I make an excuse about needing to go to the chemist and I'm off.

Chapter 11

Simon gets a lucky break.

'OK sir let's start at the beginning.'

'But officer…'

There was something going on above me but then it's gone. I'm sure I saw a man up there. But in my state it could have been anything. The policeman is starting to ask a series of questions. I can see this leading to the tricky issue of me, the car and alcohol. I'm on a loser here. One breath test and I'll turn the little crystals a shade of green usually reserved for cow fields Then it's back to the station, Q & A, blood test, banged up and then charged. Day in court and goodbye license. Shit.

I try the *'It ain't drink but the flu routine.'* I claim I've not been well. I had to come into work. I got caught short on the way out. Needed to vomit. Nice try but the smell of booze is a bit of a living thing around me.

Second shot. The booze smell - now noted by the officer - was here when I chucked up. Someone else must have thrown up here last night. I had chosen, against all the odds, to vomit in exactly the same spot. Incredible but hard to disprove. The officer's stance suggests that I'm not really treading virgin territory with my excuses.

Ok - third angle. I wasn't driving. When I needed to chuck up the man behind the wheel had nipped back in to the office and left me. He will be back shortly. The policeman smiles. I know I'm lost.

The radio on the officer's tunic crackles. A message is fed into his ear piece. He looks up and a police car crawls into view with a whoop of its siren. Moments later there are two policemen above me. My hope rises. They don't seem to be that interested in me. Something about someone falling from the roof. The name George is mentioned.

George? George our maintenance man? George the maintenance has fallen off the roof. Tragic. I'm so sorry. I'm sure you need to investigate. Can I go now? Brilliant.

I listen. Fuck, it seems no-one has actually fallen. Just a report that someone saw someone hanging from the roof. Not George though. Someone else. The first officer looks down at me.

'Put the car back in the garage and go home. I need to attend to this other matter.'

One nil. Final minute of extra time. Back of the net. Last gasp. I'm off the hook. Y'dancer.

I ignore the hangover and take the advice at speed. I jump into the car and reverse it back into the garage. I clip one of the concrete posts on the way in. I don't care. I see the two policemen follow me in the garage. I start to panic again. Stay calm. They are looking for the door that leads to the lifts. I feel magnanimous and decide to show them the way.

Chapter 12

The penny drops with Simon.

Mistake. It was a mistake to ride up in the lift with the policemen. The smell of booze is amplified in the small space. I may just be giving them a reason to re-appraise my early release from their custody. I try and hold my breath. This doesn't mute the stink from my clothes or my skin, my shoes, my... come on lift get a move on.

The first policeman turns to the other. He holds his nose in his best Buster Keaton style. I smile weakly. The second policeman listens to something on the radio. He crinkles his nose in sympathy.

The lift slides to a halt at my floor. I pour out with relief. The door closes and I hear the words 'Thrown not jumped.' I freeze. No context to the words. Except.

My blood temperature drops twenty degrees.

'Thrown not jumped.'

Breath catches in my throat. I stare at the floor. My headache gone. Thoughts zip round my head like a fly on steroids. No they couldn't be that stupid. No-one could. Not from the roof of our own office. That wasn't the deal. That wasn't the fucking deal.

I run to my office. I rifle through my desk and grab a key. I pull back a panel in the wall. I reveal a small wall safe. I insert the key in the lock. All the time I'm thinking no-one could be that dumb. No-one.

I open the safe door. I pull out one of the 'Pay As You Go' mobile phones lying there and power it up. It takes a few seconds to get going. The provider flashes up on the screen. I pull out my wallet and remove a battered business card. Scribbled across the face is a mobile number.

I should really phone 'the Voice'. This call was supposed to happen only in emergencies. This is an emergency. I dial the number. I wait for the connection. All the time I am praying that no-one could be that dumb. I mean who would….

The phone rings in my ear. After five rings the recipient picks up.

'Tell me you didn't throw our friend off the roof of this fucking building,' I shout.

The voice at the other end hesitates. I hold my breath. Then he talks. He assures me that he has done no such thing. Air rushes from my lungs. I fall into my seat. He tells me not to phone this number again. I hang up.

I fiddle with the phone for a second before deleting the outgoing call from the record. I remove the battery and pull out the sim card. I place it on the floor and grind it with my heel. I root in my drawer and pull out a cloth. A little more rooting and a roll of plastic sandwich bags joins the cloth on my desk. I wipe the phone and battery clean. I drop them along with the battered sim card into three separate bags. I'll dump them on the way home.

My headache returns. I welcome it. For a moment I thought the man falling from the roof was Leonard Thwaite. From our roof. From the same bloody roof that the two policemen are now heading for. I am shaking. Not with fear. With anger. I reach into another drawer and pop four more headache killers. I lean back hoping the pills work fast.

I fall asleep and I'm woken by a knocking on my door. The tablets have kicked in. I open my eyes to see someone standing in the door frame.

It's Leonard Thwaite. I'm slightly flustered and re-assured at the same time. Here is living proof that Dumb and Dumber didn't throw Leonard from the roof.

'Didn't think you would be in today. Not after last night,' he says.

Leonard had been at the party last night. He left early. He is nothing if not a party pooper. That and a fucking thief.

I say hello and ask what he wants. He looks at me with a cockeyed leer. He tells me that he needs to run over a few things. I tell him to go take a running jump. He shakes his head and walks into my office. He closes the door behind him. He has an envelope in his hand. He tells me he was going to leave it for me to read. I smile. He hands it to me. I drop it on the desk.

I ask him what the hell he is on about?

He slumps into the chair opposite mine. He places his feet up on my desk. I throw him a look that says 'get your feet back on the fucking floor.' He ignores it. Leonard is forgetting his place. I stand up to swipe his feet from the desk. The hangover still has some force and I drop back to the chair. I let rip with a mouthful instead. The normally timid Leonard doesn't flinch. He puts his feet back on the desk.

A little disconcerting I must admit. I spit out a few more choice words. Leonard looks like he is on brave pills - he smiles. I tell him to get to the point. He smiles again. I tell him that I am going to come round and play squash with his balls. His smile wavers. He nods at the envelope. I pick it up. It has my name and P&C written on it. He's an arse. In this office P&C is equivalent to CC All. I tear the envelope open. There is a single typed sheet of paper inside. I pull it out and begin reading.

Dear Simon

Having been your accountant for some ten years now I am sensitive to your moods and I have noted a slight change in your attitude of late. As such I'm fairly sure that you have discovered the small discrepancy between the money in two of your bank accounts and what you would expect to find there.

I look up at him. His feet are waving nervously. Small. Yeah if you can call two hundred thousand small. I return to the letter.

If you haven't discovered this yet then consider this letter a pre-emptive strike.
I'm fairly sure that you are not going to take too kindly to such accounting discrepancies and as such I have put a little insurance in place should you decide to pursue matters in an inappropriate manner.

Inappropriate. What like a knife in your fucking gut?

As of last week I have sent several electronic copies of accounts concerning certain of your business transactions to some key strategic locations.

I look up again. He has stopped smiling. But his feet are still on the desk.

All the accounts are strictly protected by a password. If the individuals are not given the correct password when contacted, the accounts will be sent directly to the authorities. If I die or vanish, the strategic locations have instructions to release the accounts to the authorities within forty eight hours.

I have also taken the liberty of confiding in a work colleague who has placed a hard copy set of the same accounts in a place of his own choosing.

I have no intention of facilitating the release of the accounts if we can both act in a reasonable manner. After all as your accountant I will not be without blame and the thought of prison terrifies me. Equally I do not want to die and if you take a sensible approach to this little issue we can both live long and healthy lives.

Regards

Leonard

P.S. I hereby tender my resignation as your accountant.

I finish reading. My brain is in a flat spin. Leonard's smile returns as he drops his feet from the desk. He stands up. He turns and walks out of the office.

I pick up the letter and re-read it several times. I shake my head. I never thought he had it in him.

Leonard has been our accountant for ten years. He knows we have some dodgy business practices. But he is paid well. Paid very well. A little extra compensatory payment on top of the official Cheedle, Baker and Nudge fees. For this he is expected to turn a blind eye at key moments.

Two days ago I discovered that he had been dipping his fingers in the till. Sod it, he had been dipping his hands and both bloody arms in the till. Hence the contract killing that Dumb and Dumber were working on. Now things were a bit more complex.

Leonard is a clever swine. Over the years, in an Enron inspired move he has created a number of so called tax efficient vehicles to wash our cash through. Trouble was that with each rinse cycle a little leaked out into his pockets. As far as I can work out he is more than two hundred thousand to the good. And now the gormless fucker has set up some Machiavellian scheme. A scheme to protect his fat backside.

I read the letter again and then once more for luck. I push my chair away from my desk and lean back. I stretch my legs out in front of me. I reach

61

into my trouser pocket. I pull out a cardboard tube and rob it of two pills. I pop them. Indigestion killers this time. This needs thought.

This needs serious thought.

Chapter 13

The gorillas go ape.

I pull open the fire door and then Jim is through in front of me. Time is of the essence. The maintenance man is unlikely to stay quiet for long and someone will find him when he starts banging around. He might not know what is going on but he has seen us and he knows we got the wrong man. He even knows the name of the right man.

And then there is the impostor on the roof. If he comes round he might struggle to the door and get help or someone might stumble onto him or he might croak. The latter is a real bad news story. But there is fuck all I can do about any of that. Let's keep it simple. Find Leonard. Deal with him and get the hell out of here.

We drop three flights of stairs, passing the cupboard that holds the maintenance man. Thankfully there is no noise coming from behind the door yet. We exit the stairwell and head for the lifts and I press the call button.

The lifts have indicators above telling you what floor they are servicing. The one on the far left is on floor thirty two and rising, the other two are much lower down - so we walk over and wait in front of the due lift.

I look round at Jim who is humming a dirge and tapping the index finger of his right hand against the palm of his left. The lack of concern on his face goes some way to explaining why he can be useful on jobs like this. He is the original Mr 'Point and Shoot'. He also exhibits little or no regret at events. He can happily beat the crap out of someone - regardless of age or sex and once done walk away with an air of total indifference. I've been told that he is slightly psychotic and this may be so but I also think he was too far down the queue when the brain cells were being divvied up and this has more to do with the way he acts than being psychotic.

The lift has one floor to go and I step forward anticipating the doors opening. They slide apart and I start in and stop as two policemen exit. They look at me and Jim. I smile at them like a recent escapee from a mental institution. Jim says hello.

There is a moment when they stand in our way, blocking entry to the lift. They look at us. Jim nervous, me entering panic.

Common sense calms my panic. This is an office. We are both wearing business suits. Good quality business suits. Why shouldn't we be waiting on a lift in an office block? The police can't know what has happened. Can they?

There was no one else on the roof but did someone spot us from another building? Unlikely - the building we are in tops out anything else nearby by ten floors.

The smaller of the two policemen steps back to prevent the lift door closing and then they are asking questions. *'Have we seen anything suspicious?' 'No'. 'Have we been up on the roof?' 'No'. 'Do we work here?' 'Yes'. 'Where?' 'Cheedle, Baker and Nudge.' 'What floor?' 'Twentieth'. 'What are you doing up here?' 'Seeing a client'. 'Who?' 'Matman and Sons'.* I point to an office door with a brass plaque on it.

They pause for a second and then stand aside to let us in the lift. The first policeman watches as I press for the twentieth floor and the doors close. Jim farts. He often does that when he is uptight.

How long before they find the impostor? Five minutes maybe longer if they don't cover the whole roof straight away. We need to get out of here. Leonard will have to wait. I press the ground floor button and do what everybody else in a lift does and watch the numbers drop. Jim does what Jim does and starts to hum his dirge and tap out the rhythm on his palm. At the twenty fifth floor the lift stops and the door opens to let someone in.

My jaw drops as I stare at a man who can only be described as a 'gormless fucker who looks like a pervert' walks in. He glances at us and then seeing the twentieth floor button is lit looks back at us.

Leonard Thwaite, delivered on a plate.

I can see he is trying to figure out why we are heading for his floor. Given the whole floor is given over to Cheedle, Baker and Nudge he is trying to figure out who we are.

The twenty third floor flicks past and I make a decision. I lean over and tap Jim on the elbow and nod my head towards Leonard. Jim screws his face in confusion. I haven't time to explain as the doors will be open in a second.

Twenty second floor.

I step behind Leonard and remove a knife from my inside pocket and jab it into his side. He jerks to

65

one side and with practised ease I pin his arm and pull him towards me.

'One move, one sound and I skewer your liver.'

His mouth begins to open and shut at speed.

Twenty first floor.

'Jim stand over here and help me keep him still.'

Jim is still five seconds behind the action but he dutifully obeys as the lift opens on the twentieth floor.

Someone gets in.

'Hi Leonard,' the stranger says.

Leonard says nothing and I see the confusion in the stranger's gaze.

'Leonard, don't be so rude,' I say.

Leonard turns to look at me and I give the knife a dig. I think I draw some blood and it does the trick. Leonard greets the stranger. The lift heads for the ground floor. Too slow for my liking. The police must be on the roof by now. As soon as they find the impostor they will put two and two together and we are still in the building.

The eighteenth floor.

I adjust the knife a little and try and place Jim between Leonard, me and the stranger. Leonard moves and I dig the knife in a little more and he squeals. Too much. The stranger looks round.

'Everything ok, Leonard?'

I twist the knife and Leonard nods his head and says yes. The stranger is suspicious.

'Who are your friends?'

Jim sees the danger and acts like a whippet after a rabbit. He delivers a haymaker to the stranger's head. The stranger wobbles but doesn't go down.

Knocking someone out with a single punch is a lot harder than the movies make it look. Jim throws a second punch and the stranger staggers into the lift wall. Jim's third fist finds fresh air. Thrown off balance by the air shot Jim topples into me and I'm pushed away from Leonard. Leonard swings round and I see the intention in his eyes - I have no choice but to go in hard.

Twelfth floor.

The stranger, reeling from the unexpected punches, still doesn't seem to know that he needs to defend himself and Jim regains his balance and this time his fist connects with the stranger's stomach. I hear the air wheeze out from the stranger's lungs at the same time as I lunge at Leonard.

I hold my knife hand out to one side and use my free hand to try and land a punch. Leonard leaps to one side. The wrong side. There is nothing I can do to stop my forward momentum and Leonard's eyes widen as the blade enters his guts. He looks down and I pull back.

Jim has the stranger on the floor and is giving him the good news in a big way. I should stop him before he goes too far but Leonard has my full attention. I step back and Leonard slaps his hand to the knife wound and staggers forwards, bowling me into the lift wall. Warm blood spurts between us and Leonard clings to my suit. I try and push him off but he grabs like a limpet. His face is inches from mine.

Sixth floor.

'This shouldn't be happening,' he says.

Leonard utters the words in a whisper.

Tell me about it. We have entered a whole new world of screw ups here. I shout at Jim to stop and with one last kick to the stranger he obeys. Leonard begins to slide to the floor.

Second floor.

I grab Leonard and haul him back up. I tell Jim to get to the far side and take his other arm. I pray there is no-one waiting on the ground floor.

The doors open and we get a break. The lobby is empty. I urge Jim out and we walk, half dragging Leonard between us. I look back. I can't tell if the stranger is breathing. I reach back and punch the twenty first floor. I have no idea why that floor, other than I need to gain a few seconds and leaving the stranger on the ground floor is asking for discovery. The doors slide shut.

We are in a marble palace with three lift doors on each side. Behind us there is a wall covered in a mural. In front of us I can see the main lobby.

Someone is walking towards the lift. An open shirted man with an expensive taste in shoes. I start to walk toward him and as we pass I mumble something about drinking during the day. He watches us go past and as I turn my attention to the lobby, I can feel his eyes on my back.

Twenty feet to the main reception desk. It is manned by two uniformed guards. Someone is signing in and I keep as much distance between us and the guards as is possible. We are almost level with the desk when the nearest guard shouts over and asks if everything is ok. I tell him that everything will be ok when our friend gets a breath of fresh air.

The main door is ten paces away. I haul Leonard a little more upright. Jim does the same and Leonard moans. He is passing out and leaking blood on the floor.

I push on and we hit the revolving door at pace. I shove Jim and Leonard into the first section and push the door round - diving into the next section. I hear a shout go up as the guard spots the blood on the floor.

Jim and Leonard crash to the pavement as they exit and, as I follow them out, I stumble over them and struggle to keep my feet. I reach down to grab Leonard but he is now out cold. I leave him and help Jim up. Behind me the guard is entering the revolving door.

'Leg it,' I shout.

Jim doesn't hesitate and sprints to the left. I sprint to the right. Leonard will have to take his chances. I hope he doesn't make it. I'm not going back to finish the job.

I hear the guard shout and I put the pedal to the metal and hit top speed and birl into a woman hurrying along the pavement. She looks up at me and for a split second holds my gaze and then I'm gone. I hear her shout after me.

What a fuck up.

What a right royal fuck up.

Chapter 14

Tina to the rescue?

The running man outside George's building nearly takes me down. For an instant we are eyeball to eyeball. He sprints off and I call him an arsehole. No, strike that, I call him a complete arsehole. I re-focus on getting on with the job in hand and head towards the entrance of George's building.

It's the liquid on the ground that I see first. For a second I think the man on the pavement has peed himself. But a guard is shouting and waving his hands like a man possessed and there is screaming going on from a woman holding a shopping bag. The revolving doors of George's building spin and a second guard dives out.

I'm looking down at the man on the pavement. The liquid is way too thick and way the wrong colour for pee. Blood. I have never seen so much blood. I had no idea that people contained that much blood. I watch, transfixed as it spreads slowly towards me.

The first guard is on his knees. I'm not sure he knows what to do. He fumbles at the guy's neck and then fumbles around his wrist. The second guard hovers above - equally useless.

'Ambulance,' I say as I step away from the advancing blood. The second guard looks at me, pauses and then it dawns on him what I mean and he is off back into the building.

I step round the man and the guard but I can't decide if I should try and help or keep with plan A. The guard makes my mind up for me when he looks up and asks if I know anything about first aid. I don't. He asks if I have something to stop the blood. Hasn't he? His eyes are pleading for help. I pull off my cardigan and hand it to him. He takes it and bundles it into the man's stomach. I suspect I may never wear my favourite cardigan again.

Around me the world is beginning to focus on our little tableau. At a discreet distance pedestrians are beginning to congregate. Rubber necking. Whispering to each other. People are such shitheads. They are forming a tight circle with me, the guard and the man on the pavement at its centre. In seconds the circle is two or three deep. There is nothing like a crowd to draw a crowd. They all stare. Not help but stare. I hear one man say 'Can you move? I can't see. Is there blood?'

I give him my best 'tosser' look. Unbelievable. A man is dying on a public footpath and someone is more interested in seeing the blood than helping. Then the man on the pavement makes a sound like a cat giving up a furball.

I turn away and the people nearby look at me as if I'm about to say something. I do. I ask if there is anyone with medical training. A man steps forward. He is tall, painfully thin, with a suit that seems to struggle to stay on his body. He brushes me aside and bends down; informing the guard that he is a doctor.

I take the opportunity to step back into the crowd. George is back on my mind and I can see a train load of questions coming my way if I stay here and I don't have the time. George needs me. The man on the pavement has nothing to do with me. I push back through the crowd.

The second guard is back on the pavement looking up and down the street. No doubt searching for the ambulance. I squeeze past him and into the lobby.

The lobby is empty and I cross to the lifts. There is no one waiting and there is a lift on its way down. It flicks from floor six to five as I watch. Come on. The door opens and I'm almost flattened as a policeman barrels out, eyes darting.

'Did you see two men in suits? One tall. One short.'

I say no and he takes off towards the lobby and I get in the lift. I realise that I may have just lied. My gut is beginning to churn. Events are piling up in a bad way. The men on the roof, George on the roof, the push (and it was a bad push), the man on the pavement, the rushing policeman. The running man in the suit. Are they all connected? I hit the top floor button and lean back on the lift wall.

At the twenty fourth floor the lift stops and there is a man standing in an agitated state. He steps in, hits the ground floor button and sees the top button is lit. He asks if I'm going up. I say yes, he swears, jumps back out and swears some more. The door closes.

Weird.

The world has gone crazy.

Just plain crazy.

Chapter 15

Something bad dawns on Simon.

Leonard has sewn me right up. I open my eyes and pick up the letter once more. I know his scheme can't be fool-proof. No scheme ever is. But on the face of it he's done a good job. Passwords, copies of accounts, specific instructions - he has put some thought into this. I need to do the same. My hangover is not conducive to coherent thought. I decide to order a taxi. Go home and figure what to do.

I flip open my address book to find the taxi number. The alarm bell goes off in my head with the force of a World War II siren. My address book falls to the ground. My alcohol fuzzed brain catches up with the reality of what is happening.

Happening right now.

At this very moment Dumb and Dumber are under instructions to hunt down Leonard. They have strict instructions to cause him maximum damage. Fatal damage.

The same Leonard who now has me by the short and curlies.

'I do not want to die and if you take a sensible approach to this little issue we can both live long and healthy lives.'

Fuck, I need to stop them. The number. Where is the phone number? On the business card. I dig it out of my pocket. I reach for the phone then stop myself. Wrong phone. I need a phone that can't be traced. The safe. I take out the key and open it. I pull out a phone. I hit the power button but nothing happens. I hit it again. Dead battery. I pull out another phone. Dead as well. I fumble in my pocket for the battery from the first phone I used. It is the wrong make. I reach for the office phone. I have no choice. Anyway the phone I'm calling is a Pay As You Go - not traceable. I dial the number and wait. It rings and rings then cuts out. I try again. Still nothing. I try a third time and it is answered.

'I told you not to phone again. Anyway it's done. He's outside the building. Don't think he'll make it. Need to go.'

All of this was said in one breath. The connection is severed. I ring back but the line is dead. What's done? Not Leonard. Outside the building? What building? This building? Of course this building. Didn't they tell me not ten minutes ago that they were in the building?

'Don't think he'll make it?'

That means he isn't dead yet. I kick back from my desk. The chair leaves a mark in the wall that will need filler.

Outside the building. Leonard Thwaite is outside the building. Dying outside my building!

I dive through the office and hit all the lift buttons. Up and down. The lift arrives. I jump in and press for the ground. I pause. The top floor button is lit. I realise there is a woman in the lift and a second later I'm back on my floor waiting on the next lift. I look up. None of the lifts are within ten floors of me. I decide to take the stairs. I know this is irrational. Waiting on a lift will be far quicker but I need to be doing something. I hammer through the fire escape door.

The stairs vanish under my feet - three steps at a time. There are two flights of stairs per floor. At the bottom of each flight I fling myself round by the hand rail, I pick up speed. Twice I miss my footing and come within inches of a cropper.

The final flight appears and then I'm out in the lobby. I can see a large crowd outside. I rush to join them. The sound of an approaching ambulance can be heard. I squeeze my way into the crowd and towards the front. I ignore the indignant mutterings as I force myself through.

In the centre I find two guards, a policeman and a man lying on the ground. The policeman is beginning to push people back, telling them to move on. He is standing between me and the man on the pavement. I edge round to get a better look. He confronts me and asks me to move along. I try to ignore him. He gently grabs my arm and steers me away. I contemplate saying I know the man but realise that would be folly. I pretend to walk away. I then circle back to the other side. The policeman keeps moving everyone on. He notices I'm not leaving and he starts over to me. I decide to call it quits and walk off.

The frustration is immense. I need to know if the man on the ground is Leonard. I need to know that if it is Leonard then is he alive? I need to know that if he is alive then will he stay alive?

I stop walking away and make my way over to the building side of the pavement. I edge myself back to the scene. If the policeman asks I'll say I work there. Hardly a lie.

I pass by the circle of people and gain the front entrance of the building before taking a further eight or nine steps. I turn and walk back to the incident. This time the policeman is at the far side of the crowd talking to someone else.

I move in.

The guard is still kneeling down next to the man. I have to move round to get a better view. I see the blood, running from body to gutter. The man looks like Leonard from this angle. I try to get a better view. The man is curled in a ball on the ground and I can't be sure. I keep circling, my eyes fixed on the man's head. I bump into someone and look up. The policeman. *'Have I some interest in what is going on?' 'No.' 'Wasn't I told to move on?' 'Yes.' 'So why am I back?'* I'm struggling on that one. There is a retch from the man on the ground and the policeman turns towards the noise. The man on the ground spasms. His head flips round.

Leonard.

I walk away.

This time I keep going until I reach the corner of the building next to the lane. I feel numb. I'm usually cool under pressure. Now I'm not. What is going on around me is too fast and too out of control. I need space to think. To address the situation properly.

I try and take the positive from the moment. Leonard isn't dead. Not yet. I saw him move. This may not be as bad as it could be. Except I know I am in straw clutching territory. The retch was not a good sound. The spasm looked terminal. There was way too much blood on the pavement. Leonard might not be dead but he is as good as. I close my eyes and step into a quieter, more ordered world. Think.

'As of last week I have sent several electronic copies of accounts concerning certain of your business transactions to some key strategic locations.'

Several. Not one or two but several. Key strategic locations. Several strategic locations. How many is several?

'I have also taken the liberty of confiding in a work colleague who has placed a hard copy set of the same accounts in a place of his own choosing'

Who is the work colleague?

'All the accounts are strictly protected by a password. If the individuals are not given the correct password when contacted the accounts will be sent directly to the authorities. If I die or vanish - the strategic locations have instructions to release the accounts to the authorities within forty eight hours.'

That means I have two days. Two days max. Maybe less. Once Leonard's death is reported

77

what's to stop his 'strategic locations' releasing the accounts straight away?

The need for action is intense. I have to get into Leonard's office. He will have kept a record of his plan somewhere. But I need to move now. I have no idea how long it will take the police to ID Leonard. When they do they will go straight to Cheedle, Baker and Nudge's offices. I need to get there first.

I work my way back to the main entrance, through the doors and to the lifts. Behind me the ambulance is just arriving. The policeman and guard are still beside Leonard. There is a lift waiting and I ride up to Cheedle, Baker and Nudge's floor.

The reception is clean, tidy and insipid. They are not a big money operation. The receptionist recognises me. No issue there. I'm a client after all. She tells me that Leonard is out at the moment. I tell her I know. I tell her that Leonard has asked me to wait in his office. She nods. I walk through the doors to the main office. I walk quickly down the hall. I slip into Leonard's office. Leonard shares it with two other accountants. Neither is in. I close the door and think about blocking the door with a filing cabinet. I decide against it. If anyone came in, furniture-moving would make me look suspicious.

The office is old school. No Boston Legal type glass walls. Half panels of painted Gyproc at the bottom and heavily frosted glass at the top. The type of frosting that lets you see shape but no detail. The door is fake oak. The only way to see what is happening in the office is to walk in.

Leonard's desk is next to the window. His laptop is lying open on top of it. I close it and place it on the edge of his table. It's coming with me.

I start with his top desk drawer. I work my way down the drawers. I'm not sure what I'm looking for. Six drawers are opened and searched. I find nothing that looks like it might contain the details that I need. I switch to the filing cabinet. I hear soft footsteps approaching. I freeze. A shape slides by the frosted glass. The footsteps recede. I try the top drawer on the filing cabinet. It is locked. I daren't force it. Anyway the chances are that his details are on his laptop. Leonard is a bit of a tech geek. He is a Blackberry convert. I'll put twenty to one that his plans are on the Blackberry and that he backs the thing up on the laptop. I take another look round the office. Nothing.

I grab the laptop.

It occurs to me that the secretary will see me carrying the laptop out. I'm not wearing a jacket. I open my shirt and slide the laptop into the top of my trousers. It is cool against my skin. I button up. I try and fold my arm over it. I'm going for the 'natural but hide the bulge' look. I end up with my left arm stretching up to the right side of my neck. My other arm is draped across my midriff. Awkward looking but it will have to do.

I exit the office. The receptionist looks up. I ask her to tell Leonard to give me a call on the mobile. I tell her I can't wait any longer. She smiles and nods. I'm gone.

I ride the lift up to my office. When I'm back in my seat I open up Leonard's laptop. As expected it is password protected. I know someone who can crack this but not here. I gather up my stuff and put Leonard's laptop in my brief case. I take the lift to the basement. I'm still a million miles from being fit to drive a car but I have no choice. I need to get the laptop to my computer wizard as soon as possible. A taxi will take too long.

It won't take the police long to find out that I have been down to see Leonard. Once they talk to the receptionist I will become a very interesting person to the police. If anyone notices the missing laptop then my interest quotient will go through the roof.

I pull out into the lane. The Merc purrs. I moan. I nudge the nose out onto the main road. To my right the crowd has swollen again. Three police cars have arrived to join the ambulance. There are two policemen at the front door. I signal to turn left. I can see the police stopping people leaving the building. I put my foot down and pull out into the outside lane. I'm swallowed by the traffic.

Chapter 16

George escapes.

I can't breathe. I really can't breathe. The tall thug stuffed an old handkerchief in my mouth. A used handkerchief. A recently used handkerchief. The cable tying my hands is inch thick in dust and as I struggle the dust kicks up and is hanging in the air seeming to vaporise oxygen.

I'm wheezing and the world is dropping a poor shade of pale. I hate breathing through my nose - one of my nasal passages is larger than the other. My left passage is almost closed and I am breathing through my right and I can't grab enough air. I can feel myself passing out. My panic is extreme. I need air and I...

I come round lying on my side. The handkerchief is lying next to me in a small pool of vomit. I could have choked on it. How Keith Moon is that. I hear footsteps on the stairs and try and shout out but my throat is bone dry and I can barely whisper. My hands are still bound but now that I am free of the breathing panic I begin to work on the bindings and it doesn't take long to wriggle my hands free. I sit up and the world spins so I lie down again and wait. I sit up again - this time at a more sedate pace and the world spins a little less. I wait for it to slow to a crawl and try and stand up.

The world returns to carousel mode and I need to sit down. I wait for a few seconds and try again. On my third attempt I make it. I'm wobbly but vertical and I reach out and try the cupboard door handle - the light from under the door providing just enough vision to work with. It is locked and the thug took my keys.

The cupboard is one of a hundred dotted throughout the building. They are identical in size and identical in layout. Each has three shelves at the back, a power point, a single ceiling light and little else. Usually they are full of the sort of rubbish that such cupboards excel at accumulating - cleaning material, mops, tools and the like, but this one is different. This one is rarely used and is bare. I place my ear to the door but there is no sound from outside. I consider banging the door but in the back of my head I realise this is folly and get scared that the thugs will still be around. I was close to getting a real kicking and I have no intention of opening myself up to such abuse. But I still need out.

I know the locks on these cupboards are not substantial. Unusually the door opens outwards, as they all do. I wonder how much pressure I would need to pop the lock. I lean my shoulder into the door, press and build up until I am putting as much pressure on as possible but nothing gives. I consider my next move. I can shoulder charge the door but this is hardly a silent option and if the thugs are still around I'm in trouble. But I need to do something. They could come back soon and that isn't a fun story either.

I make my mind up and back up as far as the cupboard will let me and take a run at the door and hit it with my shoulder. I bounce back and my shoulder registers its disapproval in a big way. The door seems unaffected so I try again with the same result and after the third attempt I stop. Obviously the locks are a touch more substantial than I gave them credit for.

I scan the cupboard for anything of use but it is clean as a whistle. I search my pockets and come up with a small win in the shape of a Swiss Army knife. Not the daddy of the range but a faithful servant over the years.

It is about four inches long and nearly an inch thick and amongst a small array of accoutrements it has two blades - a three inch and a two inch. I flip out the smaller blade and try and insert it where the lock is located but the door frame protects the mechanism. Had I been on the outside this would have been easy. Had I been on the outside this would be a redundant problem.

I study the door frame. A protecting strip of wood is tacked on to the door frame with what look like small panel pins. I insert my knife between frame and wood at the top of the door and lever the strip away. At first the small pins hold firm but then, with a small pop, part of the strip comes free. I bend to the floor and repeat the process.

I move up the strip, prising it away from the frame until it is sitting proud a centimetre or so along its entire length. I turn my attention to the lock area and work at the strip until there is enough space to get my fingers in. I insert my fingers and try to pull the strip free from its mountings but it is stubborn. I start again with the knife at the bottom and this time loosen the whole strip another centimetre and insert my fingers and try again. This time it splinters and pulls away. I throw it behind me and insert the small knife into the now exposed gap between door and frame and with a little effort pop the lock.

I open the door but keep it from swinging free. I push my head through the gap and look out. The stairs seem empty. I open the door further and put my head round the door. Still all clear. I exit.

I head down to the next floor and I hear approaching footsteps with some speed on them. The door below opens and two figures come through. I throw myself against the wall but there is nowhere to hide. The figures start up the stair and reveal themselves to be a policeman and a paramedic. They rush past me and up to the roof. I change my mind about going down. Police upstairs. Thugs maybe downstairs. I'll go with the police.

I'm back on the roof seconds behind the police and the paramedic. There are another two policemen on the opposite side of the roof to where Charlie was being thrown off. I follow the paramedic and the first policeman over and see Charlie lying on the ground. The paramedic drops to the ground and gets to work. The policeman walks over to me.

I give him chapter and verse. No holding back. I tell him who Charlie is and he notes it all down and then makes me go through the story again. '*Was the man being thrown from the roof or did he jump.*' '*I don't know.*' '*Did the two men in suits say anything?*' '*Not much.*' '*Do I know why they might have chosen to throw Charlie off the roof?*' '*I'm not sure they did throw him off, after all wasn't one trying to save him'* *'Explain?'* I explain about Leonard. *'Who is Leonard?'* I tell him.

The questioning runs on and I stop it to ask if Charlie is ok and the policeman asks the paramedic. The paramedic says he'll live. It's all the answer I get before the three policemen get together for a chat.

I wander over to Charlie. He is in some state. His face is bruised and his nose is at right angles to where it should be. His left ear is caked in blood. His right eye is closed but his left eye is open and active. He spots me and he tries to say something. The paramedic tells him to lie quiet but he curls the right finger of his right hand in a beckoning motion and I close in. The paramedic is loading up a syringe. No doubt something to send Charlie to dreamland for a bit.

Charlie reaches up and grabs the paramedic's hand to stop him and beckons me again. I look at him and then I look at the paramedic and the paramedic leans back to let me talk to Charlie.

Charlie whispers. So low I struggle to hear him and low enough that no-one else can eavesdrop.

'Leonard. The gorillas said I was Leonard.'

I nod. No understanding but I nod.

'Not me that was the thievin' prick. Leonard.'

I am clueless.

'Behind my filing cabinet. Take the parcel and hide it.'

I am about to ask what is going on but then Charlie moans big time and the paramedic pushes me aside and unloads the syringe into Charlie's arm and he is gone.

I'm confused.

The first policeman approaches me again and tells me that I need to come down to the station. I ask if that is really necessary but it is clear it is. We head for the exit just as two more paramedics appear with a stretcher. Right behind them is Tina. She looks in a state of total bewilderment. She rushes to me and wraps herself around me like a long lost brother. She babbles about the man getting thrown off the roof and me being pushed. A bad push. Tina can do shorthand of the mouth like no-one I know.

The policeman cottons onto to what she is trying to say and gently pulls her away and starts to question her about the incident. I hear her side of the story and I'm still not sure if Charlie jumped or was thrown.

I have time to think about what Charlie has just said to me. It makes no sense but then again the whole shooting match makes no sense. One thing does make sense is that the two men in suits clearly thought Charlie was Leonard.

'Not me that was the thievin' prick. Leonard.'

That's what Charlie had said and it sounded like Leonard Thwaite had stolen something. Maybe the gorillas were here to repay Leonard's thievery. Maybe they thought Charlie had something to do with it.

To say I'm confused isn't even half the story.

'Behind my filing cabinet. Take the parcel and hide it.'

Could this be what Leonard stole? Maybe? Then why would Charlie have it? I'm still confused.com.

86

Whatever the story the parcel must be important. Charlie was clearly in pain but he blank refused the jab until he passed on the information. The policeman is finished with Tina and I ask him if I can have two minutes with my girlfriend. He agrees and I reassure her that I am ok. I then tell her what has happened and what Charlie said.

'Do me a favour,' I say. 'Go down to Cheedle, Baker and Nudge. Charlie works there. Susie will be on reception. Tell her George sent you to pick something up for Charlie Wiggs. Me and her are good so she'll let you in his office. See if there is a parcel behind Charlie's filing cabinet. If there is can you grab it and hang on to it. Can you do that as soon as possible?'

She's not keen. Not keen at all. I don't blame her. Tina's not stupid. She tells me to forget it and tells me to say to the police about the parcel. But Charlie is one of the good guys in life. One of the guys that didn't take the piss out of my cupboard indiscretion. Good guys are thin on the ground and I want to help him. I push her to help.

Tina asks why she shouldn't pass the parcel straight to the police. I tell her that Charlie doesn't want that to happen. 'How do you know?' she asks. 'He would have told the policeman about the parcel, not me,' I reply.

She is wavering. I kiss her and the policeman steps in and tells me we need to go. I ask if we can stop at the front desk to pick up a spare set of office keys and he agrees.

I wink at Tina and hope she follows up for me. And then I'm out of there.

Chapter 17

Tina gets in deeper.

And then George is gone and I'm standing on the roof with the sort of feeling I used to get when I was stood up by my boyfriend at school. There are still two policemen and a paramedic fussing over the man on the roof. I wander over for a look but I don't recognise him. Presumably this is Charlie Wiggs but I wouldn't know him from Adam.

I chew over George's request and can think of a dozen reasons why I shouldn't do what he asked. For a start I have no idea what is going on. Bodies on the pavement, bodies on the roof. Police, paramedics and heaven knows what else. It would seem more prudent to run than get involved.

Yet I like George, I may even love him but that is a debate for much later. I want to help him but I'd also like to know what I'm getting myself into.

The urgency in George's request isn't helping. That and the cloak and dagger nature of the whole thing has me flipping like a top. Help. Don't help. Help. Don't help. I hate being like this.

They are lifting Charlie onto the stretcher and I realise that I need to make a call. Assuming that Charlie's request is tied up with the whole situation then time is of the essence. It won't take the police long to get round to Charlie's work place. I mentally flip a coin but I'm already moving before it lands. There was never any doubt that I would help.

Suzie turns out to be a little less helpful than George suggested. She knows something is going on but not the detail. I tell her that George has asked me to pick something up for Charlie. She is hesitant and says she's not supposed to let anyone in the offices without a member of staff. She is lying but I nod in understanding. Part of me wants her to refuse and take the issue out of my hands. I say nothing and wait for her to make up her mind.

The phone on her desk rings and she picks up and answers with a cheery greeting. Her grin vanishes in a second and she tells the caller that she will put them through right away. After a moment it is clear that whoever she is transferring to is not in. She informs the caller of the fact and after a short conversation agrees to go and track someone down and phone the caller back.

She looks at me and informs me that that was the police. Something about Leonard and Charlie. The police are on their way up and want to talk to Mr Cheedle. No doubt the Cheedle in Cheedle, Baker and Nudge. She excuses herself and disappears into the offices. I know I should leave. Even being here will raise questions.

I look at the door to the offices, step forward and push it open. Beyond is a corridor with doors to the left and the right. I shouldn't step through but I do. The first door has a small brass plaque informing on the occupants. All the offices are signposted in this way and it doesn't take me long to find Charlie Wiggs' office. I see it is also home to Leonard Thwaite and Christine Obego.

I enter the office and see three desks. One against the window and two against the far wall. I examine the first one but there is no way of knowing whose desk it is. The second desk has pictures of kids and a picture of a man standing with the Golden Gate Bridge in the background with the words 'From Mr Obego to Mrs Obego with love' scribbled across it. Obviously Christine's desk.

The desk next to the window has a pen and pencil set and a small paperweight - otherwise it is clear. Next to it is a filing cabinet with the initials LT on a sticker above the top drawer. I return to the first desk and the filing cabinet has the letters CW. Charlie's desk.

I've been in too long already. I can feel the police approaching. I try and pull the filing cabinet away from the wall but it is heavy. It moves an inch or so and I look in the gap between the wall and the cabinet and I see a small parcel. I rock the cabinet another inch and the parcel falls to the floor. I pick it up and I'm out of there.

The corridor is clear and I head for the door to reception. As I reach for the reception door handle a voice from behind me rings out asking if they can be of help. I turn round to see a small, compact, balding man in a neatly fitting suit. I tell him I'm looking for Suzie and he asks if she is not at reception. I tell him she was but left to get someone and hasn't come back and I popped my head in to see if she was nearby. The man is not convinced by this and escorts me out into the reception.

Luckily Suzie hasn't returned and the balding man tells me to take a seat and he will find her. He vanishes back into the office and I head for the lifts. I press the button and wait. And wait. And wait. The lift arrives and I step forward as the balding man's voice rattles my ears again. I ignore it and press for the ground and the door closes.

The lobby is chaos. The police are letting no-one out until they have checked each person's ID. I have no choice but to wait in the queue, sweating as it crawls forward. Any moment now the balding man might appear and I'll be at the centre of a spotlight. There are four people in front of me and two officers working the line. Everyone is being asked for identification. A woman at the front of the queue doesn't have any ID and is asked to stand to one side while they process everyone else. She reluctantly moves over to stand in a small crowd of other people that have no ID.

It is my turn and the policeman asks me for my details. I opt to tell him that I have already been questioned by the policeman on the roof. He still asks for ID but I have none. In my rush to help George I left my handbag at my desk. He asks me to stand in the small crowd.

I stand to one side, glancing at the lifts for signs of the balding man. I contemplate making a run for it but realise the folly in this action.

Suddenly there is a commotion in the line. A t-shirt clad man is objecting to being told to stand to one side. He has no ID but is adamant that he is leaving anyway. The policeman tries to talk to him calmly but this simply turns up the dial on the man and he racks up the volume. The other policeman vetting the line steps over to give a hand. The policemen stand either side of Mr T-Shirt and face him down. Mr T-Shirt reacts by twisting the volume switch all the way to eleven. All focus is now on the developing scene and I see a window of opportunity.

A third policeman leaves the entrance and joins his colleagues in fronting up to Mr T-Shirt. I slip from the small crowd and head for the revolving doors. I expect to hear a shout but the police are pre-occupied

Out on the pavement I head for my office, clutching the parcel tight against my chest. Every step towards my office I'm waiting for a call or a hand on my shoulder.

When I get to my desk I slump into my seat still clutching the parcel. Around me the office continues with its business as it has done for years. I slip the parcel into my gym bag and try and get back to my work but it will be a long afternoon. A long, long afternoon.

Chapter 18

A brief interlude.

The blind man watches the events unfold from the coffee shop opposite Tyler Tower with mild curiosity. His white stick rests against the window of the café and his guide dog lies with its head on his master's shoes. The dark glasses the blind man wears are made of mirrored glass and reflect the world back to anyone who cares to look.

Despite the warmth of the café the blind man wears a shin length overcoat topped of with a rather OTT black felt Fedora. In front of him a mug of de-caffeinated latte sits cooling. A newspaper lies on the table next to the coffee. Although folded neatly and unread it is still a strange purchase for a man who lacks the visual tools to digest its contents.

The dog stirs and drops its chin from shoe to floor, yawning as it does so. They have been sitting at the table for over an hour and the dog, not used to inaction, is bored. It is no more a guide dog than a million other dogs but when required it has enough training to look and act like a guide dog and that is all the owner asks of it.

The blind man notes the comings and goings across the road with an eye for detail that has kept him in his trade far longer than most of his fellow tradesmen.

When he sees the two suited men and the vic emerge onto the pavement his interest rises a notch. When they leave the vic on the ground and run he shakes his head. Unprofessional. It is a word that he strives to eliminate from his vocabulary.

His reputation is built on a service second to none and the incident he has just witnessed would dip his credibility into the toilet. Steps would need to be taken. Reputations were hard won and easily lost.

He watches for a while longer as the circus gathers momentum. He watches Simon's antics as he tries to get a better look at the vic and he notes the policeman leave with the maintenance man in tow.

After a while he stands up, picks up his white cane and encourages his dog to step out in front of him. He leaves the café and takes a last glance across the road.

Serious shit is going down.

Chapter 19

Simon gets busy.

The drive home was a journey from hell. My head was full of events and headaches. My gut was a mess. I couldn't focus on what was important. I had made a call on my mobile - forced to illegally use my handset rather than the hands free. The bloody system had never worked properly since it was installed.

I arranged to meet the computer wizard at my house in one hour. Enough time to shower, change my clothes and get my crap together. I pulled into my driveway fully expecting to see a police car parked outside. It could only be a matter of time.

The doorbell rings and I am in a fresh shirt and jeans. I pop three more headache killers. I look through the bedroom curtains. A battered black Mini Cooper sits outside. No police car.

I open the door and invite the wizard in. His name is Quentin Rathbone. You would go a long, long way to find someone who looks more like a computer geek than Quentin does.

Long dank hair, starting to recede at the front. His pallor is that of a prison lifer. Flesh hangs from him like unwanted fat from cooked meat. His eyes are sunk so deep they look like small lumps of coal. His teeth are crooked, yellowed and cracked. His personal hygiene is a serious issue. Halitosis, BO, dandruff mixed with (and he tells me this crap) athlete's foot, cracked heel and crotch rot. He is wearing the same t-shirt he has worn since the day I first met him. At one point there had been a logo on the front but that has long since faded. His jeans are a patchwork quilt of varying materials. His trainers had once been white but have now achieved a shade of grey that you rarely see in clothing less than ten years old.

He carries a World War II issue haversack in one hand. Over his back a shiny new, high tech backpack sits at odds with everything else. He shuffles past me and slumps onto my sofa. He puts his feet up on my coffee table. My African Blackwood coffee table.

I pick up Leonard's laptop from the hall table. He doesn't look up as I drop it in his lap. I exit to make a coffee.

Twenty minutes later I am sipping some serious caffeine. Quentin is making mincemeat out of the security settings on the laptop. I watch in silence.

Once, long ago, he tried to explain what he did as he went along. I had made it crystal clear that I had no interest and that was that.

A small punch with a clenched fist suggests that he has cracked the laptop's secrets.

'Wha' ya lookin' fur?'

Translated he was asking me what I was looking for. I tell him. I have no worries about Quentin knowing intimate details. I had made it my business to have his balls firmly in my hands long ago. He knows his place. Besides he would be amply rewarded for his efforts. He knew better than to shit on his own doorstep.

Another quarter of an hour rolls by. The keyboard is battered to death. He unslings the new back pack and extracts a printer. He powers it up. A few seconds later sheets of paper begin to print off. When the printer finishes he passes the paper to me. He switches off the printer and repacks it.

'T' lot.'

Translated that means - 'That is the lot'. There are three sheets of paper. Each is crammed with words and symbols. None of it makes any sense to me.

'What the hell is this?'

'Code.'

'Can you break it?'

'Maybe.'

'Well?'

'K.'

He opens his haversack. He takes out what looks like a kid's toy laptop. For the next half hour he flips between the laptops. Then the clenched fist appears again.

'Wanna details.'

Did I want the details?

It was so tiresome with Quentin but he was good at what he did. I let him rabbit on for ten minutes. I do my best to decipher what he is talking about. The gist is as follows.

Far from 'several strategic locations', Leonard had sent the accounts in electronic form to only two recipients. As far as Quentin could tell there was no reference to who had received the hard copy that Leonard had referred to. I would get to this later.

Leonard is, or was, a clever bastard. Each recipient has been sent an encrypted file with a simple set of instructions. If they suspect any foul play they are to click on an embedded link on the e-mail. This will send a message to Leonard's inbox. All they then do is wait. If within forty eight hours Leonard replies to the e-mail with a special password then all is sweetness and light and nothing happens. If on the other hand Leonard does *not* respond to the e-mail within forty eight hours then the recipient's inbox will perform two functions. Firstly it will unlock the file to allow the recipient to read the attachment. Next it will make a copy of the file and despatch the copy to an unknown address. Quentin's best guess is the Financial Services Authority. In this way my dirty little secrets will be out.

As a safe-guard Leonard can also send a second password to the recipient. If the recipient opens this e-mail then a programme gets to work and cleans out the original e-mail and all traces are zapped. Quentin seems to think this is quite impressive given the current state of anti-virus software. I don't care. If, however, the wrong password is sent then the file is sent to the authorities. All in all a clever piece of work.

The killer, as far as I am concerned, is that there are no records of any passwords on Leonard's machine and Quentin is fairly sure that it will not be easy to work them out.

'Min twenty 'ix chacs. Prob?'

A minimum of twenty six characters. Probably?

I ask if he could crack this and he nods but then adds.

'T four, four eight - no sure.'

Twenty four hours or forty eight. I'm not sure.

I ask would we know when someone clicks on the link to send off the enquiry e-mail. He says as long as no-one interferes with the system then yes. I tell him to get working on the code. I look at my watch and tell him to inform me when he cracks it or as soon as someone clicks on the link.

I ask him if we could ID the two recipients. He shakes his head - both are hotmail addresses and this makes it tricky. He suggests sending an e-mail from Leonard. The e-mail might force them to give us some idea of who they are. I reject this. If news of Leonard's accident reaches them at the same time as an e-mail then they will almost certainly pass the e-mail straight to the police. I need the stolen laptop to stay in the shadows.

I know I can't rely on Quentin cracking the code. If Leonard is dead then both recipients could easily pass on the original e-mail at any point. The files might be encrypted but the police wouldn't take long to crack them.

I need the identities of the two recipients. Then I need to eliminate them as soon as possible.

I tell Quentin to surf through all of Leonard's contacts. I tell him to compare names with the hotmail addresses. He smacks the keyboard. The screen fills with addresses.

The hotmail addresses are a mix of letters and numbers that have no relation to any name or a company in Leonard's address book. I had to figure that Leonard knew the contacts well. I had to figure that the contacts would be sitting somewhere in the laptop. I tell Quentin to dig deeper.

After a further half an hour Quentin has five possibles. All are company e-mail addresses. With a quick burst on Google all turned out to be local to Tyler Tower.

Three of the companies are accountants. One is a legal firm. One is a security firm. I ask Quentin how he has short listed them as possibles? He starts to talk about voids.

After a little translation I get the idea. Leonard has had regular e-mail dialogue with all five of the 'possibles' up to a week ago. Then it had ceased. To Quentin this was suspicious. He suspected that Leonard had deleted in and out bound records to the five addresses over the last few days. This was what he meant by a void. I ask why five 'possibles' when only two have been sent the documents. He doesn't know. I tell him to get cracking on the code. I take the five e-mail addresses and retire to my study.

Once seated I open the bottom drawer on my desk. I remove another Pay As You Go mobile. I hit the power button. This time I am greeted by a working battery. I dial a number from memory. An answering machine kicks in. Ten minutes later the mobile rings. There is no caller ID.

'I've another job I need done. But after the cock up today I want some assurances,' I say.

'the Voice' informs me that changes are being made. He assures me that normal service will be resumed. Then silence. Clearly I am expected to buy this re-assurance. Either that or hang up. I have no choice. I pass on the five e-mail addresses. I explain what I need done. Then the phone is dead.

I return to the living room to find that Quentin had spread out. My sofa and floor are now a mass of laptops, small black boxes and other assorted paraphernalia. I sigh, swear and leave to make another coffee.

My next task is to identify the work colleague that Leonard has passed the hard copy of my accounts to. I am sure it is going to be one of his office buddies - Christine or Charlie. I can't risk going back to their office so I pick up the office phone.

I dial Cheedle, Baker and Nudge. Bouncy Suzie answers only she isn't too bouncy. I ask for Leonard. She tells me that Leonard is not in. She refuses to divulge anything else. I guess she has been told about Leonard's 'accident'. I ask if Charlie or Christine are in. Not unusual as they sometimes pick up Leonard's work when he is off. I'm informed that Christine is on holiday. A bit of digging forces Suzie to tell me she has been away for nearly three weeks. Charlie is unavailable. I push for more. She comes up blank. She sounds distraught. I wonder if something had happened to Charlie. That starts my head spinning again.

I hang up and a lead ball settles in my stomach. Then a thought forms. Could the man on the roof have been Charlie?

'Tell me you didn't throw our friend off the roof of this fucking office?'

He hadn't. What he didn't tell me was they had tried to throw Charlie Wiggs off the roof. That was why he paused. There was a physical resemblance between Leonard and Charlie. This was turning into amateur dramatics week.

It couldn't be Christine that had the other set of accounts. Not unless he had given them to her before she went on holiday. I dismissed her. The evidence on the computer pointed to a more recent planning process than this. He could have given them to Charlie. But if he had, was Charlie dead or alive?

I fire up my computer. I log on to bbc.co.uk and then on to the local news.

'Man stabbed in Glasgow.'

'A man has been found with fatal stab wounds on one of Glasgow's main streets. The man has yet to be identified. He was found outside Tyler Tower on West George Street at around ten thirty this morning with a single stab wound and was pronounced dead on arrival at Glasgow Royal Infirmary. Police are following up a number of leads and are asking any witnesses to the incident to come forward. No name has been released yet.'

'In a second incident another man was found on the roof of Tyler Tower suffering from multiple wounds thought to be the result of an assault. Police are not saying if these incidents are linked.'

There was a picture of Tyler Tower and a contact number for the police. Charlie had to be the other man in the news story.

So Leonard was dead. Charlie might be dead or Charlie might be alive. If he was still alive I might still have a chance of getting my hands on the documents. That is if he has them.

I grab the Pay As You Go and re-dial the number. The answer machine fires up again. Ten minutes later the phone rings.

I explain my new request. 'the Voice' tells me that it will not be possible until at least tomorrow. If I want it done today I will need to make a choice between my previous request and this one.

I need both done.

'the Voice' offers me a new option. I don't like it and my first instinct is to say no. The offer is to put Dumb and Dumber back on the case. Either that or wait until tomorrow. After their screw up with Leonard I didn't want the Dynamic Duo on the case. I swear. But needs must when the devil is booting your backside. I give the details I have on Charlie. The phone drops dead.

I contemplate my next move. I realise that I am redundant. Quentin is trying to crack the code. He will inform me as soon as he breaks it or if someone triggers the forty eight hour button. There are people on the street about to give a whole mountain of bad news to the 'strategic locations'. Dumb and Dumber are on the case with Charlie. All in all stuff is going down.

All of this would come at a high cost. Neither Quentin or 'the Voice' were cheap. I have no choice. If this can be sorted - any price would be worth it.

I wander back in to watch Quentin at work. I soon get bored. I go to lie down.

Chapter 20

Charlie has a lie in.

I'm not sure how long I've been unconscious. An hour, a day, a week? The roof of the building seems an age ago. I'm lying in a hospital bed in a private room. It is dark but as to whether this is due to the thick curtains covering the window or time of day I have no idea.

Pain seems to wash my body at regular intervals like a bad tide. I do a check and the first thing I feel is strapping on my left arm. I can't feel my fingers. My face has a bandage running top left to bottom right and I can only see from my left eye. My legs are bandage free but it feels like someone has been playing football with my right one.

I take a deep breath and pain shoots through my chest in three different places. My guts feel twisted and bile rises in my throat. So far there is nothing positive about this experience. I try to sit up but either I'm too weak or the required muscles aren't working.

The dregs of the knockout drug are washing round my system and I want to drift back to sleep. The door opens and a nurse walks in and asks how I am. I tell her I feel like, well you know and she smiles. Good she says at least you feel like something and with that she presses a button above my head and a few moments later a doctor appears. After a brief examination he explains that they have already x-rayed me and fortunately the only broken bones are a couple of ribs on my left side.

This is a new meaning for the word fortunately that I have missed in my life. I ask if they have caught the person who did this and the doctor says no but there are two policemen who want to ask me some questions. Do I feel up to it? I don't but I ask him to send them in anyway.

When they enter I can feel their suspicion enter with them and the questioning reflects this. I take them through the sequence of events but there is one moment they keep coming back to.

'So you say they threw you off the roof and then at the last minute changed their mind.'

It wasn't they didn't believe me. George the maintenance man had been there and according to the police he had helped pull me back from a long fall - I don't remember that bit.

They go over the same ground a dozen times. *'Did you know the men?' 'No.' 'Did they tell you who they were?' 'No.' 'Have you any reason to believe that someone wants you dead?' 'No.' 'Why would they change their minds about throwing you off?' 'Don't know.'* And so it goes on.

I don't tell them about the parcel and the brief conversation with George. I don't tell them about Leonard and the *'thievin' prick'* line. I want to know if Leonard is alright but I can't think of a good reason to bring his name up. Suspicion is still rife with the two policemen and I don't blame them. I could mention the case of mistaken identity but Leonard is a good friend and I need to know what has been going on before I drop him in it. So I keep quiet.

The police leave telling me not to go anywhere. Like I'm going to up and run the hundred metres anytime soon. I close my eyes and start to drift off. I know I need to talk to George and Leonard but first I need more sleep.

Chapter 21

Another mission for the gorillas.

Bally says we've got another gig. That was quick. Last one seemed to go well apart from the mad dash at the end. But hey that's the way things go in this business. He says the vic is the same boy we tried to throw from the roof. Not the boy we should have thrown from the roof but the boy we tried to throw from the roof. I'm not sure I follow this. I ask why he saved him and he mutters something about me getting too big for my boots and I should learn my place. Not sure what he means.

This time we've just to get some info - not top him. Just as well we didn't throw him from the roof I say. Bally throws me a look. I have no idea what is going on. He tells me the vic is in hospital. No surprises there. A get in to the hospital, beat the info out of him and get out of the hospital job. A get in, beat up, get out. A GBG or as I like to call 'em a HeeBeeGeeBee.

We did one a few months ago. The vic was in an old folks home on the coast. Hardly Fort Knox. We broke in at two in the morning but things went a bit sour. I got the wrong room. It wasn't my fault. I have trouble with my sixes and my nines. Anyway we are laying into this old geezer; who doesn't look like he would last to the morning even if we didn't lay a finger on him. He keeps gibbering in some foreign lingo and Bally is getting madder by the second.

We are getting nowhere when a male nurse bursts in. Boy he was a tough bugger. It took both of us to bring him down. Bally got back to work on the old geezer and he was wheezing like a good 'un and I reckoned he was about to blab when I spotted an envelope on the desk. I can't read very well but the name didn't look right. I told Bally who went ballistic.

Wrong guy. Can you believe we've done the same thing twice in a couple of months - mistaken identity - but the boy on the roof wasn't my fault. Bally can't pin that one on me. Anyway we eventually found the correct old codger but even that didn't work out. He was stone cold - having died earlier that night. No point in us beating up on a dead guy. Wasn't our finest moment but we got paid and we got the roof gig. Can't be all bad.

Bally tells me we are going to the Royal Infirmary. I ask if we should wait until it is dark but Bally says there is a rush on. I ask how much. A grand. I'm happy. A grand from the job this morning topped up with another grand this afternoon - that's good cash in anyone's books. I tell Bally I never done a HeeBeeGeeBee in hospital and he shakes his head.

We have little info on the vic's whereabouts in the hospital but Bally is good on that stuff. Although not that good or we wouldn't have been doing a Mikey on the wrong guy earlier today.

We get in Bally's car and he starts grilling me. What did I mean by *'thievin' prick?'* Why was I videoing the vic? What did I know that he didn't? God is he going for it. I tell him I know nothing. The *'thievin' prick?'* line was a lift from an episode of The Sweeney I was watching on Dave last night. I tell him I thought it sounded cool. He throws me another look. Always looks with Bally. He asks about videoing the Mikey. I tell him that now and again I like to video the vic. I watch it back later. He tells me I'm an arsehole and that if I'm caught with the videos I'll be banged up. I tell him I know this but I like them anyway.

Bally can be a right pain when he wants but he comes up trumps on the job front and I need the cash.

We park some distance from the hospital and walk in. We approach the Royal and I remember that I don't like hospitals. I tell Bally this and he asks me what I want him to do about it. Tetchy git.

Hospitals make me feel ill. Right down in the pit of my stomach ill. I went to see my mother in law in hospital last year and by the end of visiting I was lying across the foot of her bed moaning my head off. I'm told it is all in my head but I know it is all in my stomach.

We walk through the main hospital entrance into reception and Bally asks the nurse at the desk where Charlie is located. She doesn't know but she gives us directions to someone who does. Her directions will take us back out the main entrance and in another door.

I need the air. I feel sick already.

Bally tells me we can cut through the hospital instead. I ask if we can go the way the nurse said.

Bally ignores me. I traipse behind him like an ill lapdog, moaning at every step.

He doesn't understand these places. You can taste the illness in the air. It can't be good for anyone to walk around with the air full of so many bad germs. Every time I breathe I can feel the little buggers sliding down my throat. I can feel them starting to breed.

We pass an examination room and I look in. A pile of surgical masks are lying on a table. I nip in and grab one, put it on and catch up with Bally. Better. At least the wee swines can't get to my throat but I can still feel them everywhere. Landing on my suit, touching my face - it all makes me squirm. We turn into a new corridor and Bally is striding forth fixed on getting to the vic.

We pass another room and I notice a white lab coat lying across a table. The very thing. That'll keep the little shits off my suit. I grab it and slip it on. Much better.

We pass a few hospital staff and they stare as I pass. I don't care. My aim is to be germ proof and they can stare all they want. I feel an itch on my scalp and alarm bells go off. My hair. Sneaky gits.

I look round. I need one of those plastic hat things that doctors stick over their head. We pass a row of examination cubicles and I nip into an empty one and rifle the equipment trolley. Bingo. Not only do I find the hat thing but a pair of shoe covers and a whole bundle of plastic gloves. I sit down and put on hat, gloves and shoe covers and then jog a little to catch up with Bally.

I am now as near nuclear proof as makes no difference. I reach out and tap Bally on the shoulder and he turns round.

Chapter 22

The gorillas play Hide and Seek.

I feel the tap on my shoulder and I turn round expecting to see Jim.

Mother of God.

For a second I'd swear it was a doctor about to go into surgery. Then Jim pulls down the face mask and smiles. You have to be kidding. You seriously have to be fucking kidding. My mouth goes into stutter mode. I want to say six things at once and my brain can't make this happen. Jim is still smiling. My mouth works and I ask him what the hell he thinks he is doing. He keeps smiling and then goes into a diatribe about germs. I grab him by the arm and drag him in to a small room. Thankfully it is empty. I tell him to take all the shit off but he refuses. I tell him to get real. This is not a joke, we need to blend in, look normal. Jim doesn't see the issue and tells me he is the one that looks normal in a hospital. He could be a doctor.

I pull the hat off him, then the mask and push him onto a chair. Reluctantly he takes off the shoe covers and the gloves. He stands up to take off the lab coat and I stop him. Jim is planet hopping again but maybe the idiot has a point. I tell him to take off the coat but hang onto it. I tell him to wait and after a short hunt I return with my own lab coat in hand. I push Jim back into the corridor and I head for the location the nurse gave me.

Jim looks unhappy. So he should.

We reach the right department and I make enquiries with the receptionist but draw a blank. The receptionist is not going to hand out information. I explain we are friends of the vic but this cuts no ice and she tells us to take a seat and she'll get a doctor to come and see us as soon as possible. She eyes the lab coats with suspicion.

We sit down in a small ante room. The sort of room that seems to litter hospitals of a certain vintage. A series of poorly hung posters advise on everything from your rights as a patient to the tell tale signs of sexually transmitted infections. Jim seems particularly interested in this poster. It is made up of drawings of men and women's genitalia and the signs to look out for. I know Jim will be struggling to read the words but he is lapping up the pictures and I have to stop him as he starts to unbutton his flies.

The doctor arrives but he passes on little information and is more intent in finding out who we are. I tell him we are old friends and push to see Charlie. We are told this would not be possible. It is not long to visiting time and if we would care to come back then we can see him. I change tack and ask if we can have his ward number as a few people would like to send flowers. He tells me to send anything to the department and they will make sure it gets to Charlie.

I let it go and decide to retreat and figure another way to get to Charlie. The doctor is getting way too suspicious plus Jim is back at his flies again. We leave and walk a little way back down the corridor and stop at a drinks machine.

I wait until the doctor is out of sight and tell Jim to wait by the machine and tell him if anyone comes along make it look like he is getting a drink.

I walk back to the reception area but stop just short of being seen. I poke my head around a corner and note the receptionist is buried in a PC. She is facing away from me but I would need to cover about thirty feet without being seen to make it to the other side of reception and out of view. All the receptionist needs to do is look up and I'm a goner. I scan the reception and note that a phone sits on a shelf at the back. I have a thought.

I walk back to Jim to find him, trousers at ankles, examining his privates. I order him to pull up his trousers and glance around to see if he has been spotted. I tell him what I need him to do and I head back to reception.

A few moments later the phone rings on the reception shelf and the receptionist spins round to answer it and I move. I briefly look back and see Jim on his mobile talking to the receptionist. I walk across the gap, keeping my eyes firmly fixed on the reception desk.

I just make it to the other side when she slams down the phone. Heaven knows what Jim has said to her but when I look back he has a stupid grin on his face and is beginning to undo his flies again. I wave my hands in the air, point to my groin and violently shake my head. He gets the message but I have no idea for how long. I head for the wards.

Chapter 23

Charlie is it.

I come to and still feel groggy. My bladder is in major need of relief. I reach over and press the call button and a nurse appears and I tell her that I need a pee - she reaches into the cupboard next to me and brings out a plastic bed pan. She doesn't leave. Does she expect me to use it in front of her? I have trouble peeing in the gents. There is no way I'm taking a whiz in front of a girl.

I ask her to leave and she shrugs her shoulders and exits.

I look at the bed pan. It's not hard to figure how it works but I'd rather go to the toilet. I'm not sure that my number one will make an appearance without a guest stint by a number two and I'm not sure I trust myself enough not to screw up the whole operation. I put the bed pan down and pull the covers to one side and try and sit up.

My inner ear objects and does its best to stop me moving. My bladder kicks up a notch and in my physically reduced state I'm not confident I can hold it in much longer. I clench my teeth and force myself to stay seated and then place my feet on the ground. My leg aches but I push on and up and then out of the door and into the corridor.

I have no idea where the toilet is but just then another male patient exits from a door across the way and I ask him if that's the toilet and he confirms it is. I push in, find a cubicle and slump onto the toilet and let rip.

Joy.

The effort of getting here has run down my battery a little. A few moments on the pan won't do me any harm. I close my eyes and lie back.

'Are you ok in there?'

I drift back and answer with a yes.

'Are you sure you are ok?'

I answer in the affirmative again telling the enquirer I'll be out in a moment. I have no idea how long I have been asleep. I hear the door swing closed and start the struggle of getting back to my bed. I make it as far as the toilet door but I'm weak and even opening the door takes its toll. I look out and the corridor is quiet but not empty. The main wards lie to the left and there are two nurses chatting next to the entrance doors. To the right there is a man walking towards me. It takes an instant to recognise him and in my haste to get out of sight I tumble back into the toilet and fall to the floor.

The gorilla. The short one. Back for me?

I'm square in the middle of the toilet and I realise that I'm exposed to anyone that walks through the door. I crawl to the nearest cubicle and push the door closed behind me. This is not a good thing. All I can think is that the gorilla has come to finish off what they failed to do on the roof. I wish I had been more forceful when I told the police about the gorillas. Maybe they would have given me some protection?

I try and figure what the deal is? Surely he wants Leonard not me? Was I not a mistake? Am I now to be killed because I could finger him? Maybe he knows about the parcel and has come to get it? Maybe he isn't here for me at all? Too many questions and nothing like enough answers. Whatever he wants it isn't good news.

I figure I have minutes at the most before he susses my whereabouts. This is too obvious a place not to look. I feel like a new born kitten. I'm in no fit state to outrun him. I can barely stand. But I can't stay here. I grit my teeth and anything else I can grit and pull myself to my feet. I would give my left arm for a bit more energy.

I open the cubicle door and look round the toilet. Apart from the door there is no other viable way out. The only windows are high up. I consider trying to smash one but the noise would be a giveaway and I have no idea what lies beyond. I know from the view out of my bedroom that I'm a good two or three floors up. I cross to the door.

Each step is getting harder and I need to hold onto a wash hand basin to stay vertical. I pull the door a crack and see the gorilla standing outside my room door. Conveniently there is a hand written sign informing everyone that I am the current occupant.

Make it easy for him won't you Mr National Health Service!!!

I watch as he considers his next move. He reaches for the door handle and I get ready to move. I won't get far but I need to move before he returns.

117

I grasp the door handle and prepare to stagger to my death.

A voice rings out and I realise one of the nurses has spotted the gorilla. Gorilla number one take his hand off the door handle and turns in the direction of the voice. The nurse is asking what he is doing and he starts to spin a story about being a friend. The nurse asks who let him onto the ward. It isn't visiting time so how did he get past reception? Gorilla number one is free wheeling as he tries to dig himself out of a hole. He opts for discretion and tells the nurse he will come back later. The nurse isn't that easily fobbed off and asks him to wait while she phones reception. The gorilla ignores her and turns to walk away from the ward. The nurse is too long in the tooth to put up with nonsense but she also recognises trouble when she sees it. She heads back to her colleague and a phone.

I wait until she slips into the ward and then I check to see if the gorilla is out of sight. He has gone and I walk slowly to my room. I have no plan of action. No idea what to do. I'm far too weak. Just getting dressed seems like a mountain to climb and I can't make good an escape in a hospital gown - no matter how good my bum looks at my age.

I sit on my bed assuming I have some breathing space while the gorilla retires to formulate a new plan of action. The urge to sleep is massive and I place my head on my pillow. Ten minutes. Ten minutes kip and then I can think straight.

I'm gone.

Chapter 24

Tina and George get busy.

George has just phoned from the police station and asked me to go down and pick him up. I make my excuses and pull a wave of angry looks from my friendly neighbourhood work colleagues for pissing off for a second time in one day. I ignore them. They can all go and take a running jump.

I'm only worried about my boss and he is in a strategic planning meeting - shorthand for being cooped up until well gone finishing time. My car is parked in the multi storey across the road and I am half way out of the office when I remember the parcel and I have to double back to my desk.

Ten minutes later and I am behind the wheel of my venerable Vauxhall Astra. My car has not tipped the thirty thousand mark yet she is nearly thirteen years old. I'm not a high mileage person. But she is reliable, gets me from A to B and I like her. She's my friend. And that says a lot about my life.

I have three friends on this planet - George, my car and Nancy. In rank order Nancy is the oldest friend - we met at primary school. My car is next and then George. There have been others but not others that I would call friends. Not real friends.

To me a friend is not someone who you met a few weeks, months or even years ago. To me a friend is a very special person. I consider my car a person. After all she has a name - Connie. A friend is someone who has to earn their stripes in a big way over a long period of time. Except that would preclude George and, somehow, he has managed to short circuit my whole friendship rule, skipping from a stranger to a friend and missing all the pain in between. I should be suspicious of this. I'm always suspicious of other people's new 'best friends' but George is that unique object in the universe - someone who is different. With George it's not how long you have known him but how deep you have known him and I am Marianas Trench deep.

So I class him as a friend.

The traffic is the usual for this time of day - annoying. The grid system that makes up central Glasgow conspires to send me the wrong way but I have fought hard with it over the years and despite the council's best attempts to ban and bamboozle motorists, I have always managed to get in and out of the centre. I see it as a bit of a personal crusade. It's my right to use a car and until this is taken away from me by force of law I'll slug it out with the Glasgow traffic system and by hook or by crook get to work and get home again.

The police station is easy to find but difficult to park near. Double yellow lines, CCTV cameras and a lack of parking bays inform you that you are not welcome but after a few moments circling I see a Ford Fiesta slide out of a space and I slip in.

George is waiting for me at the reception and we say little until we are in my car. George is a quiet man but today he is in the mood to talk. I should really go back to work and so should George but given the events of the morning we decide to head for my flat in the West End. I'll deal with my boss tomorrow and George is counting on his trip to the police station giving him an out with his company.

He makes a quick call to his boss from his mobile and tells him how it is. He hangs up and shakes his head muttering 'fools'. He tells me that his boss wants him to go in early tomorrow to make up for the lost hours. He thinks that stinks. I think it's fair. My boss will be far less forgiving and I'm not daft enough to let the fact he is in a meeting all afternoon lull me into a sense of false security. I can guarantee that one of the many grazing bovine creatures that populate my office will only be too happy to grass me up.

With that thought I am sullen all the way to my flat but cheer up when I realise that the parking nightmare that I usually live amongst has become a sea of available spaces at this time of day. I park and we go up to my flat hand in hand. I put on the kettle while we chew through what has happened and what we need to do.

It doesn't take long before we get round to the parcel and George is all for opening it. I'm not so sure. Whatever it contains is not going to be something that will benefit us. Then again the sheer curiosity factor has to be taken into account. We throw the idea of opening it back and forth as we sip our tea, me on lemongrass and strawberry, George on monkey brew.

George ends the debate by slitting the parcel flap with his pen knife and tipping the contents onto my coffee table. A small waterfall of photocopied sheets tumble onto the table. Some cascade onto the floor.

I pick up one at random and find myself faced with a typed series of numbers in tables with rough annotations in pen scribbled at random points. George picks up some other sheets and finds the same. We sift through the rest of the contents but they are much of a muchness. George pulls out one that seems to differ from the rest.

For a start it is wholly handwritten. On the left side of the page there are a series of dates going back two years and more. In the centre, lined up with the dates are sums of money ranging from a few thousand pounds to over sixty thousand pounds. On the right, again lined up with the dates, is a list of names. George recognises some of them. He spots six people who all work in his building. There are two people from the same business on the fourth floor and the other four are all from different companies. George can't think of any connection between the companies. Some of the names he recognises seem to have a dozen or more entries on the sheet. George totals up the amounts against a man called Stephen Mulligan. One hundred and sixty two thousand pounds! I ask what Mr Mulligan does. George thinks he is the financial director of a firm called Brightmile. I ask what they do and he is unsure. Something to do with mobile technology he thinks.

The sheet has a number 4 at the top and looks like it is one of a sequence but the rest are missing. The dates stop six months ago but there could easily be sheets after and at least three before. George leaps to the word bribe and I can't think why not. He totals the sheet and whistles when he works out there is over a million pounds on this sheet alone. He searches through a few more of the typed sheets but can't make head nor tail of them.

I decide to make another cup of tea and George follows me into the kitchen. He suggests that we go and see Charlie. After all, the parcel belongs to him. If it has anything to do with his truncated flight and the two thugs then we need to figure what to do next.

The police told George that Charlie was at the Royal and I pick up the phone and dial directory enquiries. I get the number for the hospital and re-dial to enquire when visiting time is. The girl at the other end tells me and we have a couple of hours to kill before we can go visit so we sit down and talk. George opens up and I get some clarity on exactly what went on this morning and then we flip through the sheets again and talk and talk and talk.

I reach the point where I don't want to talk anymore but George seems blind to my subtle suggestions and there is no way I am going to come straight out and ask for sex. I sigh as he starts to put the sheets in page order. I play along until it is time to go see Charlie Wiggs.

Chapter 25

More bad news for Simon.

I'm half dozing when I sense that there is someone in the room with me. Quentin is standing at the doorway. Oozing geekery. I glance at the clock. It is just after five o'clock. My hangover is still hanging around in the background. Before I ask Quentin what he wants I pop another two headache killers. I rub my stomach. A stomach pill follows the headache killers.

I ask if anyone has triggered an e-mail. He shakes his head. I ask if he has cracked the passwords. He shakes his head. I ask him what the hell he wants. He asks me to come through to the main room. I follow, stepping across the jumble sale that he has going on across my carpet.

He gestures for me to sit down next to him in front of Leonard's laptop. I slump beside him but keep a respectful distance. At close range his aroma can kill.

He runs off at the mouth about some techno issue or other. I wait for him to settle down and get to the point. He pulls up a screen full of files and clicks on one. The screen fills with numbers, all neatly tabulated. I stare at them but they make little sense. Quentin tells me that these are the files that Leonard has sent to his 'strategic locations'. I ask him what they mean. He smiles. A toe-curling smile of wasted enamel and rotting gums. He highlights the entire spreadsheet with the mouse. He pulls down a drop down from the menu bar and hits the word unhide. The sheet transforms and words appear next to the numbers. I take the mouse from him and scroll across and down the sheet. I minimise the page. I open up another file and repeat the unhide function. I do this with six files. I fall back on the sofa with my head in my hands.

The calls to 'the Voice', Quentin cracking the codes, the slow disappearance of my hangover. All had lulled me into a sense of optimism. In a few seconds Quentin had undone this. A click of a mouse, a spreadsheet and a cold knife entered my gut.

I had figured that Leonard might have some details that would be bad news in the public domain. What lay in front of me suggested that Leonard was far more dangerous than I had believed possible. I had expected the files would contain some records of the money that had exchanged hands over the years as we had 'grown' our business. Oil in the wheels of commerce as Robin would say. Karen called it 'balls money'. Once they take it, you've got them by the balls.

The thought of Karen reminds me of my liaison with the HR devil. I park the thought and look at the sheet in front of me.

To understand the pit that had just opened in front of me you need to know a little about Retip.

Robin, Karen and I have a tech background - all be it not a very good one. Robin has been fired from two start-up companies for incompetence. Karen has spent a few months in a low security establishment for siphoning off funds. And me: well let's say that I have a string of broken companies hanging around my neck. All in all an unlikely trio to launch a new business. A business that has, to date, performed exceptionally well.

Retip (UK) Ltd is essentially a middle man organisation. We identify customers with tech requirements and suppliers who can service the customer's needs. Then we put them together. Not a very original model. In these days of internet search and instant communication we should have lasted all of ten minutes. In such a high tech world it is easy to cut out the middle man unless they can add value or have a little edge. We had a little edge. And that edge is called a backhander.

Across the globe there are myriad firms with people in charge of purchasing tech equipment. Every one of them falls into three basic categories. Those who take a regular bung to move a deal in the right direction. Those who won't and those who will - but for one reason or another haven't yet dipped their hand in the till.

The first group are not thin on the ground but they are cagey. Those in this group that survive cover their arse well. They do this by only dealing with people they know. Newcomers, even newcomers bearing gifts are rarely welcome.

The second lot are a waste of space to our organisation.

The third group are another small but lucrative bunch. People who have yet to feel a brown envelope. Bung Babies. Value Virgins. Kickback Kindergartners. Call them what you want. To us they were a gravy train.

126

Karen had been the queen of the market. She had a nose for it. We hit the technology tender market hard. Unlike many of our competitors we door-stepped the customer. Karen would exercise her Chitty Chitty Bang Bang style child catcher nose and we were in.

At the start we were crap at the whole game. We barely survived. As the years unfolded we got better. The key was figuring a way to lock in our customers better than a cashback offer at Marks and Spencers. Karen was great at spotting potential 'customers' On the back of this we got good at turning their greed into profit. And then we hit real pay dirt.

Out of the blue we got a call from a firm we had never heard of but they had heard of us. They knew of a tender about to pop out of the European Union money machine. They were barred from bidding. Would we do it on their behalf? For a fee of course. Legit. No backhander. No hassle. We did. And we made good cash. The second gravy train had pulled in at the station. We got on board. Our reputation for winning tenders grew. So did our legit trade. It was a great double-sided combination - bung or fee - both generated cash for us.

Then we got an altogether different call from an altogether different type of organisation. One that had need of methods to wash cash through our system. They could think of nothing better than big European contracts to clean their ill gotten gains.

Now these were serious people. Serious people with serious consequences if you crossed them. However they paid at the top end of generous. They asked few questions - as long as they got their cash and as long as their names never showed up any place they shouldn't.

It was a complex business keeping the three strands of our business working. Leonard had been a star at juggling the small bungs and the legit trade. However, as far as I was aware, he had no knowledge of the serious money laundering.

Staring at me from the computer was clear evidence that this wasn't the case. I knew at once that Robin was to blame. The lazy tosser. We had agreed he would handle the money laundering side of the business - it was all we asked of him. The rest of the time he was either buying, sailing or selling a yacht. He had gotten lazy. At some point he had handed over the laundering to Leonard. Without telling me!

The spreadsheets in front of me contained chapter and verse of the laundering operations. Names, times, amounts - a veritable smorgasbord of information that was now hours from being made public. There were twenty files in total. This told me that Robin had been shirking his duty for at least a year. I was no longer in danger of a spell behind bars. I was now in danger of a far, far worse fate. So was everyone who worked with me. So was anyone who even knew me well. If these sheets got in the wrong hands the clients would declare nuclear war. There were thousands of years of jail time typed into these sheets for our clients. I put my head back in my hands. This was shit of an altogether different dimension.

I left Quentin to his code cracking. I grabbed my mobile and walked into the garden.

I knew Robin was on his latest yacht somewhere off the south coast of France. If he was close to the coast he would have a signal. I dialled his number and waited while my call bounced around the planet. The long drawn out ring tone of an international call sounded in my ears. After five rings it tripped to Robin's answering machine. I left a message. I made it clear that pretending he hadn't checked his mobile was not something I was going to buy. I told him to give me a call right away.

I pulled up Karen's details and stared at the numbers. This was going to be awkward. I hit the dial button and started to walk in circles to calm myself down. Karen picked up on the third ring. I hadn't blocked my caller ID so she would have known who was calling.

We had a few moments of inane chatter. Then I told her we needed to talk about last night but now wasn't the time. She was surprised that the call wasn't going to be about last night. I gave her the bare bones of the story so far. Not all of it. I omitted 'the Voice' and the work he was handling. When I finished there was a predictable silence at the other end. I waited for her response. Just then my phone buzzed. There was no caller ID. I told Karen I had another call. She asked if it was Robin. I told her I didn't know. She told me not to answer it and let it go to voice mail.

So I left it.

The second call vanished. Karen took an audible breath before launching into her own spiel. She went to the heart. If the documents got out then she was sure that Robin would do a runner. I rejected that. Robin had a wife and mansion in Scotland. Correction said Karen - he has sold his house and split with Lyndsey.

When?

Last month.

And when was I to be told?

She didn't have an answer. I suddenly felt like checking the company bank account. I also felt good that I hadn't told her everything. I told Karen she needed to come round. She said that wouldn't be a good idea. A lightbulb went on - 'Et to Brute'. The phone went dead.

There are moments in your life when you wonder just what happened. This was one of them. As of yesterday I had a thriving business. I had a future that looked rosy. Now I was looking at the thin end of squat. I re-dialled Karen. Her voice mail answered. I re-dialled Robin. Zip. I walked back to the main room and into my office. I fired up the computer and waited for the mandatory ten minutes that Bill Gates steals to let me use the thing. I accessed the internet. I drew up the company on-line bank account. I pulled the password from my wallet. I went through the security procedures. I was rewarded with the current trading balance of our main account.

How much crap can one person take? There should have been the thick end of two and a bit million in the account. The balance read less than a hundred thousand. I clicked on the latest statement. Amongst all the day to day stuff were two transfers for a million each. It didn't take a genius to figure where the hell the money had gone - the Robin and Karen retirement fund. I looked up the other three accounts we held with the bank. They were bare. Strangely the first thing that came to mind was my romp with Karen. She must have known that I would find out about the cash? So was last night some sort of goodbye bonk? I tried Karen and Robin again. Nothing. I tried Karen's home number. Another blank.

Karen lived less than fifteen minutes away. I knew her husband was currently in Spain on some property deal. I'd go and face the bitch down. I told Quentin to call me as soon as anything came up. I jumped in the car - burning rubber in getting to Karen's house.

I drew up at the main gate. It was a hell of a house. Nine bedrooms. Five main rooms. A granny flat. Topped off with a swimming pool. The lawn was immaculate. The whole deal would not have looked out of place in one of those glossy house magazines. It occurred to me that Robin's house was none too shabby either. In fact of the three I was the pauper in the poor house. Why had I never noticed it before? Karen's garage door was closed so I couldn't tell if her SLK was at home. And there was another thing; Karen had three cars - none under forty thousand in value. Robin had two in an even higher price bracket. I had a single five series BMW. Top of the range but still nowhere near the value of either of my fellow directors' motorised worth. The feeling in my stomach was not getting better.

Karen has a security entrance squawk box on the left hand pillar of the main gates. I get out of the car and press the button and wait. After a few seconds I press it again. This time I hold it in for good measure. Still nothing. I try the gate but it is locked shut. I give the button one more extra long press. The speaker remains silent.

I circle round the perimeter until I'm at right angles to the main entrance. Here the wall is little more than five feet high. I pull myself up and over. I'm standing on the immaculate lawn. I make my way to the front door.

As I cross the grass I look for signs of movement from the house. There is nothing. Curtains are drawn even though it is still bright daylight outside. Before I reach the door I'm sure there is going to be no answer. I press the doorbell anyway. I'm rewarded by the distant sound of 'I'm Not In Love' by 10cc - Karen lacks taste at times. I give 10cc another couple of outings and give up. As a last throw of the dice I walk round the house. It's wrapped up tight. I decide to call it quits.

The bitch has gone A.W.O.L.

I walk down the main path and I'm just about to cut across the grass to the wall when I see what looks like a business card lying at the edge of the grass. I pick it up. It is warped from lying in the morning dew. I read it. Jonathan Brewer, Managing Partner, Grey, Littleton and Michaels. This is just such a bad news day.

I know of Grey, Littleton and Michaels. High end estate agents who rarely touch anything less than half a million. The bitch isn't A.W.O.L. The bitch is flying the nest.

I pocket the card, jump back over the wall and slump into my car. I pull my mobile out. I try Robin's mobile. I try Karen's mobile and home number. I try Robin's home number. The first three draw a predictable blank. The fourth brings an answer in the shape of Robin's wife, Lyndsey. I ask if she has heard from Robin. Suddenly, no warning, no pre-amble, it is confession time and she goes into overdrive.

How could Robin leave her? What had she done? Wasn't she a good wife? Was it another woman? Did I know if it was another woman? Who was the other woman? Did I think she could get him back? I'm his best friend - can I talk to him? Bring him to his senses?

I let her rant and when she runs out of steam I tell her I'll call her as soon as I hear from Robin. I hang up. I've no intention of phoning her back.

I start up the engine and decide to head back home. Maybe Quentin has some good news? I need some.

Chapter 26

Charlie goes for a short walk.

I'm woken by a presence in the room and I freak. Two bodies. The gorillas? My eyes focus and I see George with a girl that I don't recognise. They are standing quietly near the door. I beckon them over and note the girl is holding the parcel that Leonard gave me yesterday. I ask them to sit down but not before I ask George to check the corridor and tell me if he can see the two gorillas. George's eyes widen in fear. He asks if they are here and I say one of them was. He gets up and opens the door to look out. I can see shapes passing outside and realise that it must be visiting time. The gorillas wouldn't try anything during visiting time. Would they?

George sits down and tells me there is no sign of them. I'm not re-assured. We sit in silence for a few moments and then George introduces me to Tina and fills in on what they have been doing since I saw him on the roof. I reciprocate with my encounter with the gorilla. George agrees with me that they will probably be back. I ask George to go over the contents of the parcel again. They pass me a written sheet with a list of money and names and a sample sheet from the others. They tell me all the other sheets are typed. I scan the written list and recognise a fair few names. I look at the other sheets and recognise them as some sort of record but they lack any sort of clue as to what they are a record of.

134

I put the sheets down and Tina picks them up and puts them back in the parcel.

It doesn't take a genius to figure that Leonard had been up to something deeply dodgy. The names on the list are familiar in their own right but I'm also sure they are connected to each other in some way. At the moment I can't figure how but it will come to me.

I lie back to think and it is obvious that I can't stay in the hospital. The gorilla will return - sure as cheese is cheese. He'll also bring his mate.

I don't know if the gorillas are aware of the parcel and its contents but assuming my introduction to flight was a mistake and that Leonard was supposed to earn his wings then the parcel could well be the object of their desire. Although how throwing me from the roof would have got them the parcel is beyond me. They didn't ask me a blind word about the parcel and at the time they thought I was Leonard.

I quiz George again on the roof top events and thank him for intervening but he insists that it was gorilla number one that had saved me. He had only helped. I was at a loss to figure why?

When George tells me that Leonard is dead I make up my mind and decide we need to leave. If the gorillas come back I am dead meat.

George gathers my clothes and helps me to my feet while Tina keeps watch. I begin the slow process of dressing. After a few moments of struggle I fall back on the bed and ask George to tie my shoe laces. I still feel as weak as a strand of candyfloss. I ask George if there is a way to sneak out unseen but he thinks not - we will have to go by reception. He muses over the idea that at the other side of the main ward there would be an emergency exit but that would mean passing the nursing station and it is definitely manned - so the reception it has to be.

I pull on my coat and lift up my collar. I stand up and George takes my left arm and Tina my right and we walk out into the corridor.

It is quiet now that the visitors are gabbing with the patients. We turn and walk in the direction of the reception but even after a few steps I know I'm little more than dead weight to my partners. I knuckle down and force some strength into my legs and try to take some weight from them.

As we approach the reception Tina has an idea. She asks if George and I could manage for a few yards. I doubt it but we will give it a go. She races ahead and vanishes in the direction of the reception desk. George and I keep walking. Well he walks and I kind of drag.

When we emerge into sight of the reception Tina has the receptionist engaged in deep conversation. Angling herself between the receptionist and us Tina moves slowly round as we crawl across the open space. It is agonisingly slow progress but we make it to the far side and seconds later Tina joins us and I thank her. There is something seriously bright about this woman.

Ahead are the stairs to the ground floor and next to them the lift. I ask if we can take the lift and they both agree. When it arrives we stand back as an orderly rolls out a lady on a dolly stretcher. We get in and the lift slides at hospital pace to the ground floor. When the door opens I ask George how far to the car. He says not far. I don't believe him.

We stagger out onto another corridor and begin following the signs for the exit but after less than a couple of minutes I ask if I can sit down. Gratefully Tina and George drop me into a plastic chair and flop into the chairs on either side. I ask for a glass of water and Tina goes off to get one from a machine a little way down the corridor. I take the opportunity to tell George that this isn't working. I'm not sure I can stand, never mind walk. Tina returns and listens to what I am saying. She thinks for a second and then tells me she will be right back. As I wait I sip at the water. It tastes warm and antiseptic. George asks where Tina is going and I shrug my shoulders. Even that takes too much effort.

Tina re-appears with an empty wheel chair - the girl's a genius. Tina and George leverage me into it and start pushing me to the exit.

We turn a corner and we are in the main entrance. The place is alive. People waiting on chairs, people standing in queues, people dying on trolleys. All walks of life are on a par here. Rich or poor, there are no shortcuts to treatment on the NHS. If you want priority go private.

Standing at the exit doors are the two gorillas. I spot them before they see us and I give George the heads up in a quick way. He wheels me one eighty and we vanish back round the corner. George figures there has to be another way out. Tina disagrees. She thinks hospitals are not far short of prison status nowadays and I think she might be right. I have an idea and tell Tina to get a blanket. She nips off and returns two minutes later without a blanket but with a nurse in tow asking what the hell she is up to.

I tell the nurse that I was cold and that I am on my way home. She looks at me and I can tell she thinks I'm way too ill to be heading out. She starts into question mode and we have a shed load of the wrong answers but then again this isn't a police state so I tell George to get me out of here. What about the gorillas he asks? Just go. He shakes his head, ignores the nurse and pushes me back into the chaos that is the entrance. He keeps his head down and pushes straight for the door but we have a ranting nurse acting as an escort and we become the grand centre of attention double quick as the nurse tells us to wait in a loud and authoritative voice. George ignores her and I look up just as gorilla number one spots us.

I tell George to put his foot down and we exit the hospital at a full tilt. George swings me to the left and Tina rushes out behind us - followed by the nurse. Ten seconds later and the two gorillas are out as well. We are moving at speed parallel to the hospital and George is aided in his pushing by a slight downhill and keeps up a pace. I spot a police car parked at the bottom of the hill. Two policemen are talking next to it. Tina catches up and turns my wheelchair in their direction and forces George to make for them.

We slide to a halt a few yards short of the chatting police. I have no idea what Tina is doing. I look round and see the nurse still standing at the door but the gorillas are right on our tail. Tina coughs and excuses herself and one of the policemen turns round. She points to the two gorillas and, casual as you like, says that they seem to be following us. The policeman cocks his head and makes her repeat what she has just said. The second policeman turns round, surveys the three of us and then looks in the gorillas' direction. The first policeman asks what she means by following us and Tina turns round and points at the gorillas. 'Ask them.'

The gorillas put on the full brakes. The policeman shouts after them and they go into reverse. The policeman shouts again and the gorillas do the hundred yards in Olympic time and vanish into the car park. It then takes ten minutes to convince the police that we don't know who the men in the suits are.

Tina tells the policemen that we had seen them on the way in and that they had started following us on the way out. The policemen tell us to call if they turn up again and let us go. The fact we were so willing to go makes the policemen suspicious. If we were genuine we wouldn't just walk, we would have been at them to do something about the two men. I don't care. All I want to do is to get away. George pushes on and we don't look back.

Tina's car is parked a couple of streets away and as we head for it all three of us do a great deal of rubber necking to see if the gorillas are following. We get to the car and I am bundled into the back. There is no room for the wheel chair and we abandon it on the street and Tina takes off.

George wants to go back to his flat. Tina disagrees. I'm with Tina. If the gorillas have picked us up since we left the policemen the last thing we want to do is lead them to one of our houses. Tina drops on to the M8, heading for Edinburgh. We pass a couple of junctions and then with no warning, she throws a left at the last moment and screeches up the next off ramp. At the top she jumps a set of red lights, turns left and hauls the car into the car park for the Fort Shopping Mall. She cuts through the car park and at the far end finds a space and pulls in.

She orders us out of the car and George seems surprised at her abrasive nature. George and Tina haul me to my feet and drag me, under Tina's directions into a nearby Starbucks. I'm pushed into a mock leather armchair and Tina tells George to order up three anythings. He ambles off and Tina sits in the chair next to me. I sense a conversation coming on.

Chapter 27

A gorilla goes for a wander.

I ain't up to this running lark anymore. Bally might be but this is too much like hard work. That and the close shave with the pigs. None of it adds up to easy money.

Bally is breathing hard next to me. I'm down on my haunches and he is looking back to see if we were followed. We had hit the car park and then kept running and only stopped when we got to the cathedral. I look up at the building. I'm not big on churches. They don't agree with me but this one is nice enough. I don't know much about it other than it is called Glasgow Cathedral and the monks who used to live here started life brewing beer. Seems like a good idea to me. Not sure how churchy it is but booze is never a bad idea. I know that Wellpark Brewery is not far from the cathedral. Now there is a place that would be worth a visit. Home of Tennent's Lager - my drink of choice. 'Brewed in Glasgow since 1885'. See I told you I was good at remembering things. I wonder if they do tours and I ask Bally. He looks at me with that 'piss off and die' look that I seem to get on a regular basis. I can't see the issue. We've lost the vic and might as well do something useful.

Bally stands up. His breathing is heavy but easing. Mine will take a bit longer to calm down. There is a museum in front of the cathedral but it is closed for the day. I read the sign - St Mungo's

141

Museum of Religious Life and Art. A pity it is closed because it is bound to have a cafe and if I can't get a pint I could go a cup of tea. Bally is off for a wander and I look across the road and see an old, old house.

Now I know about this house. I do. I just need to think and it will come back. There is something special about it. It is very old and has a small door and three rows of three windows on the side I can see. It's a kind of rickety affair; plain at the front but a bit more arty at the back if I remember correctly. I can't think what the hell is so special about it but if I wait it will come back.

Bally is soon on the mobile phone. I hear one side of what sounds like an argument and then he hangs up. He tells me we have to sit tight. I ask what for and he blanks me. So I get up and walk to the pedestrian crossing and across the road. Bally doesn't stop me.

I go for a wander round the old building and my memory kicks in. Provand's Lordship - strange name for a house but it is the oldest house in Glasgow I think. See I am good at remembering things. I find a plaque on the sidewall. It reads:

ST NICHOLAS GARDEN
1995
PROVAND'S LORDSHIP
1491
Built by Bishop Andrew Muirhead
for the chaplain of the nearby
St Nicholas Hospital
Admission Free

I'm not sure if that means the garden was built by the bishop or if the bishop built the house. Even I know it can't be both. There is over five hundred years between the dates. Not unless the old Bish was a time traveller or, maybe there are two Andrew Muirheads. One around today and one back in 1491. Of course there could be an unbroken chain of Andrew Muirheads going back in history or maybe you only get to be a bishop if your name is Andrew Muirhead or maybe you have to change your name to Andrew Muirhead if you become bishop or maybe it is the same guy and he just hangs around so long that everyone else dies and he keeps going, the oldest man in the world and the oldest house in Glasgow. Maybe this is his house and he just lets people wander round it to avoid paying the council tax.

It *says* it's a museum but maybe that's just a cover. Maybe deep down, out of sight of the tourists there are a whole set of secret rooms where Andrew lives. Maybe he has a whole family and they are all over five hundred years old and frozen at a certain age by some strange power that the house holds. Glasgow could be sitting on the fountain of youth and not know it. I bet if you know just what to do and just what to say you can get a bit of the old youth magic yourself.

I think about it and then I have an idea. I bet the plaque is a clue. Now I'm good at these things. I used to be good at Cluedo. At least I was good at the kids' version.

So let's figure - the old bish feels guilty about being so old that he has put the secret in plain sight.

If you can figure it out then the jackpot's yours. I read the sign again. Let's see - St Nicholas Garden 1995 Provand's Lordship 1491. So if we take 1491 away from 1995 we get? Shit I need a calculator - I'm crap at sums.

I pull out my mobile but it takes me five minutes to figure out where the calculator is on the damn thing. I hate maths. After I check the sum a few times I get five hundred and four. This is so Dan Brown. Not so much the Da Vinci Code but more the Provand's Lordship Cipher. I'm not sure if cipher is the right word but it sounds good. The Provand's Lordships Cipher, the PLC.

I squat down in front of the plaque and let my mind wander. I like letting my mind wander.

So we have 504. I count the letters and numbers in the plaque and get 124 if I ignore the Glasgow Museums logo at the bottom. So I add this to 504 and get 628. I then add the six, the two and the eight and get 16. Now there is a thing. Today is the 16th and if I add the one and the six I get seven and this is July - the seventh month. The plaque says the garden was built for the nearby hospital and we have just been to a hospital. It also says Admission Free and I bet that's code to let you know that anyone can have the secret if you can crack the PLC.

I lie down on the ground and stare up at the plaque. I'm onto something here, I just need to think.

Ta-Da. I've got it. The plaque contains instructions. If I go to the hospital, which I have just done - I'm assuming the Royal and the St Nicholas mentioned in the plaque are one and the same - and walk round the garden 1995 times and then round the house 1491 times on the sixteenth of July, I get the magic.

Seems a bit much though. I'm not sure how long that will take but it isn't going to be a short walk.

No the bish is cleverer than that. My maths is wrong. Maybe I need to change tack. I add up all the numbers in the first date and I get twenty four. Add the two and four of twenty four and I get 6. Add up the numbers in the second date and I get fifteen and add up the one and the five and I get 6 again. Six is the magic number. If I walk round the building and the garden six times on the sixteenth of July I get free admission to the youth club - for ever.

I stand up - there is no time like the present. I pick a start point and off I go. Forget your couple of grand for a hit - I'm going to live forever. The bish is a smart old coot. I bet no-one else has cracked the old PLC.

I feel good.

I'm on my third circuit when Bally shouts from across the road. I ignore him and keep walking. I'm fairly sure that once you have started the laps you can't stop and Bally vanishes from sight behind me as I round the corner. I keep walking and as I start my fourth lap Bally appears behind me and tells me to get my backside in gear. It seems we have a potential address for the vic. I blank Bally and keep walking. He gets mad so I tell him, while still walking, all about the PLC and I can see he is struggling - but then again he's just jealous that he didn't figure it out. I tell him I only have two more circuits to go and he starts to shout. I walk on.

One and half laps to go. Bally is now trailing me threatening me with a range of consequences from loss of earnings to severe physical harm but the prize behind the PLC is too great for me to be diverted. I tell him I have only got to go round one and a bit times more and he can shout and scream as much as he wants but I'm finishing it. I see his shoulders slump and I know I've won. Ten minutes later I finish.

I'm disappointed. I expected at least a flash of light or the sound of thunder. Something to announce my new found eternal youth. All I get is more gobbing from Bally but I know it has worked. I'm sure it has worked and with a spring in my step I follow him to our car.

As I walk I wonder what the world will be like in five hundred years from now.

Maybe I should keep a diary.

Chapter 28

Tina has had enough.

'So why the hell should I help you?'

I'm mad as hell. Strange though, because I was almost calm when we left the hospital. Even when the two idiots were after us I simply thought this is something we need to get through. When we got to the car I was nervous, apprehensive, uncertain but not angry. It wasn't until the conversation got round to how going back to my flat was a bad idea that the anger started. And it built as we headed along the motorway and now it is at full boil and there is no off switch.

What in heaven's name am I doing involved in all this. I don't know diddly squat about Charlie Wiggs. George doesn't know much more than I do and yet we are being chased by thugs. I have a dodgy parcel in my handbag, my house may not be safe and for what? For Charlie Wiggs? Why? For heaven's sake why?

I ask Charlie the self same question for a second time and it is clear that Charlie doesn't have an answer. How could he? What do I expect him to say? "Please Tina you have to help me - we've been friends for nearly an hour. How can you let me down after all this time?"

Instead he looks at me and says

'You shouldn't.'

This stops me in my tracks. It's hard to know where to go when the air has been let out of your tyres so effectively. He repeats and repeats the phrase until his head drops and somewhere my off switch is hit and I drop from boil to simmer and then down.

It's not just what he said, it's his whole demeanour. He oozes pathetic. His face is half hidden in a bandage and what you can see of it is either black with bruises or white with shock. He is slumped in the chair and is struggling to keep himself upright.

To add mustard to his last reply he gently kicks me between the tits when he says I should go and he will sort it out.

He could no more sort this out than my two goldfish. The last of my anger slides away and pity replaces it. I look round wanting George to be there with three mugs of coffee. But he is still in the queue and I find myself lifting my hand and placing it on Charlie's lap. He tries to smile but even that seems to sap him. I have to lean forward to catch him as he passes out. Luckily the chair is big enough for me to push him back. I stand up and use my coat as a pillow and try and make him comfortable.

People are looking but I ignore them and settle Charlie before sitting down and waiting for George.

When George comes back he has three enormous cups of something frothy and high in caffeine. He looks concerned when he sees Charlie but I'm counting on the fact that Charlie is asleep and not sliding into some form of coma.

We sip the coffee in silence and I look around at the normality that I have suddenly been divorced from.

Next to us two older ladies are chewing the cud and trying to divvy up a slab of what looks like solid chocolate. Next to them a mother is breast feeding her kid and next to her two business types are sitting in front of two open laptops trying not to spill their coffee on the keyboards.

The queue at the till is a cross section of Glasgow life - all waiting to order their Venti De-Caff Wet Skinny Latte's or their triple espressos. Beyond the glass window the shopping mall teases me with more normality.

A couple of hoodies are being quizzed by the police. A mother is dragging a child behind her in that time-honoured manner that all children know and hate. An old man is sitting on a bench - at work mining his nose for whatever contents it might give up and next to him a young girl is staring in fascination at the old man. He retrieves something and pops it straight in his mouth and the young girl squeals in delight and shouts for her mum to come over.

There are now two worlds. Old and new. This morning I was a resident of the former and at some point I was evicted and now wander in the latter. I wonder how I can get the eviction order overturned but one look at Charlie and I know it won't be anytime soon. I ask George what we should do and then have such a blindingly obvious idea that I feel maybe I can gain re-admission to the old world.

'We should go to the police,' I almost shout. 'Tell all and we are clear.'

So simple. So obvious. So right. Just go to the police and tell them everything and let them take care of it all. OK, so George would have to admit lying to them the first time round but I've watched enough Law and Order to know that the police are well used to the odd porky.

We pitch up at the local station. No better still we pitch up back at Glasgow's main police station. George bares his soul and throws himself upon their mercy. I tell them that it was me that made him see sense. We hand over the documents and they can put Charlie back in hospital and give him a guard until the two thugs are caught. We skip free and I'm back in the normal world.

Suddenly the coffee tastes wonderful. The man excavating his nose is repellent but it's his nose. I want to tell the two hoodies to get a life and the two men with laptops to get a life. I even want to tell the two old biddies to get real and buy a slice of cake each rather than cheaping out.

It is a stunning fact of life just how quick things can change. I smile at George and then Charlie wakes up at my shout and chucks a bucket of cold sick on my magic moment.

'Can't go to the police. Can't. Leonard isn't the only one that has his hands dirty,' he says.

The living dead speaks. Obviously he wasn't as out for the count as I thought. George leans over and asks what Charlie means.

It's not a long story but it takes a long time to tell as he drifts between full consciousness and somewhere near sleep. At times he stops speaking for so long I think he has passed out again. George makes a second trip for more coffee and this time forces a double espresso down Charlie. It seems to help and we get to the end of his story.

He slumps back and closes his eyes and I look at George and mouth the word 'crap'.

It transpires that our Charlie is not as innocent a bystander in all this as we thought.

Chapter 29

Charlie owns up.

I finish telling George and Tina my little revelation and I feel so bad that I want to lie on the floor and just drift off but the caffeine is still getting to work so I close my eyes and go over what I have just said.

I knew the names on the list were familiar and I knew there was a connection. I knew I had seen them before and now I knew where.

Leonard is, or rather was, a workaholic. In before me. Out after me. Weekends were just additional work days and I can't remember the last time he had a holiday. I could never figure why. We weren't overloaded. I had as much on as he did and I knew it. Our regular monthly meetings were designed to re-distribute work load around the department if it looked like someone was sinking but in all the time I had been at the firm I can't remember Leonard calling out for help. Still I assumed he was putting in the hours to get by because he had to and every time I brought it up at the monthly meet he would dismiss it all and tell me that we all had our own way of working. I would shrug and tell him it was his grave he was digging. He would shrug and smile. It pissed me off.

Leonard played stuff close to his chest. As a result it was a bit of a surprise when mid last year he turned turtle and threw up his hands and admitted he needed a bit of help. He told me a client had just landed him with a shed load of nonsense and he needed to off load a little of his other work for a short period. I told him to bring it up at the monthly meeting. To say he wasn't keen on this suggestion would be an understatement. He said that he didn't want to let the others know and then asked me if I was averse to a little homer or two.

I wasn't. Nobody in the firm was. It was strictly against the rules and therefore everybody did it. Only they did it very quietly and very carefully. There is nothing like prohibition to spur on enterprise.

Most of my homers were family and friends - if you were smart this meant more friends than family - it is hard to charge your family for advice. In the main it was tax advice and the occasional piece of investment advice.

Leonard opened up a little and it transpired that I was in the lower divisions on this front and Leonard was aspiring to the Premier League. He told me he was doing a little extra curricular work for Retip Ltd and would I mind covering the day to day on their core business for a while. In return he would cut me in on the deal he had with their management but if anyone asked I could, with a clear conscience, tell them I was doing work for, and billing for, Cheedle, Nudge and Baker. I asked what the other work was - but he blanked me and when the brown envelope turned out to be worth a thousand a month, who was I to complain? The most I ever made from my own brown envelopes was a few hundred quid.

In this way I got to know Simon, the Managing Director; Karen - HR and Robin - the FD, and from the off I didn't like them. Everything about them smelled like old cheese in a well worn sock but like a good boy I put my head down and did the work avoiding them as much as I could.

All went well until Leonard was hit by an industrial bout of man flu. He tried to keep up work from home but his man flu turned real on him in a bad way. Robin was on the phone to him daily but eventually Leonard had to call it quits and told Robin that he would be back in a few days and could he just park what he could till then.

The following day Robin appeared in my office. His face was flushed and he said that he couldn't get a hold of Leonard. This wasn't surprising since Leonard's wife had taken Leonard's mobile off him and confiscated his laptop and Blackberry. Robin had even gone round to his house but Leonard's wife had blanked him. I was obviously the last resort.

He asked if I was able to access Leonard's system and I said I could but I wasn't allowed. In an instant he produced a wedge of cash and dropped it on the table. There had to be close to five grand in two bundles. I stared at the cash and then at Robin. He told me he didn't want to dick around. He needed some info and only Leonard had it. The money was mine if he could log onto Leonard's machine for ten minutes. Ten minutes max and then he would be gone.

I'd love to say I hesitated and had a moral crisis but I didn't. I fired up Leonard's machine, logged on and went back to my desk. Robin was as good as his word and after grabbing some sheets from the printer was gone in less than ten.

I went over to close the machine down but out of curiosity I decided to see what he had accessed. I also wanted to make sure he hadn't gone surfing into anyone else's accounts. I breathed a little easier when I found out that he had simply opened up some Retip Excel documents and printed them off.

I clicked on the documents and was rewarded with a list of names and a bunch of dates. The same names that were in the parcel that Tina held - only this time the names were accompanied by a list of company names. Company names some of who were all good Cheedle, Nudge and Baker clients. Clients who were in receipt of backhanders if the list in the parcel was anything to go by.

I told George and Tina that I had closed down Leonard's computer and went back to work happy with my five grand on my hip and an additional grand a month in undeclared income. To date I was now fourteen thousand pounds to the good and there was no way that I could claim that I knew nothing was amiss in Leonard's dealings. At the very least Robin had the five grand over me. I couldn't stop George and Tina going to the police but it would be without me. I told them that I needed to sort this out but I knew, as I said it, that this was just plain beyond me in my present state.

I wasn't sure how they would react. George is a passing acquaintance and I only met Tina an hour ago - and yet I had just confessed to fraud and deception. George said he wanted to chat with Tina and they got up and went outside. I saw them sit on a bench in the middle of the main mall drag and start to chew each other's ears with serious vim and vigour. I drifted in and out of sleep and was wrestled back to the real world by the sound of raised voices.

I looked out at the mall and Tina was standing over George, hands on hips giving him a right doing. George was head down taking it like a man.

Chapter 30

George also owns up.

Tina is going off at the deep end. Big style. Around us the shoppers have come to a halt. There is nothing like a couple having a screaming argument to bring out the nosey in you. I'm staring at my feet and yet I can tell that there is not an eye in the place that isn't focussed on Tina and me.

I was only trying to get everything out in the open. 'Fess up' as my brother's kid would say. Tina seems to have gone into stuck record mode. She just keeps screaming *'What'* like some crazy burglar alarm. I reach out and try and touch her leg. She jumps back but at least she stops shouting. I count to ten and look up and she is standing about six feet away. Her face is flushed red and her eyes have a wild look that I've never seen before. She is framed by the steel and aluminium edifice of a Next shop and as I look left and then right, there are still a fair number of people fixated on our little scene.

I feel like standing up and telling them to mind their own business and then I wish the chair was a James Bond prop and that it would sink into the mall floor to be replaced by an identical but unoccupied copy.

The ball is in Tina's court and I wait to find out if she is going to slam it into my privates or just flip it skywards and walk off. She does neither. She walks forward and slumps into the seat next to me.

The world around us switches frequency and we are old news.

'Why?'

She looks at me. OK so here's the rub. After Charlie had confessed to his little misdemeanour we had come out to figure what to do next. Tina - in the middle of an act of self preservation - says we should still go to the police and if it dropped Charlie in it then so be it. I was less than keen. Partly because Charlie was one of life's good guys and hadn't taken the piss out of my indiscretion in the cupboard, partly because I had fed the police a line of nonsense less than a few hours ago but in the main because I maybe wasn't as clean as I might be.

Now don't get me wrong I know nothing of the whole Charlie/Leonard/Retip thing. All of this is news to me but there are certain things that I would rather stayed in the darker corners of my life. I'm no career criminal but I have a nice little side line going down at Tyler Tower and it is not the sort of side line that I want the police sniffing around.

It started in a small way. People asking me if I knew where they could get their hands on small everyday office stuff - paper, pens - you know. It was easy. Most of the offices had their own stationery suppliers but some of the offices used me as a source. The smaller offices found that I could provide a very reasonable service at prices substantially below the market norm. I also provided them with a paper trail that indicated a far higher selling price than was the case. I'm happy and they are happy.

In time this developed into other areas. Tickets for concerts - all because my brother wanted to off load a couple of Neil Diamond tickets. CD's and DVD's - high quality copies - no rubbish. Small electronic items - I'm a whiz at the cut price iPod - to larger items - white goods are becoming a speciality. I became the source for many a thing in the building. To date my biggest deal was on a Volkswagen Golf Plus at a very non VAT price. All in all the transactions earn me a nice little supplement to the pitiful wages my firm think I'm happy with.

I see myself as providing an essential service. Unfortunately the service involves less than kosher gear and no mention to my tax man. Not that I feel guilty about this. I mean it goes on in every corner of every part of this planet. In Italy tax dodging is the national sport and you tell me how many real Rolexes you find on the street corner when you next visit any one of a dozen Far East cities.

It was when I passed on this info to Tina that she hit the roof.

Next to me she was talking again and trying to tell me that we could still tell the police about Charlie et al and I could keep quiet about my entrepreneurship. Cool I say until I tell her that Retip and by Retip I mean Robin and Karen are two of my best customers. Drop them in it and they won't hesitate to pull me down with them.

Especially as Karen is sitting on the hot VW. A pressie for her niece. And Karen is more than aware that it is an oven glove special. Well heeled and moneyed up as she is, the chance to get a brand new car at the same price as a third hand, high mileage model was too good to pass up.

Tina tries to argue that no one is going to admit to receiving stolen goods. I don't buy it. Robin is into me for forty iPod nano's - last year's Retip client Christmas presents. Forty for the price of ten. He currently has another order for fifty and a friend of his wants the same again twice.

Tina still doesn't think they will bother with me.

I play the trump card. The aforementioned iPods are currently sitting in my little cubby hole in the office along with three docking stations, ten pairs of Parasuco jeans - not quite from the original manufacturer - a good few hundred CD's and DVD's - unfortunately the DVD's are of films that have yet to make their cinematic debut, a range of brand name perfumes and aftershaves, a brand new set of Nike golf clubs, four Sony Vaio laptops, ten sets of Wusthof kitchen knives and a veritable pot pourri of small but eminently desirable objects. Even if Karen and Robin stay stum I need time to move the stuff out. As soon as the police start snooping and my name comes up I'm a goner - sure as eggs is eggs my little stash will be found.

A quick check of my little den and its hello Mr Sheriff.

Tina slumps back and I suspect I am no longer the perfect find that Tina thought I was. I refrain from telling her that I would have been the cream at furnishing her new flat. I'd already sourced an Aga at a very favourable price - she told me within an hour of meeting about her desire for an Aga.

Sitting next to me, the calm after the storm, I knew she still had a few options that neither Charlie nor I could take advantage of. She could just leave. Walk. Claim no knowledge. She would probably get away Scot free. Or she could also roll up at the police and drop Charlie, me and the rest in it and I couldn't see she would be in that bad a place. But I can tell she is struggling. Maybe my down to earth charm is difficult to live without?

'This is the wrong place to do this.'

With this she gets up and walks back into the Starbucks.

Chapter 31

A break for Simon.

The drive back from Karen's house did my mood no good. I slam the car door and I kick the front door for good luck. As I charge into my house I note that Quentin is spreading like a virus. The hardware that had decorated the main room has been added to by coffee cups, plates and a take away pizza box. I know better than rattle his cage but I rip him a new one for the mess. He takes the kicking in silence and begins to tidy away all his gear. He was leaving. I knew it. He knew it and he knew I knew it. I took a deep breath, went into apology mode and promised him a bonus if he could crack the code tonight. He stared at me, mid pack. I stared back.

I knew he would back down and get back to work. He knew he would back down and get back to work and I knew he knew that I knew. I left to make a coffee too many. My mobile goes off. I pull it from my pocket and check the caller but the number is withheld. I let it trip to answer machine. While I wait for the caller to leave a message I charge up the espresso machine. I press the go button and set it in motion. The phone bleeps in my hand. I dial up the answer service. It is 'the Voice'. I head for the office. I retrieve a Pay As You Go and dial the number. Answer machine. Ten minutes. Phone rings. I answer.

'We have a positive ID on one of the targets. He has been taken care of and his PC is on the way to you. We had a negative ID on two more but they also had to be removed. This will increase the cost. We are looking for the last two and will call later.'

The line goes dead. Three people dead. Even I swallow at that one. Hell of a price to pay for my peace of mind. Two to go. I hope they get them quickly. At least I was down to one electronic copy of the documents floating around out there. One soft and one hard copy.

The espresso machine lets me know it is ready to pump steam through the beans. I froth and burble my way to another hit of caffeine. I take the cup through to the den and switch on the TV. Fifteen minutes of BBC News 24. Fifteen minutes of Sky News. There is nothing on Leonard. I hit the internet. Leonard is living in cyber space.

The earlier story has been updated with his name and a note that they are looking for his family. The connection to Charlie through Cheedle, Baker and Nudge had been made. There is a rough description of two individuals the police wanted to talk to. The descriptions are vague. I doubt that 'the Voice's' thugs are quaking in their boots. I shout through to Quentin if the e-mail had been tripped. He says no.

Whoever Leonard's other electronic 'strategic location' is either haven't caught up with the news or are currently winging their way to the police to start singing. I could only hope they were news shy. I haul my arse out of the chair. I go back in to see the geek king. I tell him I am going out. I give strict instructions to contact me as soon as he cracks the code. He nods. I tell him to call if the e-mail is tripped. I think he says ok.

I leave. Fire up the car. I have a mission on. It is time to break records cutting across the city. A light rain is falling. Then again this is Glasgow - a city that really should have two hundred names for rain. My grandmother, a veteran of Glasgow's west end defended the rain by telling everyone that it might rain a lot but at least it kept the streets clean. She was right on both counts.

The traffic is thinning out on the back of the rush hour but there is still enough to frustrate me. I see a gap ahead. I squirt between a bus and taxi, raising horns and fingers. I shoot an amber light. I haul the car into the left hand lane. I strip a layer of rubber from the tyres as I round the corner. I lay my foot to metal and send a surge through the three and half litre German power plant. The road slides under me and I make the next three lights on green and the fourth zips past as it trips to red.

I am running parallel to the River Clyde. A river in transition. A river once famed the world over for shipbuilding. A river now acting as a backdrop to new offices and luxury flats. I flash past the Scottish Exhibition and Conference Centre - hugging the edge of the car parks. The wheels complain as I pass the heliport and onto the Clydeside Expressway. I plant my foot a little deeper - trying to work out a balance between excessive and legal speed.

It had been while surfing the internet that I had a blinding flash of inspiration. I knew, with huge certainty, where Karen was. I had to be quick but if luck was with me she would be ensconced in her mother's flat in Whiteinch. Whiteinch was an old feeder district for the Clyde shipyards up until their demise in the 60's and 70's. Tonight was the night Karen went to see her mum. A ritual that she held to with religious zeal - cutting meetings, phone calls and just about anything if she thought she was going to miss her seven o'clock cup of tea with dear old mum.

It had been the reference to Leonard's family on the news item that had sparked the thought. God love my mind. The sign for the Clyde tunnel looms up. I take the exit prior and down to a roundabout. I zip onto the old road to Dumbarton and over the entrance to the tunnel. I take a right. Karen's mum lives on Medwin St. Two floors up in a typical Glasgow tenement. I roar past what had once been the old swimming pool and steamie.

The steamie was Glasgow slang for the giant communal laundries that sat next to most Victorian built swimming pools. In their time they had been the street cafés of their day. The centre of local community life. Built of red sandstone they were places built in an era when space was not a restriction but more of an opportunity.

I spot Karen's 911 parked on the other side of the road. I find a space and shoehorn myself in.

Karen's mum is in her early nineties and fiercely independent. Karen had been arguing for her to move into a home for years. Her mum refuses point blank. I couldn't see why Karen was pushing so hard. I'd met her mum on a number of occasions. She had seemed in no more need of an old folk's home than me.

I can see the entrance to her mum's close. I can easily reach the car before Karen could get in and drive off. I sit back and wait.

Chapter 32

The gorillas go house hunting.

The instructions from 'the Voice' were clear. Jim and I were to drive to Charlie Wiggs, the vic's home and wait. If the vic didn't turn up by eight o'clock we were to break in. I had argued against this. Surely the vic would avoid his home if he knew he was being hunted. 'the Voice' told me it was not my decision and just to get on with it. I told him I wanted to call it quits and try and pick up the vic tomorrow but 'the Voice' wasn't someone to rub the wrong way.

Jim is trailing behind me doing his puppy dog thing but with a smile a mile wide. I have no idea what he was doing round the Provand's Lordship. I hate Planet Jim and try and stay away from it at all costs.

We go back to the hospital car park and pick up my car and I tell Jim to get out the A-Z and find the address we need. Twenty five minutes later we are entering leafy suburb land. Substantial sandstone terraced houses flash past flipping to semi-detached and then detached as the price bracket rises. We hit a main roundabout and head out towards the country. It is one of my favourite things about Glasgow. You're never far from green.

The vic lives in a new housing estate on the edge of the city. The area is a maze of houses that look like they have been poured from the same jelly mould. The pavements and the roads around here seem to merge into the one slab of block-work and at times it is difficult to know if you are driving where you should be walking.

Speed bumps and mini roundabouts abound.

After a dozen false starts we find the vic's house - a fair sized detached villa that is far too close to its neighbour for the price it no doubt costs. It is a split brick affair with darker red bricks on the bottom and lighter yellow ones on top. The décor is mock Tudor and there is a postage stamp of a lawn outside.

The rest of the front is taken up by a driveway that you could squeeze two cars into if you are good at Tetris. The garage doesn't look big enough for anything larger than a motorcycle. I choose a spot on the opposite side of the road but this is 'car in driveway' land not 'car at the side of the road' land and for all I know I might even be parked on the pavement. But fuck it we have orders and if anyone asks they can go take a running jump. At least I think that way for about ten seconds and then re-start the engine and pull away. Jim asks what I'm doing. I drive out of sight of the house and park up a couple of streets away.

I must have put on my thick head this morning. We were buttonholed this morning with the other vic. We will be on an 'all points' from the police and no doubt the current vic has been linked to Leonard. After all the two vics came from the same company. If someone reports us outside the vic's house or the police do a drive by - as they no doubt will when they discover Charlie has checked out of the Hotel Royal - we are history.

I start the car again and go in search of a quieter spot. I find it at the back of a rugby club. Typical of the area. Rugby not football. I tell Jim to get our bags from the boot and we change into more casual clothes and pack away our suits. We will need to go on rotation for this one. But with care. We can't cruise past the vic's house in the car too often. Twitchy curtains are the norm around here. We also can't walk by too often. The same curtains will be in action. So we will need to mix it up. Me in the car. Jim on foot. Me on foot. Jim in the car and so on.

We will keep fifteen minutes between passes and change between car and foot. If either of us sees the vic we phone the other and rendezvous as close to the house as we can. If we do this right there will always be one of us in the car and ready to roll.

If by eight o'clock there is no sign of the vic we will move to 'break in' mode and search the place for the documents. 'the Voice' doesn't know what we are looking for so we are to lift anything that seems relevant.

I drop Jim a short way from the house and drive back to the rugby club. Fifteen minutes later I cruise out and head for the vic's house. I pass Jim returning to the rugby club and I keep going and eyeball the target. All is quiet. I head back to the club and Jim jumps in, lets me out and heads away.

We keep this up until just before eight o'clock and then return to the car park to plan the break in.

The rain has stopped but it is still bright daylight despite the hour. At this time of year it won't get dark 'till gone ten. We have no choice but to go in when it is light and a day 'break in' is far harder than a night time one.

On the walk/drive bys I've sussed out the house. A shiny burglar alarm tells me this will be no walk in the park but I've beaten alarms before and you would be amazed how many people don't set them. Better still maybe the vic is a cheapskate and the alarm is nothing more than a decoy box.

I make a quick call to 'the Voice' and get the heads up on the latest. Not that it helped. No sign of the vic so the break in was on.

I figure there are two ways to approach the job. Neither were on my recommended list and both are on the shit end of risky.

The first is to find a weak point - a window that is unlocked (climb in the window), a key left on the inside of a door (smash the window and turn the key), a key left on a work surface (smash a window and use a bent wire coat hanger to retrieve the key) - or just smash a big enough window and you are in. This would sound like the obvious first port of call except twitchy curtains can scupper you real quick if you spend too long casing the house.

The second approach was more direct. On the last trip round I had chanced my arm with a quick walk up the vic's driveway and a tug at the garage door and I knew we were in.

It is unbelievable how many people leave the garage door open in this day and age. There is no guarantee that the internal door between the garage and the house will be open or that it will be easy to crack but with a closed garage door behind us we can take as long as we like to get in. And in my experience if all else fails brute force will eventually do the job. The tricky bit is getting us both in through the garage in twitchy curtain land.

I leave the car as close as I can without parking it somewhere that will raise questions. We walk round to the vic's house and I tell Jim what to do. This is all about speed. I can do fuck all about anyone watching other than make sure the coast is as clear as possible - after that we are down to luck.

At the driveway we turn and walk up it as if we were heading for the front door. Just two visitors to Charlie's house. I give one last check and at least there is no one out on the street.

As I pass the garage door I reach down, twist the handle and with a pull lift it clean open. Jim dives under and I follow. We are in and I close the door. I wait for a shout but that doesn't happen very often. People just phone the police.

The garage is a shrine to neatness and tidiness. The floor is brilliant white. The two walls either side of us are empty but the wall at the back is racked and stacked with garage stuff. The internal door sits at the far right of the back wall and looks very promising.

It is a white wooden six panel door. The sort that you meet every day inside a new house. As such it isn't a security door. Mistake.

The door opens in towards the garage so I need something to lever it open. I search the racks and come up with the very fellow - a crow bar. Some people must think they are invincible.

I stick the sharp end of the bar in at the lock and put pressure on. The door creaks and then, with a splinter, it gives. I push back on the door trying to keep any alarm contacts still connected. If there is an alarm we will need to move quickly once the door is opened. If not - well hallelujah.

I look round and make sure Jim has the two holdalls we brought with us and tell him I am going to open the door. I take a breath and pull the door a fraction. As soon as I do I hear the tell tale beep, beep, beep of an alarm telling the owner to input the correct code.

'Move,' I shout.

I grab a bag from Jim and we sprint in. Jim heads for the stairs and I take the first door on the right. It is the kitchen. A sterile world of stainless steel and granite - not cheap. Checking my gloves are secure I pull out all the kitchen drawers but there is nothing but culinary gear.

At the far end of the kitchen there is a double door and I push my way through it and into a dining room that opens out onto a conservatory at the back. Then the alarm goes off. I ignore it. I could try and knock the box from the wall but nowadays alarms are designed for that. Anyway the internal alarm keeps my mind focussed on getting the job done at speed.

The dining room has a sideboard and one of the drawers reveals some papers. I sweep them into my holdall. I check the conservatory is clear, exit the dining room and enter the main room at the front of the house.

A giant plasma TV dominates the room and the rest of the furniture is arranged to pay homage to the telly. There is a book shelf filled with

Waterstone's finest top ten and I brush them all off but there is nothing hidden behind them. I can hear Jim upstairs going through the place. There is no subtlety in burglary. You trash without prejudice. You don't look under a bed; you simply turn it over. You don't rake through drawers; you pull them out and tip them upside down. Speed is of the essence and we needed a hard on full of speed.

The alarm continues to howl.

The front room proves to be a washout and I leave, cross the hall at the bottom of the stairs and through the door opposite. It is the toilet. I trash the medicine cabinet and the towel bin but nothing. There is one door left and when I push it I know I am in jackpot land.

The study is neat. A desk with a laptop power plant on a table faces the sole window. I pull the curtain shut and work my way round the room. I tip any likely papers into the holdall until I have everything except the contents of a filing cabinet. I sprint back to the garage and pick up the crowbar and hear Jim's feet on the stairs.

The alarm is still keeping us company.

I re-enter the study and wrench the filing cabinet open. There is no way we can carry all the contents so we need to sift rather than grab it all. I start at the top and pull the files out and throw them to the floor if they looked useless. The top drawer is the A to F of household and it ends up in a pile at my feet. The second drawer is the G to Z and it joins the growing mound. All of the third drawer looks relevant so some goes in my holdall and I shout for Jim and empty the rest into his bag. The fourth and bottom drawer is full of porn magazines. Jim's eyes light up and he half inches a pile until he realises it is Gay porn and he throws it to the floor.

We are history. Out through the internal door to the garage and then up with the garage door. A quick check of the street, out, close the door and head down the driveway and back towards the car. Behind us the alarm rings away and in twitchy curtain land not a curtain moves. Go figure.

I keep my eyes open for any movement but there is nothing and five minutes later I sling my holdall in the back seat of the car, as does Jim, and we are away.

I have instructions to meet up with a Blue Ford Mondeo that will be parked up less than a mile away. I get Jim to pull the A to Z and we head for the drop off point.

Chapter 33

Charlie wants to goes home.

Tina walks back into the Starbucks with a face like thunder on a mountain ridge. I am still struggling to keep awake but I know that staying here is not an option. She sits across from me and unloads about George. I can't pretend I am surprised at what she tells me. I was an iPod and twenty DVD's to the good through George's supply network. Like it or lump it we were in this together.

Tina then drops a bomb shell. Like someone looking in on a fish tank she sees the whole picture. The gorillas. Retip, Robin raiding Leonard's computer - see the connection. Like a flashbulb in my head I'm there. Blindingly obvious is not the word. I see it in an instant - Leonard has turned over on Retip and Retip has turned over on Leonard. This is a step well removed from where I thought we were. My flight, Leonard's death - all down to Retip. Retip were dodgy but I didn't think that they endorsed killing.

I try to figure what Tina will do next. Will she run? Will she grass me up? She keeps up a monologue and it dawns on me that Tina had no more intention of dumping George, and hence me, than she does of stripping naked and going for a run in the car park.

I tell her I want to go home and she vehemently disagrees. She tells me what I already know - that the gorillas will hardly overlook my house. I shrug, or at least I move my left shoulder about a quarter of an inch. I need rest and I want to go home.

She is after me like a dog with a bone and gives me a dozen good reasons why going home is a crap idea. I agree with them all and still say I want to go home. A couple of hours shut eye, pick up some clean clothes and figure what we need to do.

Tina is not for letting go. George comes in from the mall and she tells George what I want to do and he says it is a bad idea. Tell me something I don't know.

Tina comes up with a compromise. They will check me in to a hotel and go back to my house, pick up my stuff and then we can go figure. I'm too weak to argue any longer so hotel it is.

The walk back to the car is a long one and the check-in at the hotel an awkward one.

We choose a shiny Holiday Inn Express in the centre of town. I don't look like the sort of guest that they are building their clientele around but some sweet talking from Tina and I'm in a room with the most inviting bed in history. I kick off my shoes, crawl under the covers and it's good night Vienna.

I dream. Some weird mix of me as patient and me as doctor. I decide to operate on myself without the benefit of anaesthetic. I need a brain transplant. It seems the current one isn't working too well. I (the doctor) tell me (the patient) that this won't hurt and as the first incision is made I wake up in the hotel room screaming. The clock next to the bed tells me that I have been asleep for a couple of hours.

I'm thirsty and need a pee and not in that order. I roll out of bed and am delighted to find that I now feel only part rubbish and not the full on variety of rubbish that had been hanging around me earlier on. I hit the toilet, let rip on the porcelain and cringe at the too dark yellow fluid filling the bowl. Dehydration.

I pick up a glass from the sink and unwrap the plastic cover that is supposed to re-assure me that the glass is sterile. Who's to say that they don't just rinse the cup they find in the room and wrap it in plastic to fool us? I let the water run but even though it is cool the water has a metallic taste to it. That takes some doing. Glasgow water is usually great. Soft, clean water from the hills to the north. I force myself to drink more than I want and go back and lie down and wait for the liquid to worm its way through my system.

I am dozing when I hear a noise at the door. I sit up but if it is the gorillas there is little I can do. I pick up the plastic glass and get ready to throw it. If the gorillas are coming for me at least they might die laughing.

Tina and George come in and close the door behind them. George sits in the room's sole armchair and Tina balances on the edge of the bed. I listen as they tell me what they found in my house. Tina thinks most of the damage is superficial. George thinks they were after the documents and tells me about the piles of paper and magazines on the study floor. At the word magazines I cringe. I say nothing but I can see that George is looking at me with different eyes. It looks like my house has received a good trashing but according to George and Tina the house is more of a midden than a disaster area. I can cope with midden. I do midden well.

It also seems that my alarm has been as about effective as a chocolate fire guard. Not only did no one seem to notice but it has also failed to flip to silent and, according to George, it is still merrily ringing away. No doubt the neighbours will complain about the noise at some point but it will never occur to them that maybe they should phone the police to see if my house has been broken into.

I pick up the hotel phone and dial my home number. As soon as the answer machine kicks in I enter a four digit code and follow the female voice's instructions and re set the alarm. I have no way of knowing whether this has worked or not. It was an added extra when I got the alarm fitted and I've just never got round to testing it.

We sit and chat for an hour getting nowhere and I send them both out to raid the local MacDonald's for some temporary respite for my growing hunger pains. When they are gone I crank up the TV and watch some nonsense that seems to involve letting the local fruit-cases in to decorate your house for a tenner. The presenter is a three B's - blonde, bimbo and bloody useless. She is sitting in a front room of some decorative disaster zone talking to Mr and Mrs Intelligent. I can't figure if this is the 'before' or the 'after' part of the programme but 3 B's is wittering on about the importance of knowing your customer when trying to choose the right look and feel.

'If you don't know what is going on in their head - then you can't do a proper job,' she says.

Aye right and if they were to discover that you have two brain cells it would be on the ten o'clock news as the lead story.

Something clicks in my head. The drugs have all but worn off and the fug seems to have lifted to be replaced by a nagging pain across the top of my skull. I'm fairly sure that I need a check up from a doctor but that will have to wait. I look back at the TV screen and I have a plan. Or at least the start of a plan.

'If you don't know what is going on in their head...'

When George and Tina return resplendent with three Big Mac meals and three fries I take them through my thoughts.

My plan is simple but needs some steel balls.

First we need to wrestle back control of the situation and time is not on our side. The two gorillas will no doubt find us at some point and if they don't the police will. Neither situation is a 'good to go' at the moment. Secondly our only bargaining chips - the documents - are all but useless because we only have half the story. If we can at least understand what it is we are being chased for then we might be able to turn it to our favour. I ask Tina to dig out the parcel and we go through the contents.

The list of names and money is easy. It is a list of backhanders or some form of underhand payment. Other than that I might as well go fish. The other sheets are simply a mess of numbers. Big numbers to be fair but this means little. There is some order to the whole thing but what it is, is beyond me but I think I might know how to figure it.

Leonard's laptop would crack this problem in seconds but it will be a goner by now. It's the first place whoever is behind the gorillas would look. But what I know that they don't know is that Leonard is a data back up freak. He is permanently running scared of losing data and has a hundred ways to keep his data safe.

When we first met up, me a newly recruited graduate that knew next to nothing, and him in the same boat, computers were something of a rarity but even back then Leonard had some steam driven monster loaded with programmes such as Harvard Graphics, Lotus 123 and the likes. Word, Excel and Power Point were yet to take over the world.

Over the years Leonard has kept dancing on the sharp end of technology. Upgrading with purpose at every turn. His house is a Mecca to all things digital and there was rarely a day when he didn't throw a shadow over my desk and talk technobabble until I told him to use the River Clyde as a landing zone.

His latest trip had been to subscribe to an on line data backup scheme but I struggled with the idea he would place the dodgy material on it. It might claim to be secure but a couple of passwords, the use of his laptop and anyone half bright would be home and dry.

His current old school back up was an ageing portable hard drive. A one hundred gig box about six inches by four by two that he slavishly plugged into each night.

He hid it in the bottom of the department stationery cupboard - hidden below reams of never used coloured A4 paper. It was hardly a state secret but he didn't care. He simply wanted to know that a copy of his life existed in a place that no self respecting thief would go. If I could get a hold of the hard drive we might be a few miles further down the road to a solution.

Tina was dead against going back to the office for the hard drive for a whole host of reasons. Not least that it would, no doubt, be being watched. George was on a different tack to Tina. He was more than a little keen to clean out his little warehouse before the police decided to pay a visit and was all for going back.

I told them that we needed to go tonight. By the morning the authorities were bound to step it up a gear and I didn't want to give the gorillas any more time than I had to. In addition the office would be empty and that would mean George would be able to clear out his stash without being disturbed.

Tina gave in and we agreed to give it until eleven and then hit the road.

Chapter 34

Simon falls in love.

I almost miss her. I was seconds from dozing off. A passing car grinding its gears brought me back to the job in hand. I rub my eyes. Karen is leaving the close. I am out of the door like a rocket. I sprint across the road and she sees me coming. She tries to jump into the car before I can get there. I kick it up a notch. I have the momentum and slam into the driver door before she gets there. I stand before her. She smiles at me. I smile back.

'Simon,' she says.

'Karen,' I reply.

I point at my car. She crosses over the road. If I expect resistance I get none. Seconds later she slides into the passenger seat. I sit next to her, holding the steering wheel for comfort. The silence stretches. She pulls down the sun visor and checks her Polyfilla is intact.

Karen is good at silence. It is her weapon of mass distraction. She understands the intimate power of saying nothing. When it is used to its full effect it has a way of drawing people out - making them talk - when saying nothing would have been a better option. She uses it well in identifying whether a person was up for a bung. I've seen people made an offer of undeniable dubiety. Then Karen will switch off her mouth. She watches their reaction. Nine times out of ten she has them sussed in that moment of silence. A taker and she is in for the kill.

A refusenik and she backs off with dexterity. Leaving the target confused over exactly what they have just been offered.

She shuts the visor and sits back.

Waiting.

Well I can wait as well. It is her turn to do the talking. I finger the leather cover on the wheel. I run my fingertips across the stitching. Outside the light is starting to fade. I reach for my mobile to see if there is a message. Nothing. Quentin is still in mid code-cracking mode. I flip on the radio. The sound of Orchestral Manoeuvres in the Dark fills the car. They are telling me it is eight fifteen and that was the time it has always been – 'Enola Gay' a favourite track of mine.

I switch it off and look at the clock on the dash. Andy McCluskey, the lead singer for the group is a couple of hours out. I open the ashtray and fiddle with the loose change. I stop fiddling and close it.

I am about to open the centre console for a rummage when Karen swings round. She leans over. Too close. Her face is inches from mine. In a well practised move she reaches out. She grabs my head, pulls it towards her. We kiss.

I want to pull away big time. To stop this insanity. I don't. I know I should but I don't. Instead I slip my tongue into her mouth. I am beginning to enjoy this. Then she's gone. Snapping back in her seat, eyes straight ahead. Tears burst onto her cheeks. She sobs like it hurts deep down. Her breath comes in lumps. She looks on the edge of hysterical. I'm at a loss as to what to do. The kiss, the crying, the unexpected enjoyment - it all adds up to a hill of confusion. Then she stops, turns round to me. A dam breaks and she goes into talk mode in a big way. The speech is an intense soliloquy. She expects nothing back from me until she runs out of gas. When she is finished she opens the car door and gets out. I expect her to cross to her own car. Instead she pulls out a packet of Marlboro Light and does the dirty habit thing.

My head is spinning at the outburst. I try and piece together what she has just told me.

It seems that Karen has had the hots for me for some years. Me being as thick as the proverbial two by four missed this on a regular basis. As such she had being seeking solace on a number of other fronts - including one Leonard Thwaite.

Leonard and Karen had been an item for six months. Not that I would notice. According to Karen this was not good because I was supposed to notice. The affair had come to a grinding halt yesterday morning. Leonard had fronted up to Karen on where things were going. Leonard had plans a plenty. Mostly revolving around marriage, kids, a mortgage. He also desired thirty years of slippers and tea.

Karen was as far from this vision of hell as was possible. She had told him so. Leonard did not take this information well. After a row of biblical proportions he had threatened to expose all our dirty little secrets. Karen had returned the threat with knobs on. The whole thing had gone down the toilet with an extra pull on the flush.

Putting two and two together explained why Leonard had turned rogue. Clearly the fall out with

Karen had heightened his sense of exposure. Fearing a backlash he had set up the system of document dispersal as insurance.

During the whole thing there was no mention of the missing millions.

I was now in a new world. A world where I had to factor in:

a) Karen's feelings towards me
b) My feelings towards Karen
c) Where next?
d) Where was my fucking money?
e) Our clients that would certainly kill us if the documents went public

I allowed a small smile on my lips. You can only take so much. Leonard's document time bomb. My potential love affair. A fatal and very premature end to my life. All in all this was some kind of strong shit.

I watched Karen leaning against the car, feeding her nicotine habit. I had never looked at her as a woman. A fellow director yes. A woman - no. She was wearing a loose fitting jumper and a pair of faded jeans. Her boots were high in the heel. At five feet and no inches Karen used high heels to their fullest extent. Her hair was cut in a short bob and she wore make up in an obvious way.

Her face was just the wrong side of plump. Her eyes were too wide apart to let her face work in a beautiful way. I had rarely seen her out of her business suits.

She exhaled. I abhor smoking but it made her look cute. Now there is a word that I never thought I would use in conjunction with Karen. Cute and

Karen were mutually exclusive terms in my book. As she stood there, make up smudged from crying, I could easily say she was cute.

I tried to remember how far things had gone last night. The alcohol fairy had stolen my memory and I knew I would have to ask Karen at some point.

I now have to decide how much I tell Karen. I can't think that the full bhoona will be a good idea. It's not as if she doesn't know about our dealings. But I also have to remember that she has just robbed me of a million quid as well.

I make a mental call. The big house, the fancy cars, Robin being her brother - even sleeping with Leonard - the architect of my current down fall - all add up to someone to treat with kid gloves for a little while longer.

Karen finishes the cigarette and gets in the car. We start kissing.

I could get used to this.

Chapter 35

George does a little night work.

Tina is dozing at the end of Charlie's bed and the hotel alarm clock has just tumbled from 10:59 to 11:00. I stand up and look down on a sleeping man and wonder if I should leave him be. The bruises on his face are taking on a multicoloured hue and when he moves in his sleep he moans. I think about heading off myself and sorting out my end of this mess. If I was quick and dumped all the stuff from my cupboard maybe I could get back before they woke. After all Tina and I would be off the hook. Slip out, remove the gear, return, grab Tina and walk. Easy.

The thought takes on some solidity. There is real potential in it. The owners of Tyler Tower keep a Ford Transit in the basement car park. It's not just for my building. It is used all over the central belt of Scotland for picking up and dropping stuff. It was dropped off two days ago and is due to be picked up tomorrow morning. I have the keys and the petrol tank is full. It is even sitting right outside the freight lift, nicely placed to load up.

I take my mobile from my jacket pocket and finger the keys. I have a friend who will, for a small consideration, take all the hooky gear from me and flog it. I'll lose out financially on a few items but in the rounding I'll break even and I won't have a shed load of red hot merchandise with my name on it.

187

I call up his number from the address book and my thumb hovers over the dial button. I lay my skin on the smooth lump of plastic and rub my finger back and forward, applying ever so gentle pressure at first and then increasing it stroke by stroke.

If I make this choice Tina won't be happy but she'll see the sense in it later. Why would she want to stay involved in this nonsense when we can both get out?

She is lying on the bed; snoring - her mouth hanging open. Her head is lying between Charlie's feet and she looks… well she looks vulnerable. But it is not her that is vulnerable. Not really. It is me. I've only known her a short while but she has the sort of spirit and fortitude that I'll never have. She should be flying career wise but her feisty nature long ago pulled the plug on her ambitions with her current employer. She should move on and get a better job. I haven't brought the subject up. It's not easy when your own job is so bad that you have to sub it with flogging stolen gear. If she gets in any deeper in this mess then it will be goodbye to her future - regardless.

I press the dial button and wait for it to connect.

Charlie rolls over and his good eye opens. The head bandage has slipped a little and I lean forward and give him a hand to re-arrange it. He should be back in hospital but that's not going to happen anytime soon. Tina stirs and smiles at me. I hear a voice on the phone speaker and I depress the cancel button and I know that I'm not doing a runner. One way or another we are all in this for the long haul.

Charlie seems a little brighter and once he has showered, (not easy with a bandage around your head) and changed into fresh clothes he radiates a bit more life. We take the lift to the ground floor. The receptionist doesn't even look up as we leave.

The night is cool and the sky a murky mix of cloud and red, the Glasgow lights reflecting from the underside of the sky. We cross to the multi storey car park and have to dodge a couple of lads hanging around the ticket machine on the blag for loose change.

Tyler Tower isn't that far away but Charlie is in no fit state for a walk. Although to give him credit, he is moving well given the way he walked not a few hours earlier. We want the option of a quick getaway should the world piss up our leg so we'll take Tina's car.

The plan is to cruise down the back alley and I'll open up the underground car park. I know the over night security guard well so there should be no issue. A couple of iPods and he will be sweet. A couple more and he may even arrange for the CCTV to lose a few hours. The system is forever screwing up anyway so it's hardly a risk.

I'm also praying that the police will have left the scene by now.

I'll load my gear into the Transit with the help of Tina while Charlie will retrieve Leonard's hard drive and then we are out of there. I ask if Charlie is up to this and he says yes.

Tina works her way round the Glasgow grid and onto West George St. We do a fly-by of the Tower - looking for the gorillas and/or the police but if they are there we can't see them. We circle onto the square behind the Tower and then slip down the lane. I jump out of the car, remove my keys from my coat pocket, open up a small panel on the lane wall and enter a six digit code. From within there is a clunk and the steel shutter rattles up.

The noise is like a drum roll in a church and my eyes dart around expecting someone to appear to see what is going on but the lane stays empty. The shutter slams into the roof and I get back in the car and we slide into the car park. It should be deserted but I see that, along with the Transit, Simon's BMW is in its slot. My breathing ceases. Tina asks what's wrong and I tell her who the car belongs to.

She is for turning right round and leaving. I disagree. For a start I know Simon was in this morning and maybe he left the car. Tina tells us that she saw the police in the lane with what looked like the same BMW and a man lying in the gutter this morning. I tell them that Simon had been at a party and thrown up in the office. Maybe the police gave him a break and told him to put the car back and go home?

'We should go. There is no way that Simon isn't in on this?'

You have to give it to Tina for verbalising the blindingly obvious.

It is a thought that has crossed my mind a few times today. Since Tina's revelation about Robin it occurred to me that Simon might be involved. Now here was his car sitting in the garage and we were on our own. If the gorillas were with him we were walking right into their arms - dead meat ripe for the mincing machine.

We argue. Tina is still for getting out. I still disagree. If we don't get the upper hand in this whole sorry affair then running will fix nothing. Our only hope is to get the hard drive and pray it holds the answers we need. Tina reverts to type and wants to go to the police once more. She tells me that a few stolen goods are zip compared to a couple of contract killers. Charlie chips in and makes our minds up.

It is simple. If we go to the police what do we have. We have no evidence to link Robin or Simon to Leonard's death. We have a bunch of documents that may or may not relate to illegal dealings by Retip - that is it!

Charlie's right. Even *if* Charlie and I could ID the gorillas and *if* the police caught them what is the tie back to Retip? What's to stop a fresh set of thugs being despatched once we are out of sight of the police. No, we had to get a grip. If Simon was in the building we would simply have to deal with it.

Tina is still unsure but I persuade her by saying that I'll check out with Tam, the security guard, on Simon's BMW. If it has been here since last night then we can proceed. If not we think again. With that I take the emergency stairs up to the ground level. If Tam is on the ball he will have seen us driving into the garage and be expecting me.

I enter the reception area conscious that a bright Managing Director of a successful company might have asked Tam to give him the head up if anyone comes in the building. The reception is empty. I suspect that Tam is on his rounds. He does two full rounds a night. All forty four floors. It takes him the best part of two hours and he could be anywhere right now. It could take me as long to find him.

If I want to be sure Simon is not here I only have one real choice and that is to go up to Retip's floor and check for myself. I head for the lift, get in and I am about to hit floor twenty four when it occurs to me that anyone watching the lifts will see it coming. The alternative is to hike twenty four floors of concrete steps. That will take a while and both Tina and Charlie will wonder where the hell I've gone so I risk going up to twenty and walk the rest.

I get out at twenty. I'm tempted to nip into Cheedle, Baker and Nudge and see if I can find Leonard's hard drive but Tina and Charlie will be waiting so I push on.

The stairs come out near the far end of the Retip office. Unusually the space is not an open plan desert like most of the floors. Every staff member seems to have their own small office - privacy is something the company seems to revel in. Simon's office is at the far end and I can still smell the stale alcohol from the party the night before. Only the reception light is on and I have to walk slowly across the main office for fear of walking into an open door in the dark.

About ten yards from Simon's office I stop and peer into the gloom. If someone is around they are sitting in the dark. The place feels empty. I walk forward and try the door to Simon's office. It swings open. I look in. The room is empty so I head back to the stairs.

I choose the stairs and as I drop down flight after flight I hear the lift fire up. Probably Tam on his rounds. I reach the basement and see Tina's car sitting where it was. I get in the passenger side. Tina asks where the hell I have been and I ask why there is no Charlie. Tina tells me Charlie wouldn't wait and he was willing to take his chances with Simon and the gorillas if they were there.

I thought I had been gone no more than ten minutes but Tina said it was nearer half an hour. The lift I heard was probably Charlie on his way up. I decide to start clearing the gear from my cupboard. I tell Tina to wait and I get out the car. I cross the car park. I take the van's keys from my key ring and unlock the Transit. I open the back doors and head for the freight lift. The lift needs a key to operate it and when I insert it the floor number light kicks in above and the door opens onto a lift interior that would take a small car.

Tina joins me and we ride up two floors and I show her where my cupboard is. Against one wall is a two wheel trolley. The sort with prongs at the base for wheeling around boxes. I pull it out and load up the trolley with the iPods, push it to the lift and unload them onto the lift floor. I push the trolley back and repeat the process. Tina is standing like a spare spanner and I tell her to lift anything she can and stick it in the lift.

In my head I had this down as a quick job but there seems to be far more crammed inside my cupboard than I recollect. It takes us half an hour to empty it, transport the stuff to the lift, take it down to the basement and fill up the van.

I check on Tina's car twice during this time but there is no sign of Charlie. I wonder what is taking him so long.

With the van full, I lock the Transit and Tina and I go back up for one last check round. I do a complete sweep of the cupboard to check I have left nothing in some darkened corner. In the distance I think I hear a car engine growl into life but apart from that the building is a ghost town.

Happy the cupboard is bare, I take Tina by the hand and we go down the stairs to reception to see if Tam is there. I tell Tina to wait in the stairwell and go to find Tam. The reception is still empty. He could still be on his rounds. I can't wait and I decide to phone him later on and see if I could arrange for a little editing of the CCTV coverage.

Two things were apparent when we got back to the basement garage. Firstly there is still no sign of Charlie and secondly Simon's BMW is a goner. The combination of these two facts does not bode well. I tell Tina to wait and take the lift all the way to the Cheedle, Baker and Nudge offices. I push past reception and into the corridor beyond and down to Charlie's office but it is dark. I scout around the whole floor but there is no sign of life. I sprint back to the lift and ride up to the Retip floor but it is as empty as it had been not an hour since.

I drop back to the main building reception and look around but Tam is still missing in action. I run down the stairs to the basement and tell Tina the bad news. She looks pale and I put my arm around her but she pushes me away. I can hardly blame her.

I have two heads on now. One says bugger this - call the police and be done with it. The other says dump the stuff first and then make the call. The last thought makes more sense. I can't leave the gear in the van as it is due to be picked up in the morning. I ask Tina what she thinks we should do and she says the police. I decide she is right - but only after I dump the stuff and bring the van back. I try my mobile for a signal. I need to let my friend the fence know I am on my way but buried under forty odd floors of concrete the phone is dead as a Dodo. I'll make the call on the way and tell Tina to follow me in her car. Dump the gear then contact the police - that was the order of the day and with that thought I start up the Transit and head for the exit.

Chapter 36

Simon finds Charlie.

The kissing stops. It had been just about to gear up to something all too more inappropriate for a car in a public street. My phone rings. I curse and excuse myself and answer it. The ID says Quentin. Good news I hope.

And it is. He has cracked the code. He babbles on about how simple it was. He yacks something about had it been him he would have used double Boolean Schwarzkopf para logical dissection in an irregular form to encrypt it. I blank him. I don't care. I ask if we can pre-empt the last 'strategic location' without them knowing. Quentin says there is no way. The recipient needs to open the e-mail.

I consider the options if we send an e-mail from Leonard. If they know he is dead they will open it out of curiosity. If they don't they will think it is an update to the last e-mail. Either way they will open it. I consider if I should cancel the contract on the last two e-mail addresses. I decided against it. What if the 'strategic location' goes straight to the police without responding to the e-mail? I tell Quentin to send an e-mail from Leonard's e-mail address with the correct password, shut up shop and leave the laptop for me to dispose off.

Karen listens into the conversation. I realise I should have taken the call outside the car. In for a penny, in for a pound I decide to tell her the works.

I wasn't going to. Shit happens. Lock, stock and four dead bodies coming up.

She quizzes me with the prowess of a professional interrogator. By the time I am finished - I am really finished. I slump back in the driver's chair feeling almost relieved. Karen doesn't look half as surprised as she should. She gets out of the car and lights up. Another contribution to a future hospital visit. She paces away from the car. Then she turns and comes back. She leans in the window. She asks me another couple of questions and starts pacing again.

Ten minutes drift by. She returns to the passenger seat. We are going for a ride I am told. Back to work. We will clean out all traces of the recent transactions. Empty computer files, trash paper files. Get rid of as much as we can. We can then e-mail all the live contacts in the money laundering side and start the process of exiting all deals. This will take weeks to complete I say. She agrees but if we trash the evidence at our end tonight then it would take a financial genius to track down the customers. I'm not sure it will be that easy. She says we can start the e-mailing in a day or two.

Karen goes into control mode in a big way. She wants the number for 'the Voice'. Now she is making me nervous. I tell her that he won't return a call from anyone but me. She tells me to give the number to her anyway. I hesitate. Karen makes it clear there is no option. I hand her the phone and the number.

She tells me straight that there are two things that we must possess if we are to get out of this. Leonard's colleague's files and the 'strategic locations' files. I tell her I already know this. I tell her that 'the Voice' is on the case. Karen doesn't seem to listen. She wants to up the ante. Cost isn't an issue. She wants to offer a substantial uplift to get the job done as quickly as possible. I don't see how this will help. 'the Voice' is hellish expensive as it is. A few extra grand won't cut it with him. Curiously she doesn't ask how I got to know about 'the Voice'. Something smells bad.

As Karen fiddled with my phone I thought that 'the Voice' was an odd connection to make in the first place. Robin put me in touch. We had been bidding on a tricky Euro tender. One that had revealed a competitor of ours was in the driving seat by dint of their track record. The contract was a highly technical software build. The competitor had delivered three similar systems in the last three years. Needless to say we had no track record. We were counting on a substantial backhander to a Euro official to swing the show. Word had come back from our official that his hands were tied. He told us that he had no way to influence the final outcome of the tender. That was a bastard as we were down to the last two.

We were in the swamp. It had cost us the best part of thirty grand just to get this far. We were in the hole for twenty more regardless. On top of this the contract was earmarked as the way to wash a serious wedge of cash from our biggest customer. To add to the pain I had already told the customer it was in the bag. Unless we could get the competitor to pull their interest there seemed no way we could win.

Robin told me he knew someone who might help. It wouldn't be cheap. It would need another thirty grand to fix it. Given the alternatives I asked for the contact and made my first call to 'the Voice' (I had no clue who he was so the name 'the Voice' became my shorthand for him) and set the wheels in motion. A week later and we were informed we were now the sole bidder on the contract. Our last remaining rival had decided to remove their name from the final tender list. We won the contract and 'the Voice' became a source of help on a number of occasions. An expensive help, but a help all the same.

I tell Karen what to do and she dials the number from my phone, waits for the answer machine and hangs up. Ten minutes later my phone rings and she answers it. To my surprise 'the Voice' doesn't hang up at the sound of a strange voice. Karen opens the car door and gets out to hold the conversation.

When she gets back in she says 'the Voice' was close to resolving the remaining two potential 'strategic locations' so she has left well enough alone. She has arranged additional resource to be put on the case for Charlie. She hands me back my phone. She instructs me to head back to the city

The light is beginning to fade as we drive. Half an hour later we are in the offices. Why do I suddenly feel like I have become the tea boy?

Karen seems to have a fairly comprehensive plan of action. The plan suggests this wasn't the first time she had thought about doing this. I am relegated to following orders. She will take care of the digital trashing. I will take care of the dead wood trashing.

We have an industrial shredder - three thousand pounds worth - a HSM 411.2 Professional Shredder. Maximum security so it says. I get to work and soon have a sweat on. The last of the paper disappears into the machine just before eleven. Karen is finished and is closing down all the systems. We tidy up; haul the sacks of shredded material to the lift and down to my car. I close the boot. Karen is waiting at the car door when the main door shutter cranks into action. I run to the far side of my car. Karen follows. We duck down as a Vauxhall Astra comes in. It parks near the lifts. I watch as George the maintenance man gets out. He heads for the fire stairs. There are two more people in the car. I let two minutes tick and then circle round the back of my car. I use the pillars as cover. I make my way to the Astra.

As I close in the figure in the back stretches and turns profile to me. The light from the lifts highlights the face. There sits Charlie Wiggs. I nearly choke. Charlie seems to have a bandage wrapped around part of his head. The driver is a woman. I don't recognize her. I go back and tell Karen our luck is changing. We debate how we can get Charlie from the car. We are just about to go for the direct approach when the car door opens. Charlie gets out and walks to the lifts. He calls one up and gets in.

There is only one passenger lift in the garage and I'm sure the girl in the car can't see the lift doors. I tell Karen to sit tight.

I run, hand against the wall, to where the lifts sit. I crouch down. Slowly I crawl up to the pillar that sits in front of the lift. I put my head to the ground and look round the base. The car is hidden from view. I move to the lift, keeping low to the ground. If someone comes out the fire door or the lift arrives I am dead to rights. I crawl right up to the lift door. I look back. I still can't see the car. I reach up and press the call button and wait. The lift is at twenty. Charlie is working late.

The lift arrives and I crawl in. I slide up the wall of the lift and hit twenty. I'm away.

As the door opens on Cheedle, Baker and Nudge's floor I flatten myself against the wall. When the doors are fully open I place my hand on the door to stop it closing. I look out. The reception area is empty and a single light burns over the receptionist's desk. Beyond this I can see light in Charlie's corridor. I head to the door beyond the reception and into the corridor.

The light is coming from the main office. I would have expected it to come from Charlie's office. I make my way towards the light. With a gentle push of the door I reveal Charlie scrabbling around in one of the cupboards. His back is to me. I step in. At the same time I pull a pen knife from my coat pocket. The blade is too small to inflict serious damage. I'm not planning serious damage. It will have to do.

Charlie is still scrabbling around in the cupboard when I walk up behind him. I place the tip of the blade at the back of his neck.

'Do as I say or I open your fucking jugular.'

Charlie freezes. I tell him to move towards the door. He obeys. I nudge him towards the lifts. He tries to turn his head. I press the knife a little harder. Skin splits. A drop of blood oozes out between blade and skin. I push him forward.

'Simon?'

I use my free hand and smack him across the back of the head. He shuts up. I note that his walk is stiff and slow. The bandaging on his head is quite extensive. The result of Dumb and Dumber's intervention no doubt.

I kill the office light and note that one of the lifts is moving. I usher Charlie back into the office.

We wait

There is a lot of lift movement so the waiting goes on.

Once I'm sure the lifts are no longer moving I force Charlie to move.

We descend in silence. The doors open. I push Charlie to the floor. I force him to crawl until I'm sure we can't be seen by the girl in the Astra. I keep the knife tight to his neck. He is struggling but I don't care. I force him along the wall and into my car's back seat.

I notice that the transit doors are open and that it is half full.

Once in the car I hand Karen the knife. It looks tiny and ineffective in her hands. She tells me that the girl and George are loading up the van.

We need to get out of here before they return. Karen pushes the knife towards Charlie and he tries to talk. I smack him again. In these situations you need to remind people who is in charge.

I want to question him here. Ask him where the documents are. To tear the bastard's throat out. I take a breath but I can't risk George or the girl spotting us so I gun the car into life and squeal my way out onto the lane.

My role of inquisitor is usurped as Karen turns round and asks him about the documents. He blanks her. I nearly drive the car into the lane wall as she lifts up my pen knife and slams it into Charlie's lap. Charlie screams like a stuck pig. It takes all my control to get us onto the main road in one piece.

She asks about the documents again but he is screaming too much to answer. She pulls the knife out, lifts it up in the air and Charlie raises his arm. He shakes his head. She ignores him and sends the knife into his other leg. Charlie's vocal chords sound like they are going to tear apart. He collapses into the well between the front and back seats. He howls.

I tell Karen to ease up. She tells me this is nothing to what will happen to us if we don't clear up the mess. I look round and see Charlie trying to make himself as small as he can in the back seat. He is scrabbling at the door handle only to find that the central locking is on.

Karen opens the glove box and takes out the car manual. What the hell is she going to do now - teach Charlie how to change a tyre? The manual sits inside a hard plastic protective shell. She turns round, raises the manual high and brings it down on Charlie's head. He screams. It's hard to tell if the scream is part of the on going screaming from the knife wounds or as a result of the new assault.

This is a whole new side of Karen I have never seen. Her eyes are on fire. I look away. This is turning me on. She looks stunning when she is running in full anger mode. I could pull over now. Make love right in the middle of the road. I smile. I look back at her. She has no eyes for me as she reaches over into the back. She manhandles Charlie into the seat.

I can see blood, lots of blood. This is going to be no two hundred pound valet job when it comes.

She asks him about the documents again. He says nothing. She slams the manual into the bandaged part of his head. Screaming. More screaming. He howls for her to stop. He lets his mouth run. He tells her that the documents are with George and some girl called Tina back at our office. I tread deep on the brakes causing a virtual choir of horns behind me to let loose.

I can't U turn in the space so I three point even though the road is busy with traffic. Under a storm of abuse I force the car across the road, flip a v at the other drivers and reverse back, clipping a Vauxhall Frontera on the back bumper. Before the driver can react I accelerate away - no doubt with my number plate being memorised.

We are less than five minutes out from the office. The one way system and the compulsory Glasgow lights make that ten. By the time we race back into the underground car park the Astra is gone. I notice that the Transit has gone as well. Karen curses like a good one and smacks Charlie over the head with the car manual. Charlie simpers. He has a hand over each leg - trying to stem the flow of blood. She asks him where the girl lives. Three smacks later and it's clear that Charlie barely knows her. She asks about George's address. He has no idea.

I tell Karen to wait. I leap out of the car. I shout I'll be back in five minutes. The lift takes an age to get to our floor. I burst from the lift doors before they are fully open. I rifle the reception desk and find the emergency numbers. George's home number is on it. I scribble his number down. I think about phoning the number but George won't be back for a while, assuming he is planning to go home anytime soon. I return to the car. I tell Karen what I have been doing. She tells me to give her the number. She gets out the car and walks to the exit to get a signal on the mobile.

When she comes back she throws me a scribbled piece of paper with an east end Glasgow address on it. I ask how she got it. She throws me a deaf ear and tells me to drive.

I aim for the alley to the sound of Charlie losing fluid.

This is a mess.

Chapter 37

Tina goes home with George.

I can see George in the rear view mirror but I need to let him overtake. I have no idea if he is going home or not. I pull over as we cross the city and he takes the lead in the van. We enter George Square. In the centre there is a marquee being put up or taken down - it is hard to tell. The City Chambers slide past and we head east along George Street and onto Duke Street and into Dennistoun.

George lives on one of the streets that fall from Duke St and before long we are outside his house. He gets out and tells me to leave the car and jump in the van. A few seconds later a man with the dress sense of a badly advised tramp gets in. I'm not introduced and glare at George for the slight. However a few moments in the man's company and I don't feel like I want to know his name. He smells of curry and soap and badly needs a haircut and a shave.

His eyes spend a lot of time on my cleavage and I take an instant dislike to him.

George heads off and we drive along the main road for a couple of miles before we hang a right into a small industrial estate. At the back of the estate are four rows of garage lock ups. The friend tells George to pull up at the last-but-one on the third row and gets out and opens the garage door. Inside is an Aladdin's cave of miscellanea - all wearing a badge that says 'handle with tongs only'!

It takes us twenty minutes to transfer the van's contents into the garage. Money changes hands and we drop the friend at the end of George's street and I fail to say goodbye to Mr Khorma and Dove.

George suggests a cup of tea and I can't think of a reason why not. He is in a far better mood now he has divested himself of the van's load. We drive back to his flat and walk up the tenement stairs to the third floor.

I drift through an array of emotions. Disgust at George's revelations about the hooky merchandise, trepidation at the thought of what may have happened to Charlie, fear at what might happen to us, weariness at the pace of events and finally anger at being mixed up in it all. The anger is a living thing as I enter the flat and begins to stretch its muscles, much as it had done outside Starbucks. George vanishes to make tea, leaving me to wrestle with my growing rage.

I walk to the large picture window and look out on the street below. To my left is a primary school that cuts across the road - dead ending it. George had told me that at one time there was no school and the road flowed from Duke Street in the south to Alexandra Parade in the north. To my right the view looks back on Duke Street. The night is full on but in a few hours the sun will make its early summer rise and suddenly my rage is gone and I feel tired, bone tired.

George returns with the tea and we drink it in silence. He tries to bring up the subject of Charlie but my mind can't get beyond sleep. I suggest a couple of hour's shuteye and then let's see how things look. I expect resistance but George looks shattered and agrees.

It is a funny time to sleep with your boyfriend for the first time but there was no debate over the sleeping arrangements. We simply slip off our clothes and climb into George's double bed. George yawns and I yawn and it is a funny time not to make love to your boyfriend for the first time.

Chapter 38

Another interlude.

The blind man sits in the dark, sipping a large glass of Glayva over ice. The sweet liquid coats his tongue and the alcoholic kick is putting on its boots. An array of phones sit on the table next to him and the PC is on standby - a single orange light flashing. He puffs on an over sized cigar held in his left hand and in the dark a perfect ring of smoke lazes its way to the ceiling.

He watches the glow from the end of the cigar as he inhales and considers his situation. Not good was a fair call. Heading towards deep shit was another way of looking at. None of the phones ring and this annoys him.

The plan had been a good one. A simple one that had gotten way too complicated. Five people, five deaths but put the blame on someone else - easy. Leonard had been the tool to achieve this. Crude but effective and Simon the patsy should it go wrong.

The release of the documents had all been part of the plan and it had served its purpose - giving Simon a genuine reason to want the recipients dead. Planting the five names and e-mail addresses on Leonard's laptop had been easy. Convincing Leonard to set up the scheme had been a bit more difficult.

The blind man had known that Leonard had been on the fiddle but it was of little consequence to him until he needed leverage to force Leonard into action. A couple of rogue e-mails and he had convinced Leonard that Simon was aware of his growing stash of cash. The cream on the cake had been the Karen/Leonard blow up. Who knew she had been shagging him?

The scheme involving the documents was all Leonard's, all be it with a little help from a colleague that Leonard trusted. The colleague, a fellow accountant in Cheedle, Baker and Nudge, had been primed to help Leonard with his scheme. What had not been foreseen by the blind man was the choice of material that Leonard would use as black mail. The original suggestion had been to use Simon's tax details - more than enough to push him over the edge. Leonard's use of the Retip documents had complicated things but, if all had gone well, not unduly.

Leonard's colleague had suggested the password protection plan and Leonard, a techno geek of the first order, had leapt on it like a dog to a bone. The five names on the list (two to get documents, three blanks) were suggested by the colleague and with the password in hand the blind man could always erase the electronic files at any point. The voids were easy to arrange and he had to hope that Simon was smart enough to figure it out. If not he would have been given a hand.

Simon's contract to kill Leonard was just grist to the mill. Normally all contact was routed through one of the blind man's array of Pay As You Go mobiles but by giving Simon Bally's number direct it would implicate Simon in the whole thing. Bally was dispensable - as was everyone in the blind man's world.

The hard copy given to Charlie hadn't been in the plan but retrieving it would have hardly been a problem until Bally and Jim had screwed up. It would have been better for all had they killed Charlie. Instead they had scared him into running. Now Charlie was on the run with the maintenance man and his girlfriend and the documents. They probably knew their worth by now and maybe even the detail of their contents.

Less than half an hour ago he had learned that the last of the five names on the computer were dead. None of the deaths could be traced to him but they could all be traced to Simon. The electronic documents were retrieved and only Charlie and his copy stood between a perfect plan and one that could easily unleash death and destruction.

The blind man had people staking out Charlie's, George's, Simon's and Tina's homes but this was stretching his resources. It was also stretching his nerves as he had expected one of the phones to ring with an update and the silence offended him.

He stood up to stretch his legs and the phone nearest him let rip with a ring. He picked it up and answered it. A few seconds later a second phone rang.

Things were moving.

Chapter 39

Gorillas go in.

Bally has just made a call on the mobile. We are parked up in some god forsaken side street in the east end and I just want my kip. We dropped the paperwork from the vic's house as requested and were told to stake out the maintenance man's house.

I am bored stupid and tired and I ask Bally what we were getting for this gig and he told me that payment would come in the form of legs that would not get broken.

Bally hangs up and tells me that Charlie, the flyboy, is on his way to Simon's house.

We have just watched the maintenance man and a girl toddle up to his flat. Bally says we have to break in and do 'em over for some info. It seems we are after more paperwork. What is it with this paperwork? I want to go home. It's the middle of the night and I don't work well this late on without some decent shut eye. But I like my legs the way they are so I suggest we get on with it quick.

We are getting out the car when a gaggle of girls on their way home from a night out appear. We dodge back into the car and wait. The girls pass the car and stop at the street corner.

There are six of them - dressed to impress but all looking a little worse for wear. None of them are what I would call lookers. MDL's I tell Bally and for the first time today he smiles. MDL's - Mutton Dressed as Lamb.

You see them all over Glasgow on any given night. Old enough to know better. Short skirts with legs that have gone corned beef from years of MacD's and fish suppers. Make up applied by Blue Circle and dresses that cry out for a size ten body but are accommodating a sixteen.

Not that there is anything wrong with this in my opinion. I quite fancy two of them. The bottle blonde and the short dark haired one. Given other circumstances I would be chancing my arm right now. Drunk women are my specialty. Bally doesn't buy into my way of thinking. He calls it the Spanish waiter approach. He tells me that when he went to Spain in the eighties, Spanish waiters would keep trying with as many women as it took to land one. I like this approach. Who the hell ever died of a knock-back and as my old man said a million times - if you don't ask you don't get.

The girls are going nowhere fast. I can't be arsed waiting but Bally doesn't want witnesses if it all kicks off. Especially if we need to drag the maintenance man and his girlfriend down to the car.

The light in the maintenance man's flat goes off and I see Bally tense up. They could be on their way down. I've done enough of these to know that if they get in their car it isn't good news. Bally is always drilling into me about being in control. 'Know the lay of the land'. I think he means do the job where it is safe. Fat chance. It's never safe in this business. But I don't fancy a Keystone Cops car chase so I keep my eye on the tenement close. Bally also has his eyes glued to the entrance.

The girls are winding up the noise and one of them is sharing out a quarter bottle of something with the others. I return my gaze to the bottle blonde and when it is obvious the two vics ain't emerging I get out the car. I hear Bally shout at me but I'm bored and if the vics have gone beddie byes there is time for me to chance my arm with the girls.

I walk up to the girls and they stop talking. I use my best opening line. It fails - big time. I go to plan B and try my second best opening line. I bomb again. I go for broke and ask if any of them fancies a quick shag. This goes down like a jobby in a builder's lunchbox. I haven't got a plan D and Bally leans on the horn to let me know he isn't happy. Like I care. I turn and walk away from the girls and get back in the car and Bally gives me an earful. Like I REALLY care.

The girls move on. They keep looking over their shoulders at the car. Maybe they think we are going to stalk them or maybe they quite fancy me and expect me to follow. I suggest this to Bally and he blanks me. Like I REALLY, REALLY care.

Once the girls are gone Bally tells me to move and we are out of the car and across the road in double quick time. We slip into the close, a wally close as my mum would say. Tiled from roof to floor. I like wally closes. Kind of reminds me of when I was wee and used to visit my gran.

I run my hand along their cool surface letting my fingers bump along the joins just as I did as a kid. We climb the stairs and reach the maintenance man's landing. The flat has two oversized wooden doors that are tight shut. Behind them will be the front door. Bally tries the handle and finds the doors locked tight. He curses. Most of these doors will have floor bolts as well as locks. If the door is locked tight you would need a battering ram to get in. Bally steps back to consider the options.

I walk up to the door and press the door bell. Bally gasps. I can't be arsed hanging about. I stand in front of the left hand door and after a few seconds I can hear noise from within. Bally is right behind me telling me that I'm a dickhead.

There is no other way out from the flat so ringing the door bell has to be worth a shout. If they open the door even half an inch then I'm in.

The noise behind the door fades and I know they are wondering who is at the door at this time of night. I ring the bell again and Bally smacks me on the back of the head and pushes me out of the way.

The door remains closed. Bally turns round and pushes me down the stairs. We reach the floor below and he puts his hand on my shoulder and tells me to wait. I slump to the floor, back against the wall and take out my mobile. Bally is watching the stairs and I find Tetris and let Bally worry about the vics.

It must be twenty minutes later when we hear the click of a lock being turned. Bally kicks me and I put the mobile away. He points down the stairs and gives me a shove. As I drop down to the floor below Bally eases into the space between the front door and the storm doors of the flat directly below the vics. If he stays in the shadow they won't see him until it's too late.

I know my job. If they run for it I'm the one that needs to deck them. I reach the floor below and hear more sounds up stairs and then the sound of feet on the stone steps. A scuffle breaks out and then a shed load of shouting. I want to run up and join in the fun but decide to wait and see what happens next.

A short silence breaks out and then more footsteps on the stairs. Closer this time. I crouch next to the stairwell and wait for the owner to arrive.

If there is one thing that I have learned in all the years of doing this shit it's that nothing ever goes to plan. I mean never. The simplest jobs have a habit of fucking up in a way that you never see coming. I have a history of royal screw ups and none of them were my fault. Never my fault.

I mention this often.

The owner of the footsteps hits the landing and I am on to the job at hand with real speed. I jump up to grab them round the neck. Only they aren't there. At least their head isn't where it should be and I grab thin air. The girl rushes under me and I'm heading for the wall. I hit tile and stars break out. I go down like three stone of potatoes and let out a howl.

Above me there is more nonsense and another set of footsteps are hammering towards me. I try and stand up but I'm gubbed and can't get up. I see the maintenance man fly past and a few seconds later Bally is on top of me yelling. My personal collection of stars make understanding him hard and he opts to pull me, collar first, down the stairs and out into the night. He looks left and right and drops me on the path and I hear him swear, swear and then for good measure swear.

I stand up and look around but there is no sign of the pair.

Bally goes back into the close and I follow.

Broken legs. It's the only words I can think of. Then I pick my nose.

Chapter 40

George and Tina meet the gorillas once more.

The doorbell is ringing in my dreams and I don't want to answer it but Tina rolls over and whispers

'It's them.'

'Who?'

'My guess is the gorillas.'

I wake up fast. For a second I am disorientated and then I realise that I am lying naked next to Tina - who also happens to be naked. The doorbell seems a distant thing in comparison to this revelation.

I couldn't have been asleep more than ten minutes but Tina is standing up telling me to get dressed. I hesitate. Not because I don't understand but because in the dim light of my bedroom my girlfriend is standing before me in her birthday suit and she looks damn fine. I smile and she smiles back and then bends down, picks up my clothes and throws them at me. She starts to get dressed and I wish she would undress and bend down again. I swing my legs out and start to dress beneath the covers. I'm not quite ready to reveal myself to her yet.

Tina leaves the room and I hear her walk to the door. The bell rings again and she comes back and I am up and ready except for my shoes. I agree it has to be them and I suggest we sit tight for a moment. The storm doors are rock solid but I pick up the phone ready to call the police all the same.

Ten minutes go by and there is nothing. We can't stay here - sitting ducks would have a better chance. I go to the main window and drop to the carpet and push my head up between curtain and window and look down on the street below. There is no-one to be seen.

Maybe they have gone? I tell Tina we need to get out of here and she agrees. We wait another ten minutes and then I open the front door and unlock the outer doors. The click of the lock echoes across the landing. I look out, half expecting someone to bring a bottle down on my head. There is no-one there and I signal Tina to follow.

I walk over to the stairwell and look down but there is little to be seen in the gloom. With Tina in tow I drop down the first flight of stairs and stop. I fall to my knees and I can see the landing below. It looks empty.

I decide that open stupidity is the order of the day and grabbing Tina's hand I plunge down the next flight of stairs and straight into gorilla number one. We all go over in a heap. I yell, Tina screams and the gorilla swears. Tina rolls clear and I take the opportunity to kick at the thug. He shouts out and Tina gets up and disappears down the stairs.

I am in a world of trouble. I see the gorilla start to stand up and I know that he does this kind of thing for a living and I don't. I do the only thing I can think of and I rush him, head down and catch him with my forehead on the top of his chest. I hear shouts from below but there is nothing I can do about it and scrabble to my feet and head for the stairs.

I barrel down the three flights and see the tall gorilla lying against the wall. I ignore him and keep heading down. I am about to fly out the close and onto the pavement when I'm grabbed from behind. I turn with my arm up waiting for a punch and see Tina. She pulls me into the dark that lurks at the bottom of the stairwell. She indicates that I should hunker down and then joins me as the two gorillas rush past and out onto the street beyond. The small one towing the tall one.

I watch as they stop and the small one drops the tall one to the ground and begins to look up and down the street. No doubt looking for us. The taller one gets up and joins him and all I can think of is what will happen if they corner us down here.

The short one searches the street for a few minutes more and then turns and walks back to the close entrance. Tina freezes beside me and I grip her hand. As much for my benefit as hers. The tall one joins his shorter cohort.

They are standing less than ten feet away. Two feet closer and even in this dark they can't fail to see us.

The short one is cursing with every second word. The tall one seems less worried and begins to pick his nose. The short ones take out his phone and dials. I hear a short conversation. Partly about how we had done a runner before the thugs had arrived. Inventive but not true. Then he hangs up and turns to the tall one.

'The wee man has now got Charlie over at his house. 'the Voice' wants us to go over and see what's what.'

With that they cross over the road and I hear a car start up and then fade into the distance.

We emerge from the shadows and I hear a door open above us. God love our neighbours. If I had dropped a milk bottle on the step or fumbled my keys in the door they would have been out like a shot. On the other hand the sound of a fight and no-one appears until the coast is clear. Bugger the 'help your neighbour' philosophy around here.

Tina asks what they meant by the wee man and Charlie. That one is easy. The wee man and Simon, Retip's Managing Director, are one and the same person. It's a standing joke in the building. Simon is a big one for heels, hats, bouffant hair dos - anything to add to his height. Not that he's that small but he has a thing about it. Hence the wee man.

So Charlie's vanishing act and Simon's disappearing BMW at Tyler Tower were connected. The picture is beginning to clear. Somehow Leonard's documents cost Leonard his life and nearly Charlie's. Simon is smack in the frame for the arrangements and he is now onto Charlie for the documents that Tina still has in her possession. No doubt Charlie is being encouraged to divulge the document's whereabouts and that can only be bad news for Tina and me.

'Police. Police.' Tina says the word twice for effect.

I can't think why not except by the time we convince them of the whole sordid story I wouldn't give tuppence ha'penny for Charlie's chances of survival. Anyway we seem to come up with the police option at every turn and I'm beginning to think the longer we ignore it the harder it will be to use it when the time comes - if it comes.

The alternative isn't much better. Run away and spend the rest of our life looking over our shoulders. Whatever is in the documents is not something that Simon is going to let go. We could hand the documents back to Simon and hope he is in a forgiving mood. Or…

I look at Tina and dismiss the thought but after five minutes chatting the thought is back. It sounds simple. It really does - if we were in any way professional at this game? Rescue Charlie, finally take the police option, confess all and pray Simon, the gorillas etc all get caught. It is the last bit that gets me worried. Even if we could rescue Charlie who's to say that Simon and the gorillas will be caught or at least caught before they get to us.

Tina comes up with another build on the idea and I look down in admiration. I quiz her about it but the more we talk, the more it appears the only option. We agree on a course of action starting with the highly implausible feat of extracting Charlie from the clutches of Simon.

George and Tina to the rescue - don't all laugh at once.

Chapter 41

Charlie in prison.

Both legs are screaming at me and I'm facing a dilemma - no matter how hard I press on the wounds the blood still seeps between my fingers but the more I press the more it hurts. I've pulled myself back on the car seat but every time we turn a corner I'm thrown against one of the doors. I can't let go of my legs to grab a hold of anything and the blood has turned the back of the car into a red ice rink.

The car brakes once more and I slide forward, slip back into the seat well and decide to stay there.

Outside the landscape is changing and we seem to be heading east.

Simon hits the hands free and the phone rings. It trips to an answer machine and he hangs up. Almost immediately the phone rings and Karen picks it up, listens and hangs up.

'George and the girl have flown the coop. The girl's house is covered but just in case I want to ask blood boy here a few more questions. Head for yours.'

There is no argument from Simon and we hang a sharp right. I smack my head off the door handle, yelling to no-one in particular. The orange of the street lights has turned my blood black and I'm aware I've lost a lot of fluid and I'm not heading for the hospital anytime soon. The strobe effect of the lights passing by is winding up a headache and the bandage around my head is loose and all but useless.

I try and steady myself while we are on a stretch of straight road. I reach out and try the door handle but the central locking is still on. Karen spots me at the handle and gives my head the business. No-one is designed for the punishment I have received in the last twenty four hours and I pass out.

When I come round the car has stopped and the front seats are empty. I push up to look out but the effort sends a pain express across my temple telling me to stop. I reach down to my legs and touch both wounds. They are still agony but at least the blood seems to have stopped flowing. I pull the bandage from my head and unravel it. I rip at it with my teeth and produce two bandages for my legs. I tie off the left one and then the right one. There is too little material to do a proper job but maybe it will be enough to stop the wounds opening when I move.

I hear a door slam and then shadows cross the car windscreen. The rear passenger door opens and hands reach in and grab me. I'm pulled from the car and land on a large blue plastic tarpaulin that has been laid out next to the car door. Simon grabs one end of the plastic sheet and bundles it up into a knot using the whole thing as a rough travois. Karen pitches in and they drag me into the garage.

Once inside Simon hits a button on the wall and the garage door winds down with the whirl of an electric motor from above. Karen flips on the ceiling lights and my eyes close momentarily against the brightness.

The plastic moves again and I'm pulled towards a door at the rear of the garage. Simon reaches out and kicks the door open and I'm dumped into the small toilet beyond. The door slams shut, missing my head by millimetres.

I hear scraping and something heavy is dragged across the outside of the toilet door and the light from the gap at the bottom vanishes. The garage light goes out and I hear a door close.

I lie for a second taking in the silence while checking the wounds - both bandages seem dry. The toilet is windowless and a small red light high on the ceiling, probably a fire alarm, throws off enough light for me to see the layout. It's a basic toilet bowl and small quarter sink set up and little else.

I prop myself up against the wall and lean on the toilet bowl. It smells fresh and not used much. Not unusual - this house probably has more toilets than most homes have rooms.

There is a breeze blowing on my cheek. It seems to be coming from an extractor fan next to the fire alarm light. The fan is dead but the wind outside is blowing through the slats, dropping small gusts on me. The world is quiet. I consider shouting but I have neither the breath nor the energy. I'm also scared to hell that Karen will reappear - knife in hand.

I try and order my thoughts.

How the hell do you think in a circumstance like this? How can you function when you have someone like Karen in the wings - a woman who seems to show no remorse, indulges with no hesitation - and will, I'm certain, be back for more.

Whatever way I look at this I'm dead in the water. What do they want with me? I can't tell them anything else about the location of the documents, no matter how many knives they stick in me.

What is also beginning to tear at my gut is the fact that they will ask if I know what is in the documents. It's a bloody obvious question and once they know what I know - I'm history. They're hardly going to let me go? I might not know the detail of what they are up to but I know enough to make things awkward. The assault on me, the gorillas and their antics, the documents and my suspicions, Leonard - any or all of this would be enough to bring the police in.

I'm making myself more and more dispensable by the moment and sure as bears drop in the woods they will be planning their next step. It doesn't take a rocket scientist to figure what that will be. Extract what info I possess and dispose of me - simple really.

I put my full weight on the toilet bowl and push myself to my feet. Both thighs telegraph a 'don't move' message but I push on. Once upright I take the small step required to get to the door and turn the handle. The lock clicks open and the door moves a half inch before hitting whatever it is that they put in its way. I turn my back to the door and try and gain some leverage. I push and there is a little give but with my legs in the state they are there is no strength in the effort but I'm sure I can move the blockage if I can get some power into the bloody action.

I slide down the door and place my feet on the base of the toilet bowl, my legs are curled up and I lean into the door and try and straighten my legs.

The pain in my thighs is a living thing but I feel the door move another half an inch. I can feel dampness and the warmth of fresh blood down the side of my left leg as the wound re-opens but I just have to get on with the job and I lean into the door with what force I have left. Whatever is holding the door closed shifts and screams as it is forced over the garage floor.

I freeze, waiting for Karen or Simon to come running. I count to twenty and with no sign of life I push at the door again. This time the door moves a little more and the object beyond slides with less protest. My legs are straight but the gap between door and frame is too small for me to squeeze through yet. I straighten my back and curl my legs up to give a final push but the blood on the floor gets under my shoes and my legs shoot away from me. I try again but all I'm doing is spreading my life fluid. It's like a bloody Torville and Dean routine from a horror movie.

I lean up and grab the toilet roll and with a pull start it unfurling. I grab handfuls of the paper and wipe up as much as the blood as I can from the floor before my leg adds it back. I wipe the soles of my feet and try for one last push.

The door resists and then the object gives up the ghost with a howl and I fall backward into the garage smacking my head on the concrete floor. I lie on my back, chest heaving, leaking blood like a sieve and nursing the return of an OTT headache.

I can't believe that no-one heard the noise. I might have only seconds to get moving. In my spent state I ought to be down and out for the count but God loves a good 'un and I roll onto my front and haul myself to my feet.

The garage is swathed in all but a curtain of black. I try and focus on where I saw Simon hit the door control and I head for it. I can see a vague light under the door that leads into the house but there is no way I can exit that way and the garage door is Hobson's choice.

I grope along the wall and find a box with a rocker switch on it. I flip it and the electric motor in the ceiling kicks into life. The door starts to rise and the garage starts to light up as the street lights take hold. I am moving before the door is an inch clear of the ground. I drop to the concrete and grasp the underside of the door trying to force it up quicker.

I risk a glance back but the door to the house is still closed. I dare to think that no one is aware of my escape yet. The garage door is about two feet in the air when I roll under it and onto the driveway. I stagger to my feet and stumble forward.

A pair of arms catch me and my heart falls like a stone.

'Going somewhere?'

Simon pushes me to the ground and for good measure kicks me.

He gives me a punch to the face and drags me back into the garage. I try to struggle but my strength is gone. He hits the switch and the door closes. The door to the house opens and Karen walks in switching on the light.

'Time for a chat,' she says.

For the first time since I was three years old I piss in my trousers.

Chapter 42

Tina and George to the rescue.

George has dropped quiet on the way to Simon's house. I let him drive as I need to make a couple of calls and get my mind straight on what we need to do. Timing is everything and we are at a severe disadvantage. I don't know Simon's house and that would seem a bit of a pre-requisite if we are to get Charlie out. My plan also has more holes than my favourite pair of jeans and to top it all we are, as far as I can see, about to take on people who see killing people as a minor hobby.

The night holds Glasgow a prisoner as we drift through the suburbs. I've walked these streets for nigh on most of my life and still they hold a mystery at such a dark hour. Cars flash by and I wonder where they are going at this time. A boy of no more than ten is standing alone on a street corner and I almost ask George to stop and find out why he is out so late but as I watch he turns and vanishes up a side road and we are moving on.

I run through the next steps in my head. I'm in alien territory here. If this was telly then the plan would be exact and extensive - mine is inexact and brevity itself. We will case - even the words feel wrong - Simon's house and look for an opportunity. If one doesn't present itself I hope plan B works.

We lose the city and after ten minutes of country we enter Simon's village.

House prices have only gone one way in Glasgow's satellite villages, even given the recent economic turmoil, and Simon's village is no exception. What few cars we see parked on the road are all fresh out the wrapper in the last three years. The houses are set back with hedges and walls to give privacy. Only the centre of the village looks inviting, courtesy of a short burst of pre World War II terraced housing coupled with the compulsory corner store and local pub,

George checks his wee black book and confirms the address. I don't have Sat Nav or a street map but the village isn't that big and we cruise, checking out the road signs. George tucks his book into his pocket. He told me at the flat it is the one thing he would save in a fire. Every contact, deal and customer is hidden in its scrappy pages. It is the only reason we know Simon's address.

George feathers the brakes and slows down to read the next road sign. He brings the car to a halt, backs up and turns into the avenue. The houses are further apart now and the road lights stop a couple of hundred yards ahead. We head towards the darkness and old homes give way to new builds. Custom builds at that. George points to a mono blocked driveway and whispers 'Simon's house'. It is the last on the street.

We drive past the last streetlight and into the night. We pull into the entrance to a field and George kills the engine and the lights. I open the door and let the cold in and George does the same. The house is a hundred yards back towards the village and we walk up to the edge of the first pool of street light and stop.

The house for all its custom build still looks like a thousand that I have seen in estate agents' windows. The mock Tudor makes me smile and ask the question 'Why? What the heck did the Tudors ever do for Glasgow that requires such homage?'

There is light behind the large double window downstairs and a small security light highlights the front door.

We wait and I wish I had brought a thicker coat. Even in summer Scotland doesn't like to hang onto the heat too long. George suggests we try and get a look at the back of the house when our attention is drawn to the garage by a screeching noise emanating from inside. There is a pause and then a second noise.

A few seconds later the garage door starts to move up. We watch, stock still, as a body rolls out under the rising door before it is even half open. At the same time the front door opens and Simon emerges. The person from the garage stands up and stumbles forward. Simon rushes to catch the falling form and I catch a glimpse of Charlie's face. Words are said and Charlie is pushed to the ground and Simon kicks him. I almost stand up to shout but George grabs my arm and holds me close. We watch as Simon drags Charlie back into the garage and as the door closes the garage light flicks on. Then there is silence.

George nudges me and points at the front door. It is open. Well we wanted an opportunity and this would seem to be one. I stand up and George follows me and we jog down the driveway and up to the front door. I stop and listen. There are some sounds from the garage but nothing else.

I push the door open a little and stick my head in. With a deep breath I take a step and enter the hallway. George waits outside and keeps an eye on the garage. I come to a halt and try and catch any more sounds but even the garage noise has stopped. There is a large room to my left and I walk forward and look in. There is no-one there and I signal George to follow me. We both enter what seems to be the living room.

The room is well decorated but a little sparse for my taste. I'm in no mood to hang around writing a feature article. I want to find somewhere to get my head down and work out the next move. I point to a door at the far end of the room and we cross the room feeling expensive carpet beneath our feet. There is no light under the door and I open it to find myself on the edge of a large farmhouse kitchen.

There is the noise of a door opening from deeper in the house and I push George forward and rush into the kitchen closing the door behind me. I can hear voices and in the dark I try and find somewhere to hide.

'He'll not get out a second time.'

It sounds like a woman's voice.

To my left is a glass panelled door that seems to lead to the back garden. Next to it is another door and I hope it is the utility room. All big houses have utility rooms - don't they?

I urge George towards the door. The voices are getting closer. I open the door and smell clean laundry and we enter just as the door from the living room to the kitchen opens and the light goes on.

We hover in the small utility room and I am sweating. Next to me George is breathing heavily and I'm scared he'll be heard. I put my hand to his mouth and then my finger to my lips and mouth the 'shhh' sound.

There is a door behind me. I ease the handle down but it holds fast. Locked. If anyone walks into the room we are caught.

The utility room is a simple affair. Along one wall lies a washing machine, dryer and dishwasher. The opposite wall to the machines is blank save for the entrance door. The room is narrow, less than eight feet wide and the door I have just tried is the only other object of note.

George and I take up most of the spare floor space.

I slide past George and try to listen to what is going on in the kitchen. I can hear two voices; a man and a woman's. They are talking about Charlie and the woman is working herself up into a lather about what she wants to do to him. The man is more restrained and I can sense caution in his voice. They want to know how much Charlie knows. I hear my name and George's mentioned in connection with the documents and then the woman's voice says they will deal with us later.

I'm not too keen on the phrase 'deal with us later.'

I hear the whisp of the fridge door closing, a clink of glass and then the light goes out and the voices leave the kitchen and return to the living room. George whispers the word 'Karen' and in the dark gives me a little background.

Things are not looking good and I decide we need to get out of the utility room. We are no use to man nor beast in here and if Charlie is still in the garage then that is where we need to get to.

I'm counting on surprise. I can't believe that Simon or Karen will expect us to turn up. If we can catch them unawares we might be able to grab Charlie and get out. I wish we had parked the car closer to the driveway but hindsight is a wonderful thing. I open the entrance door to the utility room and look out. I can hear voices from the living room. I look round the kitchen and wonder what the price tag is on it. My car was probably worth less. In fact three of my cars would probably be worth less.

Next to a huge double doored US style fridge there is another door. It is the only other way out save going into the back garden or back into the living room. I grab the handle and then place my ear against it. I can still hear voices but my guess is that the door leads to the hall we came in through. I nod my head in the direction of the door and George falls in behind me.

The door opens and I find I have guessed wrong. I enter a well heeled dining room with a set of French doors to a moonlit patio to my left and an archway leading towards the front of the house on my right. I can see light from beyond the archway and if I am now even half orientated, the room beyond the archway will exit onto the hall and the front door.

The door to the garage must lie in the next room. I circle a dining table that dominates the room and peer round the archway architrave. The room beyond is a sitting room. A panelled door sits opposite the door to the hall. The door to the garage? Unfortunately the door to the hall is wide open and the voices from the living room sound close.

Time for my back up plan. I take out my mobile and make a call.

Chapter 43

George has to dig deep.

Tina is on the phone but she has it cupped around her mouth and all I can hear is whispering. The conversation seems to take an age before she hangs up and moves towards the door to the hall.

She is listening to the voices and I know what she is thinking. If we head for the door that leads to the garage will we be spotted? To be frank I am well scared at the moment. This is way past any comfort zone that could ever apply to me. My heart is racing and I feel faint.

Tina has taken the lead on this nonsense and that's fine by me. At least it was until the reality of what we are doing kicked in. Simon is not someone to mess with. He can be the life and soul of a party; a veritable bon-viveur but he has a dark side and his almost casual indifference to the way he just treated Charlie is testament to that fact.

The presence of Karen just makes the whole sorry affair a damn site worse. I've never taken to her and on my few encounters she has come across as cold and hard - not the sort of credentials one would expect from a Human Resources person.

Tina creeps forward and I fall in behind. The voices from the living room are low and indistinct. This could mean they are at the far end of the room - good for us - or they are just keeping their voices low and are sitting next to the hall - bad for us. I try and remember the layout of the living room. There was a large four seat couch in the centre with two double seaters in attendance. If Simon or Karen are sitting on the nearest double seater we have no chance of making the garage door.

Tina is at the door to the hall and I hold a lot of breath as she peers round. Her head snaps back and she joins her thumb and forefinger in the time honoured OK sign. She pushes the door a little until it blocks the view of the door to the garage. I circle a coffee table and try the door to the garage but keep my hand on the door to prevent it clicking open. I push and the door swings in and I enter a short hall. There is a door on my left and a door to the front. I'm sure the door to the front is for the garage but I can't figure the other door. Tina is right behind me and I try the garage door and it opens.

Tina doesn't follow me immediately and I look round and catch her opening the other door. She closes it and joins me in the garage. With the doors to the sitting room closed the light is poor and Tina searches for the light switch, finds it and bathes us in light.

The garage is sparse but plenty big enough for two cars. There is what looks like blood on the floor and a trail of it heads to the garage door and then back to where a large chest freezer has been pulled over another door.

Tina moves to the freezer and signals for me to give a hand and we lift it clear. Tina opens the door and Charlie slumps out on to the floor.

We bend down and grab him but he is dead weight. His hands are tied together with what looks like clothing line. I bend down and undo the knots.

'Charlie give us a hand,' I whisper.

Charlie lays still. His eyes are closed. His trousers are stained around his crotch and he has two poorly wrapped bandages around his thighs. I grab him under the arms and heave him upright. Tina grabs his left arm and tries to support him but she hasn't the strength to add much support and I take most of the weight.

I turn him to face the garage door and cross the concrete, dragging him every step of the way. Tina lets go and looks for the garage door switch. I reach the door and Tina finds the switch. She hits it and returns to the door before killing the over head light. The electric motor is too loud and Charlie is too heavy. The whole thing is wrong.

The door takes an aeon to open but I can't move until it is fully up as I am barely supporting Charlie and bending to get under the door is impossible. The door clicks home and I summon up what little reserves I have and carry Charlie out the door and onto the mono block.

Then a storm arrives.

Behind me the garage light goes on and this is followed by a shout. I put my head down and carry on. There is maybe twenty feet of mono block left to cover before I hit the pavement. I expect to be dragged to the ground any second.

Behind me there is an almighty howl and the sound of metal hitting concrete. A second scream rings out and more metal on concrete sounds.

I put my head down and grind on. Charlie is mumbling but I wish he would stop it and start stumbling.

Ten feet to the pavement.

Behind me I can hear the sound of the garage door closing. I look up and there is now no way I'm going to make the van. My muscles are screaming at me to put Charlie down but my head is telling me to push on. I hear a footstep behind and brace myself for the worst and then Tina comes whirling up and throws Charlie's arm over her shoulder.

The reduction in weight acts like a can of Red Bull and we struggle to the van. I have no idea where Simon and Karen are but I don't care. The only thing that matters is getting Charlie in the van and getting the hell out of here.

The garage door motor kicks back into life and Tina looks back. She drops her end of Charlie and rushes to the van and flings the back door open and returns. We heave Charlie in like a sack of potatoes and then it is into the front seats.

My nerves are strung like piano wire supporting an elephant and I can't get the keys to go home. Tina shouts at me to hurry up but this doesn't help. The keys slide in and I wrench the engine to life, select first and all but stall before gunning into the night.

Behind me a set of blue lights are flashing.

'Sodding late,' says Tina.

Chapter 44

The gorillas arrive too late.

I see the blue flashing lights ahead and pull up sharp. Next to me Jim is dozing. I check the address I was given and confirm that the police car is sitting outside the wee man's house.

I pick reverse and slide back onto the main road and park a hundred yards down the road. I get out, leaving Jim asleep. He's often more use when he is dead to the world. I walk back along the main road trying to look as if I belong there and then turn into Simon's road. The police car is still standing there and two policemen are talking to the wee man. He is looking animated.

I look around for some cover to get closer but there's none. The only option is to take to the back gardens if I want to get any nearer without being seen. I walk up the broad driveway of a two storey mansion made of red brick. It looks nineteen thirties in design and the double front door is guarded by an oversize porch and some serious storm doors.

The house shows no sign of life and I skirt round to the back and enter a manicured gardener's heaven. A lawn stretches out that would substitute well for a game of football should Hampden ever fall down. There is a pond of Olympic size proportions to my left and a greenhouse like the Palace of Arts. This family have cash to burn.

I skirt the lawn - no point leaving footprints in the dew and vault the fence into the next garden.

This one is a poor cousin to its neighbour but is the Chelsea Flower Show compared to my window box back home.

Two more gardens and Simon's garden is next. I can't see the police or the wee man but the blue flashing light is strobing off the garage wall and I know they are still there.

I squeeze through a gap in the hedge and, keeping tight to the wall, creep to the edge of the garage.

The police are leaving and whatever conversation had been had has finished and Simon is on his way back into the house. The police car vanishes and I step out from the shadows as the wee man approaches.

Chapter 45

Simon meets a gorilla.

The sound of the garage door rising had been the trigger. I had popped out from my conversation with Karen for a slash. I heard it start to rise. I screamed at Karen and we dived into the garage.

I see Charlie being hauled up the driveway by George the maintenance man. A woman is standing in the middle of the floor - staring at me. I put my head down to rush her. She jigs to one side and grabs a wrench from the hanging tool rack next to the garage door button. She throws it at me. The throw is low and it catches my shin bone. I scream. I drop to the floor and clutch my leg. Karen sprints by. I hear her scream and see my crow bar tumble to the ground. Karen falls to the ground. She is rubbing her chest.

I try to stand up. The woman hurls my nail gun at me. It glances off my shoulder and I'm down again. I hear the electric motor of the garage go into reverse. I'm powerless to move for a few seconds.

Karen is trying to get up but her whimpers tell me she caught one good.

I flip onto my back and rub at my leg. I can't tell if the fucker is broken. Whatever, there will be a planet sized bruise.

I let the pain fall away a little. I try my weight on it. It holds and I limp to the garage door and hit the switch. The door rises. I step out in time to see a van disappear. Seconds later it is replaced by blue flashing lights.

I press the remote in my pocket. The garage door closes just as the police car pulls up.

I try and look nonchalant as I limp up to meet the police at the top of my driveway. I eye the road to the right. The sight of two brake lights as the van takes a corner is my reward. Then the lights are gone.

The two police get out. They approach. We go into a routine. They tell me that they were called about a break in. I play dumb. They ask what I am doing outside. I say getting some air. They ask why some one would call them and report a break in. I tell them that they are a funny bunch round here. They tell me the call came from a mobile. I say nothing. They ask me for my details. I pull out my driver's license. One of the policemen checks me out on the radio.

It's over.

The police get back in the car. I watch them go, then turn to go back to the garage.

A man steps out from behind the garage. I freeze.

'The names Tom Ball but my mates call me Bally. 'the Voice' sent me over to see if I could help.'

We have a stilted conversation. So this is Dumb - or is it Dumber. He doesn't seem the sharpest tack in the box. He tells me what he has been up to. Half way through the garage door goes up. Karen steps out rubbing her right tit.

We bring her up to speed. She calls it for what it is - a busted flush. We either get the three in the van and the documents or we are dead meat. She asks for 'the Voice's' number again. She dials it. Ten minutes later my phone rings. She takes it off me. The conversation is not a short one.

When she hangs up she ushers us into the house. She tells us both to sit down. I note that Bally is letching at Karen. She doesn't seem to notice. I feel a pang of jealousy.

Karen stands next to the fire. Legs akimbo, hand on hips. She looks good that way.

She shorthands her conversation with 'the Voice'. It turns out that someone called the police to both Charlie and Tina's houses. The watchers had to scarper. She guesses it was George or the girl that made the call. It doesn't take a brain surgeon to figure out who called the police to my house.

The stake outs will resume on Charlie's, George's and the girl's houses. Their instructions are simple. Whatever it takes, grab all three and call for instructions.

Chapter 46

Charlie needs convincing.

It's hard to convey thanks when you reek of urine and can't stop trembling but that was what I was trying to do. The smell in the van was being worked on by two open windows but it wasn't enough. I tried apologising but after the fifth time Tina told me to shut up. She had thinking to do.

I couldn't see what thinking was required. Let's go to the authorities and get this over with. 'Fess up to everything take whatever was coming and get the damn thing over and done with.

Tina was on a different page and when I told her what I wanted to do she killed it stone dead.

'Do you think that telling the police will stop them coming after you? Dream on!'

The relief at escaping from the hell of the garage had given me a huge injection of optimism. Tina had just poured a bucket of rotting fish guts on me. And of course she was right. Even at best with Simon, Karen et al locked up we had no idea who else was out there that could pay a visit to Tina, George and myself. For all I know there could be a squad ready to head out at the drop of a hat.

The police weren't a solution. We had to find another way to tackle this and as we drove into the rising sun Tina and George rolled out plan after plan and I sat in the back doing little but adding to the stench.

It was clear that Tina was no fool. She had reported robberies at all three of our houses to flush out the watchers and called in the police just before my rescue in case it went south - the girl wasn't daft.

It was reasonable to assume that the houses would be put back on watch so going home was not an option. I sat back and ear wigged Tina. If she had been smart enough to get me out of the garage and set up the phoney 'burglary' calls then she was plenty smart enough to work out plan B.

Plan B turned out to be interesting. George drove us to a spot out in the country and pulled into a lay-by and Tina let rip.

First she said, let's forget the real meaning of the documents - whatever they mean they are wanted on a desperate scale by Simon and Karen. Second, front up to Simon with a warning - back off or we release the documents. I voiced that Leonard almost certainly had tried the same trick. Tina said that this was a trade. Simon gets the documents and we stay stum.

I'm less than convinced and on the other side of the fence on this to Tina. Simon's not exactly a man of his word. Tina dismisses my worries. Look what we have on him. The documents, Leonard's death, my kidnapping.

I'm still on the unconvinced side of the fence but at least I can see a gate.

Plus, she went on, as far as he knows we have copies of the documents. How does he know we haven't committed all this to an envelope and packed it off to a lawyer? Plus what's the downside for Simon? If we hand back what he wants he walks away from a pile of shit and life goes on - we're hardly going to stitch him up if we value our lives.

The gate is open but I still need to walk through.

Who is going to do the dirty deed? Who does the 'handing back'?

'You,' Tina says to me.

'Me?'

'You!'

One doth think that she jests.

Sod this for a game of soldiers. Tina has taken point on all of this and I can't think why she wouldn't be best placed to finish it.

The answer is a stone walled cracker. It would seem that an able and fit Tina and George are best placed to run to the police should Plan B implode. I on the other hand, as a crock, would be far better doing the face to face. It would seem that being thrown off a building, kidnapped, stabbed and generally abused makes you more dispensable in life. I argue against this but short of drawing straws one of us needs to take the brave pills.

I suggest that we could do the deal by phone and drop the documents in some bin somewhere. Tina says I watch too many episodes of Mission Impossible and the only way this works is if we do it face to face. That and a little insurance she has figured out.

The gate is closing and I'm still on the other side to Tina and George. I'm not keen on being the sacrificial lamb.

George throws in his tuppence worth. We find a neutral spot. George and Tina sit in the background and we do the deal in the open. A public space where Simon isn't going to go down the nonsense route. Tina and George in plain view. Phone to ear. Anything amiss and they hit 999 and the whole deal is off.

The gate opens a little again.

George has the perfect location. George Square. You can't get much more public. I point out that a trip to hospital first might be a good idea given the severity of my injuries. I'm voted down two to one. Tina has a friend who can fix me up. A hospital would open the door to a lot of questions and this whole thing needs to be sorted before it gets fatal for us.

The conversation goes on but none of us are experts in this game and the best we can do is plan for what we think might happen and leave the rest to fate.

The gate is still open but I'm going to have to be carried through it screaming.

Chapter 47

'the Voice' makes a move.

The blind man picks up the phone and the conversation is far from satisfactory. A succession of calls later and things were little better. Sometimes in life you can make things too complicated. What seems simple gets messy and what gets messy has a habit of staying messy. And this was messy.

He pours another two fingers of Glayva and slumps in the chair. That one mistake. The one oversight. The set of documents from Leonard to Charlie that threatens to derail his life. The companies and people behind the figures on those documents are not to be messed with - not under any circumstance. Had it been Simon's tax details that were kicking around then that would have been a piece of piss.

The documents were the bad end of a bad stick and the blind man was no more immune to their release than Simon or Karen. Now the maintenance man, his girlfriend and the accountant were back on the run. The blind man swallowed a full finger of liquid and could not think of one single reason why the three fugitives were not in the process of taking the whole affair to the police.

He picks up the phone and makes a call he never thought he would ever have to make. It lasts less than thirty seconds and then he hangs up.

Life for 'the Voice' was about to change for ever.

Chapter 48

Simon wonders if this is the beginning of the end?

I took two phone calls inside ten minutes. Both were unexpected. Both changed the world around me.

The first came from 'the Voice' with a request for a meet. An unheralded moment and not one that I was fully prepared to deal with. However the request was more of a demand - in truth an order. 'the Voice' was coming to my home. One hour and be ready. I told Karen who seemed unflustered. But then again she had no relationship with the man. I did.

The second phone call came in on my home number. The sun was burning off the early morning mist and I took it looking over the fields that extended out beyond my garden. Few people use my home number. It is unlisted and a network of mobile and work numbers serve to keep my friends and colleagues at bay. My home number is known to half a dozen people. None of them would phone at this time in the morning. I listened to the voice. I ask if the caller can call back in five minutes. I hang up and tell Karen what had just been said. This time she is more than a little interested.

A trade? I had just been offered a trade in George Square at midday - the documents for the trio's safety.

Karen asks three pertinent questions.

a) Why a public trade? Why not drop the documents off?

b) What if it is set up? A trap. Police, authorities - who knows.

Good questions

Her third question is equally as tricky.

c) Why don't we just cut and run?

I'm having trouble doing any thinking. What with 'the Voice' on his way round - events are piling up like a crash on the M8. I'm not in thinking straight mode.

I have no answer to the public trade. I have a million answers to going on the run. For a start there is the missing two million. I'm fucked if I have to exit cashless while Karen and Robin head for the sun.

I need a drink but it must be a pretty distant yardarm to justify booze at this time. Regardless I head for the drinks cabinet. I pour myself a large slug of Isle of Jura. I ignore the look on Karen's face. I sit down and swallow the damn thing in two.

I put forward a proposal. We say yes to the trade - whether we are going ahead with it or not. At least that way we buy some time. If they are genuine about handing over the documents then the documents stay off the streets for a little while longer.

I also suggest that we wait and see what 'the Voice' has to say.

Karen agrees with my first point and doesn't give a shit about my last point.

My home phone rings again. I pick it up and agree to the meet.

I need a shower and a shave. I pour myself another glass of Isle of Jura and leave Karen and Bally to get acquainted.

I drop my clothes in a pile on my bed. I enter the en-suite and set the shower to stun. I try to scour the skin from my body. Every few minutes I tear myself from the pain and ingest some more of Scotland's finest.

The whole thing makes me feel a sod size better.

The door bell goes. I'm already dry and in a fresh set of jeans topped of by my favourite Tommy Hillfiger polo shirt. I head down the stairs bare foot. But not before I have aftershaved up and decontaminated my armpits with half a can of Sure.

I'm ready.

Karen has answered the door. As I descend the stairs I can hear voices. Something grabs a hold of my head and says I'm a dumb shit.

I walk into the room. Karen is standing by the fireplace. She looks good. This isn't something I would have thought forty eight hours earlier. Bally is on the mobile to someone - probably Dumber. Sitting in my favourite armchair is Robin.

I greet him with a traditional 'What the fuck are you doing here' greeting. He simply smiles. The 'I'm a dumb shit' button is still depressed in my head. I repeat the question and he says nothing.

I think about crossing the room and giving him a slap. The niggle in my head tells me I'm missing something big time.

I look at Karen and she is smiling at Robin. An industrial size penny drops. At least it starts to drop. I try and catch it and put it back where it was. This is nuts. Robin plucks a mobile from his pocket and hits a short dial. Seconds later my phone rings. He points at it and nods as if to say pick up. I play along. I hit the receive button and put it to my ear.

The world pulls a funny trick on me. In my ear 'the Voice' says hello at exactly the same time as I hear the same word from Robin wafting across my living room.

Chapter 49

A whole new world for Simon.

I watch the penny drop all the way to the ground. I feel my head unravel. Robin and 'the Voice' are one and the same person. This takes some time to sink in. This throws up some serious questions.

Robin is still smiling. Karen is still smiling. Sibling love at work no doubt. Bally has now joined the Aquafresh brigade. I'm the one with the frown. Glass in hand I decide I need a seat. I tumble into the two seater near the front window. The smiling game continues.

It is hard to fathom where to start. The idea that Robin has been my 'fixer' beggars belief. First and foremost how the hell did he become a finder of hit men and thugs? When did it start and why? To what end? With what purpose? Why in the hell…? The questions turn my head into a merry-go-round. I want to get off.

There are times in your life when you just don't know what to do. I don't mean when you can't decide if you want the Pepperoni Passion or the Vegetarian Supreme from Pizza Hut. I mean times when you can't see an answer. Times when you can't even see the question that will lead to the answer. Sometimes you can't even see the colour of the wallpaper.

Robin being 'the Voice' was so far the wrong side of the goalmouth that it was blindingly obvious. Once you thought about it that is. I mean how good can it be to get paid for fixing problems from both ends. Problems that will help a company you have a third share in.

Talk about eating your cake and having it plus an extra slice. Shit I even paid 'the Voice' a twenty grand bonus last year because he had served us well.

I look at Karen. The smiling female at the fireplace does not seem in the slightest surprised.

She knows.

And that is the killer thought.

If she knew about Robin she knew about 'the Voice'. If she knew about 'the Voice' she was in on everything. She was also...

Another fucking huge penny goes into the slot.

I had been set up. Like a royal fucking turkey at Christmas. I had been trussed and sent to the man with the big knife for a throat shave. This had fuck all to do with documents. This had fuck all to do with anything I knew about. This had a shit lot to do with something else. Something that I was supposed to be the patsy for. The fall guy. Lee Majors with no safety net.

The next half hour went past like a ball of fire falling from a mountain.

I asked a shed load of questions. Robin and Karen got busy with the answers. A brother and sister act that had me wondering how I had been so blind.

They admitted everything and denied nothing. The subtext was easy. I didn't know jack shit about what was going on in Retip. I thought we were on the dodgy end of wherever the dodgy end is and I wasn't even fucking close.

The money laundering that was so profitable was in deep with some serious people - this I knew. What I didn't know, what I couldn't know was how serious and how deep it all was. I knew we had been on the receiving end of a good year. Cash had seemed to spring forth with an amazing amount of ease. Cash that we were cleaning and making good for Robin and Karen's retirement fund.

However to make good their escape there were some people that needed to take a permanent vacation under six feet of soil. Leonard's computer had been loaded with five names. Names of people that Robin and Karen needed to take an early trip to the funeral parlour. Names that would throw suspicion on me. I was in the frame for all the deaths.

Bally was still smiling. He had no idea what was going on. He had also failed to figure out that his arse was on the line. After all why would Robin and Karen need witnesses to the whole shebang?

It looked like Leonard had dropped us all in the crap when he had handed Charlie a hard copy of the documents. Karen's hysterics in the car were genuine. She actually cared about me. But she knew she had to run.

And - and this was a big fucking and - despite the crap that Robin and Karen have dropped on me I am no more in a position to stop the documents being released than they are. Like it or not I need to work with them to get the documents back.

Had their scheme worked I would be the lead on the STV news. They would have been off into the wide blue yonder - a Swiss bank style amount of cash to the better. Five dead bodies coming down on me like rain in a monsoon. Followed by our clients.

I wanted to kick both of them into a pile of mush. I wanted to kill them. Instead I sat quietly in the chair and looked at them. Blood boiling.

It would take no effort to walk over and spend the next half hour re-arranging their molecular biology with a cricket bat.

I don't.

I can't.

I need their help to get out of this mess.

Chapter 50

George and the show down.

Glasgow city centre was gearing up for lunch. A quiet shopping morning was about to turn ugly as the workers who swarmed into the city to work every morning cut loose from the shackles and went on a food hunt.

I was standing next to Gregg's the baker on the south west corner of George Square ignoring a desire for a quick cheese pasty and waiting for the Gary Cooper moment that was due soon.

It is hard not to be impressed by Glasgow's approach to life. I'd love to say it was unique but I'm fairly certain that a washed up fishing village in Fiji could equally claim to be unique. But Glasgow just does life in a different way. The people around me have no interest in you, me or anyone else and at the same time this is nonsense. You can try and impress the hell out of the throng around you and you'll get a big fat zero. You can do something disgustingly ordinary and find you have adopted an audience. Glasgow is not a place you come to show off and I have met endless people that live, work and love here and they don't get it.

Loud mouths are a turn off, unless of course they speak with a Billy Connolly wit and even then some people will wish for your guts on a plate.

Not long ago I was a guest at a black tie function or as is the norm in Scotland a kilted function. I don't get to go to too many but on this occasion my bosses had been looking for numbers to make up a table at a Facility Management do.

As far as I could tell the function was more a money making event for the organisers than a celebration of the industry - but it was sold as an award ceremony and despite the crass capitalism by the people in charge some notable and extremely worthy people picked up some seriously poor plastic rewards for their efforts. Then, just as the show was heading for its climax, a success story climbed the stage and gave us ten minutes of his received wisdom.

Life was awful, the industry was in the crapper, no one gave a damn, no one was doing anything about it - a tirade that earned him less respect than a dog doing its business with a bitch in heat. Did he get the vibe from the crowd? Did he heck. He ranted on as if the world should hang on his every word and all that he achieved was an A+ in showing yourself up as a loser.

Did he have a point? Absolutely. But he still looked and sounded like an industrial fool. Did anyone tell him this after? Of course not? Why should they? You can lead some horses to water, you can grab their heads and stick them in the trough, you can even boot them in the privates and wait for them to inhale but they still won't drink - Glasgow knows this.

People can live for a generation and not figure out they are a prick. Some people live their lives and think they are the mutt's nuts and they just aren't. Full stop. No discussion. And that is why I live here. If you are a twat you can live in ignorance because deep down the city prefers to let its arse-wipes keep entertaining it. Deep, deep down the city is laughing all the way down the River Clyde and the best bit, the absolute cream on the bun - the tossers don't even know. Not a blind clue. I love it.

A young office type's cute rear grabbed my attention and I realised I was supposed to be on watch. I hugged the corner of the store and looked out onto the square. I was trying to keep a low profile but I was hardly a professional at this game. Hiding was also a bit redundant given the get up I was in.

Tina had suggested disguises and I had gone along. I'd always fancied myself as a young rebel, even at my age so, daft as it looks, I had pulled on a hoodie top and a pair of jeans that were four inches too big round my waist. My trainers were new out of the box - fresh from George at Asda. No Nike Airs for me - five quid and a bargain at twice the price. Under the hoodie I sported a natty line in fake designer t-shirts - Giorgio would not be a happy man if he saw the quality of the cloth that bore his name.

I was the oldest chav in town and only Tina had saved me from a Burberry baseball cap.

I could see Charlie sitting on a bench. He was one of many sitting on the ring of benches that surround the west end of the square.

The heat was kicking up a notch and the square's red concrete that had been laid by our friendly left wing council was starting to bitch back.

I laughed at the red top when they put it down. Left wing. Red flag. Red concrete. I was told that there was no political end to the acres of poorly laid material. How thick do they think we are?

This used to be a square with character. Now it's a square with the word cheap written across it. Scotland with Style is the latest strapline for the city. Pity no-one told the planning department.

Charlie was slumped a little and with good reason. Tina's friend had bandaged up the wounds and filled him with as many Neurofen Extra Strength as she thought she could get away with.

As soon as the whole deal was over Charlie was back to the Royal for a serious session with the doctors.

I couldn't see Tina but I knew she was at the far side of the square eyeballing Charlie.

The exchange was simple and smart. As soon as Simon appeared I would keep my finger over the short dial to the police. Tina would walk towards him with a video camera - doing the tourist bit.

Simon would sit next to Charlie and Charlie would open up the documents as if showing something to a friend. Tina would video, up close. Charlie would close the documents and hand them to Simon. Tina would keep videoing. Simon would get up and leave and we would all live in happy land. Simon has the documents. We have a video of the trade.

Deal done.

As my watch alarm bleeped to tell me it was midday I kept my eyes on Charlie and waited for Simon to appear.

Ten minutes roll by and nothing. Sweat is running down my neck and the top of the hoodie is damp where I am using it to mop my brow.

Fifteen minutes and it is starting to look like a bust. Charlie slumps a little more and the man next to him gives a 'sod off' look and moves along a few inches.

Twenty minutes and I see Tina's number light up on my phone. I take the call and we agree to give it ten more minutes.

Charlie does some more slumping and the man, now more of a pillow than a neighbour gets up and lets him fall over. As he falls Charlie's hand clips the armrest.

I wait for him to pull himself upright but after a few seconds it is clear that this isn't going to happen. Then there is a scream and all hell breaks loose.

A woman on the same bench had leant over to see if Charlie was alright and she was the source of the scream. She begins shouting but the traffic drowns out her words and I was on the move.

The traffic is heavy and I wait for it to clear. I see Tina crossing the square towards Charlie. I spot a gap in the cars and sprint through and onto the pavement. I round the chair Charlie is on and almost send Tina spinning as she arrives at the same time.

By now there are four people around Charlie and I have to push one aside to get to him.

'Friend of yours?'

It doesn't register the stranger is talking to me. I fall to my knees.

'Doesn't look good.'

It still doesn't register that I am the intended recipient of his words.

Charlie has his face on the bench seat. His body is twisted - his back to the sky and his legs still planted on the ground. I see a pool of dark liquid under the seat and I know what it is before my brain has time to decipher the scene.

I try to lift Charlie's head but it is like lifting a bowling ball.

'Charlie, are you alright? Charlie, are you alright?' I say.

It is clear that Charlie is anything but alright and is never going to be alright again. Unless you're a religious person. In which case you might be able to argue he has never been so alright as he is now.

Tina clues in quick and steps back. I open Charlie's jacket but the documents are gone. A man behind me asks what I am doing and I realise it looks like I am pick-pocketing. I close Charlie's jacket and stand up. I ask if someone could call an ambulance and a young girl goes for her mobile.

I am close to panic. The crowd has grown to some twenty strong and I step back and join Tina. We look down at Charlie and then take another step back. The crowd closes in front of us and we turn on our heels and leave.

Chapter 51

Gorillas give chase.

I watch as the maintenance man and the girlfriend approach the dead accountant. The rubber neckers grow in number and I tap Jim on the shoulder. He is in his own world but I don't care as long as he follows orders and keeps by my side.

The pair are leaving their friend and exiting the crowd and I can see by their faces they are not in a good place. You see that look a lot in my job.

They are both dressed to fool but they are fooling no-one.

We are less than twenty yards away but they won't see us. Not without our suits. Jim is in jeans, a fleece (too hot for a fleece Jim) and a baseball cap from the Rangers FC shop. His size thirteen trainers are a special order from the internet.

I've pulled on a woollen beany hat, a cream t-shirt and a pair of old chinos that still have white paint across the knees from a bout of painting I did before Christmas.

If the lovers look carefully enough they might remember me from less than half an hour ago, when I sat down next to Charlie, letting my copy of the Glasgow Herald flop onto the vic's knees, when I leant over to apologise, when I stabbed him, when I lifted the documents, when I folded the paper and left. Simple really.

Now for part two.

We fall in behind the love birds as they exit the square and turn up onto Buchanan St. It is wall to wall with lunch time shoppers and we have to stay closer than I would like to make sure we don't lose them. I hadn't seen them arrive but I assumed they must have a car. Either that or they made poor Charlie stagger along on his wasted legs.

I'm surprised when they turn into the glass bubble that protects the entrance to the underground. Seconds later we follow them down into the world of the clockwork orange.

Built in the late eighteen hundreds the underground system is one of the oldest in the world and one of the smallest. In a ring, that barely leaves the city centre, there are two tracks - one going clockwise and one anti clockwise. Unlike most underground systems there is no danger of falling asleep and finding yourself miles from home. Just stay on and you'll come back round soon enough.

It got the nickname of the clockwork orange in the eighties when they replaced the ageing rolling stock with tiny orange coloured subway cars.

The ticket hall is dark and the lovers are grabbing tickets from the automatic ticket machine. We hang back and then buy two tickets as they push theirs into the machine to free up the entrance barrier.

We follow them down the stairs but I flip my hand out onto Jim's chest before we hit the last flight of stairs leading down onto the platform. The platform is too small to hide on and all the lovers would have to do is cast their eyes back where they had come from and we are made. Disguised or not we would be too close to risk it.

We let some people past and hold our ground on the small landing gaining us a few choice words from those who have to squeeze by.

The lovers are on the clockwise platform and I squat down and see them deep in conversation at the far end.

The familiar rumble of the train approaching echoes around us and then with a roar it bursts from its lair and the orange and cream cars grind to a halt with a piss of air brakes and the ring of metal on metal. The doors open and the passengers exit. I wait until I see the lovers move and then haul Jim down the stairs and into the first car.

The Glasgow underground does not allow passengers to move from car to car and the cramped interior (Jim has to bend over double to get in the door) does not allow much of a view of the other cars. I'll have no choice but to stick my head out of the door at each station to see if the lovers get off.

The doors close and the driver winds up the spring and we are away. Jim is smiling again but the noise as we pass through the tunnel stops me from asking why. I probably don't want to know anyway.

Minutes later we gush into the next station, Cowcaddens and I stand up and urge Jim to do the same. No one on our car gets off and when I look along the platform no-one else has alighted. I pull my head back in and motion for Jim to sit down again.

I repeat this exercise for the next four stations - St George's Cross, Kelvinbridge, Hillhead and

Kelvinhall. At Partick our car almost empties and I'm knocked onto the platform by my fellow passengers. Ahead I see the lovers and they are already at the foot of the exit stairs. I grab Jim and drag him onto the platform, still smiling.

There is little room to move and we have no choice but to try and barge our way to the front for fear of losing the lovers as they exit the station.

We draw looks, curses and a series of 'what the f…'s as we go by but I don't care. Lose the lovers and we are dead meat. We've been told this in no uncertain terms.

We bundle ourselves through the barrier and out onto the pavement and I look around to catch sight of our quarry. The station exits onto a small square that is alive with buses and shops. I spot the head of the maintenance man as he wheels out of sight around the far corner of the square. I urge Jim into a jog and then slow down as we round on to the short road beyond the square.

The lovers are keeping up a pace and vanish left onto the main road. We follow and once we have them in sight again we hold back, keeping a few people between us and them.

I know this area well. My grandmother and grandfather lived not far from here for most of their lives.

The lovers cross the road and head up Crow Rd. I have no idea where they are going but that doesn't matter, I just need to keep them in sight until we can get them on their own.

The road runs up hill and there is a retail park on the right. Guarding the entrance is the ubiquitous

MacDonald's and the lovers cut up a small set of stairs and push their way into the land of Ronald.

Jim taps me on the shoulder and says he fancies a Big Mac. I shake my head and ignore him. Sure lets cosy up to the two lovers and share a large fries and a Coke.

The girlfriend picks a seat by the window and the maintenance man disappears to return a few minutes later, coffees in hand.

They launch into discussion and I can just imagine the talk revolving around the question of the moment - what the hell do we do now?

The girlfriend drags out her mobile and makes a call. She puts it away and they resume their chat.

It takes them fifteen minutes to down the liquid and then they are on the move again. On up the hill. At the top they cut into the left and head for a set of white multi stories. Built in 1966 my gran was the first resident of the first one built. I tell everyone that when I pass. No-one is ever interested.

At the first of the high rises the lovers stop at the entrance and hit one of the numbers on the security entrance. After a brief pause they push open the door and vanish inside. I sprint up behind them and then hit as many buttons as I can. After a few seconds the buzzer sounds and we are in. Security entrance - joke! Someone always lets you in.

I know the layout of the flats and I don't venture beyond the front door until I hear the lift doors open and close. Only then do I sprint to the lifts.

There are two lifts and they sit diagonally opposite the other. Only one is moving and I watch the numbers climb until it stops at eleven. I wait to make sure it isn't someone getting on to go higher - unlikely but not impossible. The eleven stays lit and I press the button for the other lift.

Almost immediately the door opens and Jim does his limbo act to get in the door. I hit eleven and we rise to the faint smell of piss and alcohol. A smell that I figure is an optional extra from all good lift manufacturers.

We arrive at the eleventh floor and hold back. Now it gets tricky. The corridor is shaped like a flattened Z and there are six flats on each floor. The lift we have come up on opens onto one of the flat doors. If the lovers are at this door we are made. But there is no one in front of it. Either the lovers have gone inside or they are at one of the other doors. I count to five and then peek out. I can see a second door and it is clear.

We exit the lift and I carefully look round the first corner of the Z and peer down the corridor. There is another flat entrance on the right and it has no one outside.

There is a pair of fire doors half way along the main leg of the Z and they have frosted glass meaning you can't see beyond. I tell Jim to stay put. I walk along the corridor and swing open the fire doors. The door to the flat on the right and the door further along is clear. I walk round the second corner of the busted Z and the one remaining door is also clear.

There are two scenarios. Either they are inside one of the flats or they have sussed us and headed straight back down the fire stairs. I'm guessing they are in one of the flats and suspect nothing. Their heads aren't on straight at the moment.

Now we can either wait or start knocking.

Neither option is ideal. Waiting sounds good but hanging around in the corridors will only arouse suspicion. Every door is fitted with a spy hole and everyone knows everyone in these places. Even if we are not spotted through any of the doors someone will eventually use the lift and we look as out of place as a snotty hanky in a fur coat.

Knocking is also risky. It's not as if lover boy or his squeeze are going to answer the door and give themselves away.

We retire to the stairwell. At least we can now hear if someone is coming and head up or down the stairs as need be, but on the downside once we are in the stairwell the lifts are hidden behind heavy doors and the lovers could be away before we know it.

Jim suggests kicking in each door and doing a bit of US style home invasion. I ignore him but I don't have any better ideas.

Then Jim does something I have rarely been witness to. In fact never been witness to. He has a good idea.

It takes a while for him to explain it but its simplicity is genius. I grab my phone and call Simon. He listens to what I have to say and agrees to text me straight away. A few seconds later the phone bleeps to tell me I have a text and I flip it open, select the numbers on the text and then I push Jim back into the corridor. I tell him to stay put and I head through the fire doors and hit dial on my phone. Ten seconds go by and the fire door opens and Jim is beckoning me.

I join him and he points to the door nearest to him.

The girlfriend's phone has just stopped ringing.

I'm amazed Jim thought of it but it was spot on the money. It was the girlfriend that had made the arrangements for the meet from her mobile and hadn't blocked her caller ID. Hence Simon had her mobile number on his home phone. Fortunately he hadn't used the phone since. After that all he had to do dial 1471 and text me the number. All I had to do was press and listen for the ring. Go figure. Jim came good.

We return to the stairwell to consider our next move.

Chapter 52

George and Tina get caught.

Tina's friend didn't exactly look pleased to see us. She invited us in and took us into the flat's main room. She asks if we wanted tea or coffee and I decline the offer. Tina accepts and disappears into the small kitchen and I hear the start of a conversation. I wander over to the large window that dominates the room. Beyond is a balcony with a view and half. I try the door that leads out. It is unlocked and I step out.

A railing runs the length of the balcony with a reinforced frosted glass panel beneath it. The whole balcony is a little more twelve feet long by three feet deep. From eleven floors up the view is to the west of the city, looking straight down the River Clyde.

At one time the view would have been dominated by shipyards. Wall to wall from here to Dumbarton. Red Clydeside in its prime. Clyde-built had been the by word for engineering excellence but a lack of investment, labour disputes and cheap foreign construction had driven nail after nail into the industry's coffin. But all was not lost and from where I stood I could see the BAE systems yard that had just picked up the lion's share of the two new aircraft carriers that the government had ordered.

It wasn't much compared to the thousands of ships that men and machine had built over the last two hundred years but it was a damn fine thing for the thousands who counted on ship building to earn a living.

I leaned over the railing to look at the new Glasgow Harbour development that hugged the river. Hundreds of brand new flats were going up and soon the transport museum would up roots from its home in the Kelvin Hall and move to a purpose built venue not half a mile from where I stood. A mile further up the river from that was the new riverside financial district and across from it the new digital media quarter.

The Clyde might not be the home to too many shipyards anymore but it was slowly being given the pride of place it deserved. After all where would Glasgow have been if the Clyde had run dry?

I took a gulp of air and as I exhaled stepped back into the flat. Tina and friend were still gabbing and I was sure that our whole story was getting an airing as the kettle boiled.

I needed a slash and popped my head into the kitchen to ask where the toilet was.

Having been given directions I entered a world of fragrant smells, candles and pink. I had a feeling Tina's friend wasn't sharing with a man.

I lifted the lid and let rip.

It was then that a new storm rolled into town.

The door bell rang and I jumped spraying pee onto the fluffy mat that circled the bowl. I heard Tina's friend walk past the toilet and then the click of a Yale being turned.

The crash that followed was so out of place that I turned round, hosing down the wall and the door. I tried to shut up shop but I've never been able to switch it off mid stream. I whipped back to the toilet, soaking the toilet paper on the way.

Outside it sounded like World War III had broken out. Tina's friend was shouting and a man's voice was screaming right back at her. Bodies tumbled past the toilet door and then Tina added to the din. There was a crash and I put myself away and tried to think what was going on.

The two gorillas were right at the top of my Christmas list. I could feel pee running down the inside of my leg and wished I'd shaken a little before zipping up.

The noise from the living room indicated that things were a mess. The girls were ratcheting up the screaming and the intruders were just adding to the cacophony. Another crash and I knew I needed to move.

Two ways to go. Hit the living room and wade in. Three against two and we might stand a chance. Or leg it and call for help. Given I had wanted to call for help as soon as I saw Charlie's blood providing sustenance for the pigeons in George Square I decided flight not fight.

I unbolted the toilet door and looked out. The main room door was half closed and I could see movement beyond accompanied by more shouting and more screaming.

I took hold of the door jamb and pulled myself out, around and into the hallway. The front door was still wide open - a huge scuff mark under the key hole indicating where it had been kicked as Tina's friend had opened it.

The door behind me slammed into the wall and I knew I had been spotted. I put my head down and ran. There was nothing else to do.

I exited onto the landing but reckoned without the shiny, polished floor tiles and as I tried to turn towards the fire doors and the stairwell beyond, my right foot lost its grip and I went down head over heels. I scrabbled to get up but my haste was my undoing and while I was thrashing around my head exploded in a rainbow of lights as something came down hard on the back of my neck.

I dropped to the tiles like a pair of whore's knickers and felt a strong hand grab me by the ankle. I had no fight in me. Everything was jelly slow and my tongue had dried up and filled my mouth.

Next to me I saw a shadow pass over the neighbour's door but it didn't open.

I was dragged back into the house. The door was shut, the bolt thrown and for good measure the chain put in place. All I could think was horse and stable. A hand grabbed my other foot and I took some serious face burns from the carpet as I was manhandled into the main room.

I could still hear Tina screaming but this time it was cut short with a pistol whip crack as the tall gorilla smacked her and she fell to her knees inches from my head. The silence held for a second and then the two gorillas got to work with duct tape and made the three of us comfortable on the sofa. Me in the middle.

I tried to move my hands but they were tight together behind me and my feet were taped at the ankles. Tina and her friend were trussed up the same way.

The tall gorilla disappeared into the kitchen and returned with a tea towel. He took out a pen knife and tore it into three long strips. He wrapped a strip around each of our mouths.

Tina tried to wriggle and the short gorilla took a free kick at her ankle bone and tears burst from her eyes as she yelled into the tea cloth.

I tore at the bindings and tried to lunge at him. The short gorilla raised a fist and cracked my jaw with a well practised left hook. Lights danced once more and this time I got the lesson - but I still wanted to kill him.

The short one took out his mobile and began chatting. He stopped mid sentence and asked Tina's friend for the address of the flat. She shook her head and he slapped her. He took off the tea towel and she told him that she was shaking her head to tell him she couldn't speak and he hit her again.

She gave him the address.

Chapter 53

Simon looks on.

Karen is driving and Robin is riding up front with her. I am relegated to the back. My head is still spinning from the revelations surrounding my Financial Director.

We had spent the morning working on our approach to the exchange. Robin had rejected everything and ordered Dumb and Dumber to get the documents and then call.

Bally phoned Robin when they had taken out the vic. Bally had the documents. Robin told him to follow and capture the other two. Once this was done Bally was to phone him.

When the phone rang and I was asked to dial 1471 on my phone and text the number. Ten minutes later the phone rang again.

The drive to the flats is done at speed and in silence. There is little to be said. I only want to ask questions about Robin. He doesn't want to answer any of them. Karen is stone-walling me as well.

It is clear that the remaining two vics are not long for this planet. Robin has some questions he needs answered and then they will be dropped.

The west end drifts past in fits and starts. We play leapfrog with the traffic lights. We turn off the main road and climb a hill. Robin swings the car into a small car park that sits at the foot of a white high rise.

Karen and Robin get out but don't wait for me. I have to jog to get to the main door before it swings shut behind them.

The lift struggles to the eleventh floor. We enter the landing and still not a word is spoken. Robin walks up to a flat. With a knock on the door we are standing in front of the three vics less than a minute later.

George looks a mess. The back of his head is matted with blood. He has the start of a bruise across his jaw. The girlfriend is crying. The other girl next to her is trying not to.

Robin points to the other girl. He signals Bally's partner to take her next door. It is the first time I have met the Dumber half of the duo and he doesn't inspire confidence. Dumber simply fireman lifts the girl, smacking her head off the door frame as he leaves.

Robin bends over George. He pulls the gag from his mouth.

'I'll keep this simple.'

He walks into the kitchen. For a few minutes nothing happens. George sits staring at us. His face a mix of fear and hate.

I hear the kettle coming to the boil. Robin reappears with it in his hand. He walks over to Tina and holds the silver kettle over her lap.

To George:

'You talk - she doesn't get a bath. Understand?'

George nods his head. Tina has her eyes fixed on the spout of the kettle. The steam drifts into the air.

'Question one. Do you know what is in the documents?'

George shakes his head.

Robin tips the kettle. A stream flows onto Tina's lap. She tries to howl through the cloth and roll free. Bally whips round the back and holds her down. Her body is shaking like a jackhammer as the pain digs deep.

'Wrong fucking answer!' shouts Robin.

'Do you know what is in the documents?' he repeats.

Robin holds the kettle high. Tina wrenches her eyes from the kettle. Her eyes turn and plead with George.

George nods.

'Good. Now we continue.'

Robin lifts the kettle higher. He positions the spout over Tina's head. She throws herself to the left. Bally grabs her shoulders and forces her back upright.

Robin bends over and whispers in George's ear.

'Did you take any copies of the documents?'

George nods.

'Where are they?'

I could see where this was going. So could George. With the documents out of the way, George and his girlfriend were toast and he knew it.

George hesitates. Robin tips the spout half an inch. A small stream of scalding liquid falls on the crown of Tina's head. She goes into a violent spasm.

'Tip her head up,' Robin says to Bally.

Bally does as he is told. Robin positions the spout an inch above her left eye.

'Don't fuck with me or I blind her in one eye.'

The room fills with the smell of fresh urine. Tina's jeans stain around her crotch.

'Where are the copies?' asks Robin.

'We opened a Mail Box etc account, copied them and dropped them in our mail box. Please don't hurt her anymore.'

Robin pulls the kettle away and puts it down on the coffee table that sits in front of the sofa.

'Where's the key for the mail box?'

'In my pocket,' says George.

Bally's friend has re-entered the room seconds earlier, a ridiculous smile on his face.

Robin nods at him. Jim nods back. Robin nods again. Jim nods back.

'Get the key out of his pocket you tosser.'

Jim holds his hand up as if to stay sorry. He walks over and roots around in George's trouser pockets until he finds the key. He hands it to Robin. Robin puts it in his jacket pocket. He picks up the kettle again.

'Tip her head to the left.'

Bally obeys. Robin places the spout above Tina's left ear.

'If I tip this in her ear it will hurt like fuck but that's not the bad news. I've seen it kill people. The shock you know. So I have one last question and then we can all go home?'

Tina has stopped struggling. The smell from her trousers changes. It isn't hard to figure out what she has done.

'Does…' Robin says, '…anyone else know about the documents?'

George shakes his head.

Robin tips the kettle a touch but not enough to let any water come out.

'No. I'm telling you no. Don't,' George screams. 'Nobody else knows.'

Robin smiles. He places the kettle back on the coffee table. I am stunned at the cruelty he has just shown. I realise that the Robin I have known for the last twenty years is not the man standing in front of me - and for all these years I have thought that I was the hard man.

Chapter 54

George the hero.

Tina is released by the gorilla and curls up into a ball beside me. The combination of sweat, urine, excrement and scalded flesh gag in my throat. I try to catch her eyes but she has buried her head in her chest and I can see her breathing is ragged - no doubt the water works are full on.

Robin steps away and huddles in the corner with Simon and Karen. The two gorillas take their cue and vanish into the kitchen and I hear matches on sandpaper as they both light up.

I feel a wave of depression sweep over me. I am spent. Emotionally and physically. I can see no other way that this is going to finish short of Tina, her friend and I ending up on some slab in the mortuary. It is just a matter of when.

The confab continues between the three and I touch my head to Tina's. She jerks and I pull back realising I have probably touched her head burn. Lethargy has set in big time and I pull my legs up and curl them under my backside to join Tina in the foetal position.

Robin steps back from the other two to stretch his legs. His left leg is touching the coffee table, less than six inches from the kettle. I look at the kettle and then at Robin and think what do I have to lose.

I shoot both legs out and catch the kettle square on. It cannons towards Robin and hits him just below the thigh - the lid flies open and the contents spray across his legs. He recoils and lets out a scream as the water, still close to boiling, soaks his trousers.

Simon and Karen are caught unaware and they rock back against the far wall as Robin bounces into them while trying to undo his belt to rid himself of his trousers. Robin catches Simon square in the stomach with his left elbow and Simon goes down, catching his head on the edge of the mantelpiece - slumping to the floor like a wet rag doll.

Robin continues to swirl like a dervish and Karen pushes him away. He tumbles forward. He has forgone the belt and is now trying to rip the trousers off over his shoes. Off balance he tumbles over the prone figure of Simon, hops once, catches the edge of the armchair and spirals up and over to land behind it, screaming the whole time.

Karen glares down at me and then the two gorillas hammer into the room.

I know it is hopeless but I lift my legs as best I can and lash out. By sheer luck I catch the tall one in the groin as he rushes at me. The crunch between feet and testicles is almost edible. He howls like a banshee and drops like a stone. I have hit him square in the crown jewels.

It occurs to me that for someone tied up like a Christmas present that I am doing ok but then the short one steam rollers into me and I gasp.

His momentum takes me onto Tina and then we all fall backward as we fly over the back of the sofa, tipping it onto its back. Tina flips over my head and crashes down onto the short gorilla. I lie for a second, stunned and then I try to wriggle to my left. I hear a grunt and then the short gorilla's face appears inches from mine. I do the only thing left open to me and head butt him with everything I have left.

I feel his nose crack and he yells, instinctively snapping his head away from the source of pain. Blood erupts from his nose and he rolls back and onto the floor. I lash out with my feet and catch him on the chin. His head spins away and he smashes into a display cabinet and a rain of china and nick nacks comes down from the heavens and crowns him.

But he is a hardy bugger and comes up ready for a fight only to find his rising head introduced to a falling Cuckoo clock made of solid oak. This time his eyes go out. He falls forward and pins me to the floor.

His sweet breath blows in my ear and I twist my head to see Karen staring down at the devastation. She is focussed on the tall gorilla who is still hugging his privates and then she glances at Simon - dead to the world. Above me the short gorilla has joined Simon in beddy-bye land and out of sight on the other side of the room I can hear Robin moaning.

I struggle to get the short gorilla off me. Karen sees me start to move and picks up a letter opener from the mantelpiece and starts towards me.

My luck is running out. The short gorilla weighs in at nearly two hundred pounds and I am pinned between him and the display cabinet. I shake, thrash and throw myself around but I can't get free of him.

Karen has reached the door and is stepping round the up-ended sofa - the letter opener high in the air. She takes one more step, bends over and I close my eyes as she starts to plunge the knife towards me.

Then there is another crash and voices. I open my eyes and Karen has frozen mid strike and is no longer looking at me but staring at the door to the hallway. The door bursts open and the room seems to fill with bodies. Karen is caught in the midriff by the first blue-coated body through the door and she is catapulted to the far wall.

Things get a little crazy.

Chapter 55

Back from the dead.

I am wired to the moon. Tubes to the left of me and tubes to the right of me bubble and burp. The heart machine bleeps reassuringly and a litre of plasma is drip feeding my battered organs.

I am out of intensive care but still on the critical list. I had been moved from the ICU less than an hour ago to be informed that the police had some questions for me but I told them that they would have to wait.

The door opens and in walks Tina with George on at her heels. Both look the worse for wear but both are smiling.

'How many stab wounds does it take to put you down?'

George grins like a cat as he says it.

'And do you often leave friends for dead on a bench in the middle of the city?'

I am smiling.

It had been close. I had come round on the bench in George Square knowing I was in a bad way but as the ambulance men were strapping me to the gurney and trying to stop my life leaking onto the ground I begged to talk to a policeman.

It had always been the plan to go back to Tina's friend - although Tina had found her less than a willing accomplice. I could only think that's where they would go if they weren't around.

The policeman eventually agreed to go to the address. I refused to co-operate with the para-medic unless he did.

The police had arrived at the flat to coincide with a call to 999 from a neighbour who told them that he had just witnessed a man being dragged into the next door flat.

The police had reacted quickly and broken down the door to find the carnage beyond.

Apparently they had trouble equating the punishment that had been dealt out by George given his restrained state.

George chipped up and told me his side. I was weak but the story from the flat was wild. I asked what had happened since.

Tina took up the story.

Simon, Karen and Robin were helping police with their enquiries. A forensic accountant was going through the documents and a court order had given the police access to Retip's offices. By all accounts a lot of trash and burn had gone on. But the police were confident that not everything had been destroyed and that there would be enough to go on.

The two gorillas had clammed up and were saying nothing but three witnesses from outside Tyler Tower had ID'd them and it was only a matter of time before they either sang or decided to try and cut a deal.

George had heard from one of his contacts that after the police had left the Retip offices someone else had ripped the place apart. No doubt one of the many Retip clients who now faced exposure from the documents.

Tina says the betting is that none of the trio from Retip would make a trial. Too many enemies. This might or might not be true but it is great news from our end. They are all going to be far too worried about there own future to make it worse by coming after a small time accountant, a maintenance man and his girlfriend.

George sits on my left and Tina on my right. I look at both of them and think I might have just found some friends for life.

'You know,' I say. 'When I was lying on that bench I thought this is the bottom of the well. It can't get any worse.'

George pats me on the arm and says, 'We fell a long way in a short time.'

Tina nods.

'Maybe,' she adds. 'But it's time to stop falling and start climbing again.'

I grin and look down at my bandages.

'With the state of my legs?' I say.

George starts to laugh and doubles in pain. Tina starts to laugh, bends over and hits her head on the bed side cabinet. She yells. There is a second's silence and then George starts laughing again and I just break down.

By the time the nurse comes in to see what is happening I have wet myself.

'Pain, pee and past caring,' I say to the nurse.

She doesn't smile.

'All and all it's a nice way to sum up my life at the moment,' I say.

She still doesn't smile

I slump back in my bed and smack my head off the wall. I let out a cry.

Now the nurse smiles.

I close my eyes.

Pain, pee and past caring – it would make a good epitaph for me one day.

A very good epitaph.

The End

Gordon Brown's next novel

Why would someone have less than an hour to tell their life story? Who are they? Who are they talking to? What is contained in the diary that lies on the table? As **59 Minutes** unfolds we chart the world of a criminal as he rises to the height of his profession only to have it all taken away – reducing him to begging on the street. A criminal who becomes hell bent on revenge against the man who ruined his life – a man who shows no compassion, puts no value on life and is dangerous in the extreme.

"59 Minutes" is Gordon Brown's second novel. Here is an excerpt:

Eleven-o-one. The clock on the wall says eleven-o-one. The second hand has completed another three sixty and we are now into the second minute after eleven o'clock. I know that second hand's tick intimately, lovingly, fearfully and a shed load of other adverbs that would bore you to the core. I have listened to it sweep around that clock face for such a long time but now there are only fifty eight minutes and fifty four seconds to go.

I might ask you to describe the clock to me at some point. But not yet. Not now. There are other more important things that I need to tell you in the minutes that remain to me - or rather the minutes that remain to us.

So many things to tell that we may not have the time we need.

But I will try.

Why? Why will I try to tell you these things? Because I need to. I need to tell someone and you are better placed than most, far better placed than most, to listen and understand. I need no more from you than that. Can you listen? Can you understand?

…

I was born in the west end of Glasgow. Partick to be exact. Dumbarton Rd to be very exact. Number 3 - you get the idea.

I was never the healthiest of kids. I had a tendency to monopolise whatever bug was doing the rounds. As result I missed much of my schooling. On the upside I had an in-depth knowledge of doctor's surgeries, hospitals, my bedroom, my grandmother's bedroom and a private TB clinic (and that is an entire story in itself). Suffice to say I left school with no qualifications and little prospects.

It would be nice to say I went on to make good and earned my fortune the hard way. An entrepreneur of note. But that would be a crock of crap. Yes I made money but I also managed to make a complete turkey of my life at the same time. And it was no one else's fault but my own.

Not that I didn't hold some promise in some areas. As you will see I excelled in places that others failed but ultimately I washed my life down a large plug hole. I then watched the water spin away - carrying my heart beats and my ambition to a dark place.

After leaving school, I found employment with a friend of my father. It was menial work. The sort that requires little thought, a lot of graft and small reward. My father's friend was a man called George Matthews. He owned an engineering firm on the outskirts of the city. He employed about twenty people producing spare parts for the automotive industry.

The hours were long. The job dull. Mind numbing dull. The factory had to sweat hard for its money and Saturday and even Sunday shifts were the norm for the first two years of my working life. I quickly lost contact with my school mates and found it hard to acquire new friends from work. I was, after all, far younger than anyone else in the building. My nickname was original - 'Junior' - and since the work's recreation revolved around the Lame Duck pub I was, at sixteen years of age, excluded from that particular avenue of respite.

The only reason I am telling you of this time is in relation to a certain Michael Tolt, my only friend of note from that era. It is Michael, dead these many years, that is, in part, responsible for me sitting here talking to you.

When I joined the firm I was heaven sent as far as he was concerned. In an instant the scorn the factory poured on its youngest member fell from his shoulders and dropped on mine. I think he always knew this was a shit deal and to compensate became the one person I could talk to at break time or see outside of work.

He was a fanatic for football and for Partick Thistle in particular and over the years dragged me along to a nightmare collection of games. He never tired of his obsession and was rewarded for his long term service with the club when, on the twenty third of October nineteen seventy one, against all predictions, they took on Celtic in the League Cup final and beat them four – one.

I still remember standing on the terraces at Hampden Park at half time - Partick were four up against one of the best sides in Europe. To say that there was a party atmosphere was nothing short of an understatement. There may never be a finer moment to be a Partick Thistle fan. But I had no love of the club and I was probably the least excited person on the terraces that day - but the game did bring one defining moment with it. After the match I was allowed into the hallowed halls of The Lame Duck for my first drink. I had turned eighteen the day before and the stained floorboards, dank smoky air and rank smell of a million men's farts were mine for the taking.

Are you checking the clock? **Eleven oh four and ten seconds.** Time slips past so fast. I must keep moving.

I left Matthews Engineering two months later. I simply couldn't take it anymore. The poor hours, the lack of pay and the endless insults. They all combined to force me out and onto the 'Bru' - Glaswegian for Social Security. Neither my mother nor my father were happy about this. They had been reliant on my contribution to the house to help off set the mountain of debt they had acquired.

No let's be honest about this. And fair to my mother. The debt was not theirs but my father's and my father's alone. The local bookie being the open drain he poured our cash into.

When I left the job I had intended to find other employment as quickly as possible. But Britain was heading for its worst recession since the thirties and I had no qualifications, no skills and, probably most damning of all, no connections.

I was prime meat for the local criminal fraternity and after six months of fruitless interviews and rejections Michael Tolt surprised me and stepped in with an offer that was hard to refuse.

He told me, over a pint in The Lame Duck, that a friend of his was looking for a reliable lad to run some errands. The friend needed someone who could keep his mouth shut and do as he was told. In return I would receive five pounds a week. The good news was that I could still sign on so I accepted and a week later I met Tony 'the Nose' Campbell.

Books published by Fledgling Press

Stella Maris, by Nan O'Dell   (2001)
Bag Lady, by Nan O'Dell (2001)
Gertrude, by Brian Fine (2002)
Defending the realm, by Brian Fine (2002)
Four score, by Ilsley Ingram (2002)
Soldier of the queen, by Malcolm Archibald (2003)
Horseman of the veldt, by Malcolm Archibald
(2005)
Selkirk of the Fethan, by Malcolm Archibald (2005)
Aspects of the Boer War, by Malcolm Archibald
(2005)
Everyman's Worst Nightmare, by Stacey John
(2006)
Mother Law, by Malcolm Archibald (2006)
The New Fledgling Cook Book, by Bridget
Wedderburn (2006)
Inner Thoughts, by Christine Tindall (2007)
Powerstone, by Malcolm Archibald (2008)

Forthcoming (2009):
Every Granpaw's Cook Book by Bridget
Wedderburn
The Sinkable Wife, by Jock Stubble

All available from any good bookshop, or direct
from **www.fledglingpress.com**.

Some free excerpts downloadable from
www.weefreebooks.com